I0713261

A Most Unlikely Hero

Volume 7

Written by Brandon Varnell

Illustrations by XuaHanNin

To see Brandon Varnell's other works, or to ask for permission to use his works, visit him at www.varnell-brandon.com, facebook at www.facebook.com/AmericanKitsune, twitter at www.twitter.com/BrandonbVarnell, Patreon at https://www.patreon.com/BrandonVarnell, and instagram at www.instagram.com/brandonbvarnell.

ISBN: 978-1-951904-02-9

CONTENT

Prologue: Lancelot and Morrigan

Chapter 1: Departure

Chapter 2: Arrival

Interlude: Trouble on the Home Front – Part I

Chapter 3: Merlin and Perversion

Interlude: Trouble on the Home Front – Part II

Chapter 4: Bedivere the Not So Brave

Interlude: Ingraine

Chapter 5: Avalon

Epilogue: All's Well That Ends Well... Or So They Say

DEDICATION

This page is made in dedicaion to my amazing patrons. Without them, my characters would never get lewded by so many wonderful artists:

Aaron Harris

Alarinnise

Feitochan

Jacob Flores

Jacob Wonjo

James Leon-Moore

Matthew Wallace

Max A Kramer

Michael Moneymaker

Seismic Wolf

Victor Parick Bauer

PROLOGUE

LANCELOT AND MORRIGAN

Lancelot was sitting behind his large desk as he poured over several documents. There was a steaming cup of specially brewed tea resting on a finely crafted plate with blue decorations. He would occasionally sip the tea as he read the reports that appeared on his tablet periodically.

They still haven't found Bedivere, huh? I suppose that's understandable. That fool has always been good at hiding.

It hadn't even been two days since Lancelot had taken over Winchester, the planet that his half-brother Bedivere was in charge of ruling—well, had been in charge of ruling. It was his now. Of course, this planet was just a stepping stone. The true goal that he sought was not this tiny planet.

Setting the tablet onto the desk, Lancelot's eyes swept around the room. Meagerly decorated with only a few portraits and pieces of artwork, the room was more Spartan than he would have liked. The floor was made of limestone instead of marble. He supposed it was because this planet wasn't as prosperous as his own.

Bedivere did not have what it took to rule a planet. He wasn't lazy, per say, but he never strived to create a more prosperous kingdom. His planet was a perfect example. Stuck in the status quo, the planet had not increased its revenue or expanded its trade in the last seven years since Bedivere had become the planet's ruler. It's worth hadn't decreased at all, but it also hadn't been increased.

A true ruler, a true king, is someone who is always seeking to improve his life and the lives of his subjects. Bedivere has never once followed this basic principle. That's why I'm wresting control of this planet from him, and why I won't let Arthur have his way...

As these thoughts darted through his mind, the door opened and three people walked in.

"Darling brother," the one in the lead greeted him with a smile. Soft hair darker than crow feathers framed a pale face that had enchanted many men. Dark eyes. Crimson lips. Soft features. Many people had often called this girl an angel, though he knew better. The black dress that she wore was very much a reflection of her twisted personality.

"Morrigan," he greeted, then addressed the other two individuals. "Tristan. Segwarides. I'm glad you two could make it."

"I called them here!" Morrigan said with a bubbly smile as she waltzed up to him. "Aren't I great?"

"Yes." Lancelot smiled as he patted Morrigan on the head. "You're an amazing little sister."

"Tee-hee!"

"I hope you have a good explanation for all this, Brother," said Tristan. "You might be Father's eldest son, but not even that will stop him from berating you upon his return."

Taller than anyone else Lancelot knew, Tristan was a mountain of muscle and gave off an intimidating aura. Part of that was because of his armor. The dark crimson breastplate had the depiction of a fire-breathing dragon on the front. Shoulder pauldrons clinked together as he moved. The grieves on his feet were also crimson, and they came all the way up to his knees before ending in spikes. Finally, gripped fiercely in his hand was a dangerous-looking spear the color of freshly painted blood.

"You mean 'if' Father returns," Lancelot pointed out.

Their father, Uther Pendragon, had been tasked with a quest by King Lucifer, the ruler of the galaxy. No one knew what their father had been tasked with, or even where he had gone. In his absence, his wives ruled over their solar system.

However, Father's eleven wives were very hands off in their approach. They believed it was important for their children to learn how to rule properly, and so they often sat back and let their children do as they pleased. Only Lancelot's and Morrigan's mother, Igraine, had taken a significant role in nurturing her children.

It was she who taught Morrigan to control the elements, and it was she who suggested to Lancelot that now was the best time to keep Arthur from claiming the throne.

When Arthur pulled Caliburn from the stone, it was announced that he would become king, and Lancelot had given up hope of ever becoming king himself. Why bother trying to become king when it was a foregone conclusion that Arthur would take the reins?

His goal had shifted after that. He would make his planet the most prosperous in the solar system. Then, when Arthur became king, he would present his planet as an example of what he could do and become Arthur's adviser. After which, he would rule from the shadows, advising his youngest brother on how best to rule this solar system. In doing so, he would create the prosperous kingdom that he had always dreamed of.

Then his mother had come to him, told him that Arthur was unfit to rule, that he had gone off to some backwater solar system to find Princess Gabrielle, King Lucifer's daughter, and take her hand in marriage. Arthur had neglected his duties for a woman. He was unfit to rule, to lead. Those had been his mother's words. They had convinced Lancelot that his brother was unfit to rule.

That was why Lancelot would take over. He had planned this coup with his sister. Together, they would wrest this solar system from their youngest brother.

"Do not speak with such defeatism," Segwarides said, frowning as he crossed his lean arms. "Father is a powerful and capable warrior. It would take someone of King Lucifer's caliber to defeat him."

Lean and strong, with a graceful figure that was more beautiful than rugged, Segwarides was a contrast in appearance to all his other siblings. Unlike Tristan's armor, Segwarides wore leather armor with a glossy sheen that caused light to flash off it. Further accentuating his attunement to nature, numerous leaf-shaped segments of armor studded his chest, shoulders, and kneecaps. A blaster bow was strapped across his back.

"I do not wish to speak as though he's never returning." Lancelot leaned back and stared at his two younger half-siblings. Meanwhile, Morrigan stood right next to him. "However, it has been more than a year since Father disappeared. While I hope he is safe, and that he will return home, I cannot allow myself to bask in a false hope. Since it has been so long, I believe it's better to act under the belief that he will not return."

His two half-siblings shuffled their feet, perhaps out of discomfort for the way he spoke. He did not blame them. Their father might be a bit impersonal, but all of them respected and admired him. Lancelot sincerely hoped his father was safe. At the same time, he would not turn a blind eye to the fact that it had been a year since Father set off on his quest with Gadreel, King Lucifer's first wife and the Empress of Angelisia.

"Brother. Brother." Morrigan placed a hand on his shoulder. "Perhaps you should tell them why you wanted to speak with them?"

"Yes, I suppose you are right," Lancelot said, standing to his feet.

"Considering what you've done, I believe we already know what this is about." Tristan crossed his arms. "I do not believe I can help you in this matter."

"Do not be so hasty. There is a lot going on right now that you are unaware of. At least listen to what I have to say before you make a decision," Lancelot rebutted.

"I will listen," Segwarides said. "Whether or not I will side with you is in the air, but I will at least listen to your side of the story before making a decision."

Tristan sighed. "If Segwarides is willing to listen, then I shall also hear you out."

"Thank you." Lancelot walked in front of the desk, Morrigan trailing after him, and faced his two half-siblings from up close. "I know that neither of you approved of Arthur becoming crown prince merely because he pulled Caliburn from the stone."

The two before him stiffened. Lancelot withheld a smile. The reason he called these two individuals was because out of all his half-siblings, they were the ones who expressed the most distaste. They had argued against Arthur becoming crown prince. It had gotten so bad that Father had sent them to the farthest planets in their solar system, merely so he wouldn't have to listen to them complain.

"I will admit, while I was also displeased, I believed that it would be better to support Arthur to the best of my abilities."

"Then something has changed your mind?" asked Segwarides.

"Indeed." Lancelot nodded. He held out his hand, and Morrigan picked up the tablet from the desk and handed it to him. "I'm not sure if you know, but it has been made public that Gabrielle Angelise has selected her own marriage candidate."

"We are aware." Tristan nodded.

"Then you are also aware that King Lucifer has said that whoever can steal Princess Gabrielle from this Alexander Ryker will be given her hand in marriage and become Emperor of the Galaxy?" His half-siblings nodded. Lancelot continued. "As you know, our solar system has a powerful alliance with Angelisia. It is thanks in part to this alliance that we have prospered. Years ago, Arthur was originally going to marry Princess Gabrielle, but that changed when he pulled the Caliburn from the stone. The marriage was called off because if Arthur became the Emperor of the Galaxy, he would be required to put the galaxies interests before our own, which would conflict with his duties as our king."

Segwarides and Tristan nodded. They were as aware of all this as him.

Lancelot leaned against the desk, which only squealed slightly as he put the full weight of his golden armor on it. He crossed his arms. Presenting the two with his most serious expression, he tried to put everything he felt into his eyes as he said the words that would undoubtedly bring these two to his side.

"About two weeks ago, Arthur found out about what was happening with Princess Gabrielle and has left for a planet called Mars, the place where she is currently residing. Arthur has put his own interests before his solar systems." He paused before making his final proclamation. "That is why Arthur is no longer fit to be our king, and why I would like you both to help me remove him from the position."

CHAPTER 1

DEPARTURE

There were a lot of things that Alex needed to do before he could depart with Prince Arthur and travel to Camelot. First and foremost was that he needed to clear the air with Karen Kanzaki, his former commander in the Mars Police Force, a friend of his father's, and the person who helped look after him and Alice when his father died. Since he had no idea when he'd be back, Alex wanted to at least put the issues between them to rest.

That was why he was at the Mars Police Station. It was early in the morning. At this time, Arthur should be about ready to launch his craft and was just waiting on him to finish.

Stepping into the Mars Police station, Alex walked along the tiled waiting room, past several chairs where citizens were waiting, either to file a complaint or report a problem, and wandered up to the front desk. There, a young man with brown hair, brown eyes, and a bored face sat. He was leaning against his desk, absently poking his finger at a holographic screen. It looked like he was playing a game of some kind.

"Excuse me," Alex began, "I would like to see Commander Karen Kanzaki. Could you let her know that Alexander Ryker is here to see her?"

The young man stiffened, though whether from his name or Karen's name was unknown. Looking up at him, the man blinked rapidly several times before nodding.

"Uh… yeah, sure. Just let me tell her that you are here," he said before dismissing his holographic screen and pressing a button on his console. "Commander Karen? Alex Ryker says he's here to speak with you. What should I do?"

Alex almost snorted at the question that was tacked on the end. It was almost like this man thought he was a criminal or something equally stupid. Why was it that everybody had such a low opinion of him? Well, he did cause a lot of trouble, so he had gotten a reputation for damaging property and stuff, but that didn't mean everyone should treat him like a pariah. That was just rude.

There was a short period of silence before Karen's voice came over the intercom. "Send him up."

"You heard her," the young man said. "Go on up."

"Thanks."

Spacer boots tapping against white tiles, Alex walked to the elevator that was on the desk's right side. He ignored the other people current inside. Pressing a button that would take him to Karen's office, Alex leaned against the wall and waited.

"Isn't that Alexander Ryker?"

His ears twitched.

"It is. What do you suppose he's doing here?"

"Don't know. Did you hear about what happened?"

"You mean about how he was thrown in jail?"

"Yeah, that. I heard he was obstructing justice."

"I heard her was wrongly accused."

"I can hear everything you two are saying," Alex said, staring at the male and female who were currently talking about him.

Mars Police uniforms were unisex. Everyone wore the same black and white unitard, which conformed to the body like a second skin. These two were not wearing any armor, marking them as cadets.

The two stopped talking after that, and Alex had the pleasure of not being forced to listen to people speak about him. When the elevator opened on the last floor, Alex stepped out, walked down a narrow hallway, and ended up in front of a typical sliding door. There was a button on the left that he pressed.

"Alexander?" a voice came from a speaker system.

"It's me."

"Come on in."

The doors slid open and Alex stepped inside.

A Spartan room greeted him, though that was not to say that the room was completely bereft of decorations. Situated in the center of the room, immediately behind him, were two couches centered around a table. Sitting against the wall to his left, a bookshelf was filled with numerous old-fashioned discs. Beside it, safely locked within a glass case, an ancient record of something called The Beatles hung like a prized possession. On the other side, hanging from frames and sitting on displays, were the various awards that his commander had won.

Karen Kanzaki sat behind her desk, which was in front of a large glass panel that overlooked Mars City. Blonde hair descended from her head in drill-like curls, framing a gorgeous face that screamed *"mess with me and you die."* She wore her Galactic Police Force uniform well. The white skirt wrapped around her athletic hips and revealed stunningly well-muscled legs covered in black stockings. Her white shirt with its long sleeves and black stripes gave her an air that was both professional and feminine, while the gun strapped to her side let everyone know not to screw with her.

He and Karen had not spoken with each other in nearly two weeks. The last time he had seen her was when she'd had him arrested. Since then, she had not spoken to him. However, even before that, their relationship had become precarious.

Around three weeks ago… or thereabouts, Alex had been attacked by Nyx, an assassin hired by King MacArt, who was—had been—one of Gabrielle's marriage candidates.

Anyway, Nyx had attacked and almost killed him. In response, Karen had mobilized the entire Mars Police Force and tried to have Nyx killed, but Alex had intervened. He'd moved in while the police were going after Nyx, wounded several officers, and saved Nyx's life despite Karen forbidding him from doing so.

This had resulted in the estrangement of their relationship; Karen had fined him heavily, marked this in his criminal record, and then cut off all contact with him. It had hurt, but he knew that Karen had been just as pained.

"Karen," Alex greeted as he stopped in front of her desk. He dithered for a moment, unsure of what to say.

He fortunately did not have to say anything. Karen spoke before him.

"Alex," she said, her tone softer than he remembered. "You seem to be doing well."

"As well as could be expected, I guess." Alex couldn't stop the sheepish grin from spreading across his face. "There's a lot going on right now."

"I heard. Azazel informed me that you plan on leaving with this Prince Arthur." Karen sighed. "You certainly don't do these things half-assed, do you?"

Alex shrugged. "I've recently made a decision and following through with that decision requires me to travel with Prince Arthur and help him out."

"I figured as much. What about the people living with you? Are they coming as well?"

"Gabrielle and Nyx are coming," Alex said. "I couldn't stop them even if I wanted to. However, Ariel and Michelle won't be coming with us."

They had wanted to, of course, but Alex had asked them to look after his sister instead. Alice was an important part of his life, and there was no telling who might show up while he was gone. He had told Ariel and Michelle that he was entrusting his sister's safety to them. While Michelle was probably skeptical, no doubt imagining that he was just trying to keep them from going to Camelot, Ariel had enthusiastically declared that she would protect Alice with her life.

Karen placed one manicured hand on the desk, tapping her fingers against it as she studied him. "You know, I always thought that you were different from everyone else. You never acted like a normal child. You were either serious beyond your years or more playful than anyone I'd ever seen. You had this incredible talent to make things most of us could never dream of, and whenever you put your mind to something, nothing would stop you. To be honest, I used to think you were a little creepy."

"T-that's an incredibly rude thing to say!" Alex shouted. "That last statement was completely uncalled for."

Karen smiled apologetically. "I'm sorry. I don't think that way anymore. I realize now that it's because you're different. You live in a different world from us normal folk. You're a lot like your father that way."

Alex didn't remember anything about his father, not what he looked like, or what he acted like. What few snippets of memory he had were cast in shadows.

The reason was because of the seals on his mind. Several symbols from the ancient angelisian language had been used to create seals that locked his memories away. Ariel said she could break the seal, but Alex had told her to hold off because, at the time, he had been worried that it would leave him incapable of responding to trouble.

I should have her release the seals when I get home.

"When are you leaving?" Karen asked.

"Tomorrow."

"That soon?"

"It will take about a week to get from here to Camelot." Alex shrugged. "There's a lot happening over there, and we don't really have the luxury of time. Frankly, I'm surprised Prince Arthur even suggested waiting another day, but I guess there's things that he needs to take care of that can't be dealt with while in hyperspace."

Alex assumed Prince Arthur was communicating with his half-siblings and subordinates, getting as much information as possible and giving out orders.

Communication was impossible during hyperspace, from what Gabrielle had said. Hyperspace was a region of space that coexisted within this universe. Entering hyperspace required a Hyperspace Adapter and a Hyperdrive, technology that the people of his solar system didn't have, that could allow a ship to create a bubble around themselves and enter hyperspace.

While in hyperspace, the laws of Spatial Relativity did not apply, which was what allowed for faster than light travel. During their time in hyperspace, communication was impossible. The reason was because they were "out of phase" with the rest of the universe.

Karen agreed with a slow nod. "Yes, I suppose that would make sense. Azazel has already informed me of what was happening, but I appreciate you coming to tell me."

"I thought it would be appropriate," Alex said. "But I didn't just come here to tell you that?"

Karen raised an eyebrow. "You have more you wish to tell me?"

Nodding, Alex took a slow breath before saying, "I wanted to apologize. I know that dealing with me over the years hasn't been easy. I know that putting up with my, uh, recklessness has placed you under a great deal of stress. You've done a lot for me over the years, and I repaid your kindness by acting like an idiot with a chip on my shoulders. I'm sorry."

This was the main reason Alex had come to Karen. The number of times she had kept him from getting in trouble, the number of times she had run damage control for a disaster that he had caused, were too numerous to count. Back then, he had never expressed gratitude for everything she'd done for him. He'd kept pushing his luck chasing after an unachievable dream. Even if she didn't accept his apology, he had to let her know how he felt.

To his great surprise, Karen actually smiled at him. "It seems you're finally beginning to grow up. I was honestly worried about whether or not this would ever happen."

"That… I somehow feel like I've just been given the most insulting backhand compliment ever," Alex muttered.

"Alex, be careful out there," Karen said, her smile now gone, expression serious. "There's no telling what's waiting you out there in the galaxy. Make sure not to do anything reckless and come back home."

"I will," Alex agreed. "I have a sister waiting for me, so I can't afford to be reckless."

"I'm glad you've realized that."

There wasn't much left for him to do, so Alex said his goodbyes and left Karen's office, then left the police station altogether. As he hopped onto the nearest shuttle, he thought about what would be happening tomorrow morning. Space. A new adventure. His lips curved into an involuntary smile.

He couldn't wait.

1

Alex made curry that night. He was going on a journey, with no way of knowing how long it would take, when he would be back, or even if he would be back. To that end, he had made curry because it was Alice's favorite meal.

Later that night, after making sure he had packed everything that he might need in his D-glove, Alex decided to take a shower. As he wandered into the hall and toward the shower room, the door to Gabrielle's room opened.

"Oh, Alex!" Gabrielle chirped, hugging his arm. "Are you going somewhere? Wanna watch Titan Girls with me and Alice?"

"Maybe after I get out of the shower," Alex said before he realized what he was saying. He only recognized his mistake after he noticed the sparkle in Gabrielle's eyes.

"A shower?! In that case, let me take a shower with you! We can wash each other's backs!"

"Erm… I don't think that's a good idea…"

"Why not? We're a couple now, right? You confessed to me, didn't you?"

"W-well, I did…"

"Then it should be okay!"

Just the other day, Alex had confessed to Gabrielle. He had been aware of her feelings were the longest time. However, he had refused to let himself get close, laying the blame on Gabrielle's naivety and lack of modesty. Of course, that reason had been nothing but an excuse. The real reason was because Alex had… issues when it came to dealing with the opposite sex, specifically, he had problems with his own hormones.

Ever since he turned about nine or so, Alex had begun to notice, well, girls, though it might have been more accurate to say he recognized the distinct difference between boys and girls. What's more, he had been attracted to them in ways that other boys hadn't at that age. This attraction only became worse when he grew older. By the time he turned fourteen, he'd been a walking sack of testosterone.

That was when Alex confessed to Selene. He'd been rejected. Not only had it hurt, but Alex had ignored the pain and feelings and devoted himself toward becoming a police officer. He had taken an accelerated course during primary and graduated from Atreyu Academy before heading straight into the Cadet Academy. This was despite numerous universities offering him scholarships for their science and engineering programs.

However, that hadn't stopped the lust he felt, not for Selene or anyone else. His desire to for sex had only grown with time. Alex would have wet dreams featuring Selene, Jasmine, Kazekiri, Ryoko, or any number of girls. It wasn't unusual for him to wake up most mornings with a major case of morning wood.

Matters only became more problematic after Gabrielle arrived. She had made controlling himself more difficult. Every day was a struggle to control his beastly urges. Ariel had called him a perverted beast, but she probably had no idea about just how right on the money her nickname for him was.

His lustful desires had become so bad that Alex had decided to let Prince Arthur have Gabrielle. He thought that if she was with him, then surely she would be happier than if she stayed with Alex.

It's probably a good thing Ariel put a stop to that real fast. I almost lost myself to my own weakness, and Gabrielle... I very nearly destroyed the life we have together. I'll have to thank Ariel later.

Shaking his head, Alex tried to think of what he should say to get out of this situation.

"At... let's at least wait until after our first date," Alex said. "I'll... take a bath with you then... sound good?"

"Muu..." Gabrielle puffed out her cheeks. "Okay... fine. But I'm holding you to this promise."

"Right." Alex smiled, wondering what sort of trouble he was getting himself into with this promise.

With Gabrielle placated, Alex continued on to the shower room.

It was called the shower room specifically because it was divided into two rooms: a changing room and a shower room. The changing room was sort of like a restroom, changing room combination. It had a toilet, a sink, and a rack to place clothes on. A door separated the changing room from the shower room, which was literally just a shower and a tub in a tile-filled room.

The door that led into the changing room was automatic now. Gabrielle had changed it when she was remaking the house after her sisters destroyed it. Now it opened whenever someone who was registered into the security system, another feature of hers that she added without his knowledge, was in front of it.

Alex paused as he stepped into the changing room, the door behind him sliding closed, and the temperature around him dropping rapidly.

There was already someone else in there.

Nyx, an assassin who had formerly been after his life, stood in the changing room. She was not wearing her usual black dress, or her arm and leg bands. In fact, outside of her white cotton panties, an odd choice that, she was not actually wearing anything.

Being a small girl, Nyx was not very big. She only came up about his chin. She had pale skin and hair darker than a raven's feathers, which framed a lovely porcelain face that could have been mistaken for a doll.

Alex felt his throat dry as his eyes wandered down her slender neck and shoulders, admiring her arms and delicate hands before

glancing at her chest. Somehow, she looked even more erotic with her nipples covered by the two strands of hair that trailed down to the middle of her stomach. What's more, her stomach was tantalizing. Not only was it flat, but she had abs, and for just a second, Alex imagined himself licking the sweat from that six pack after a night of passionate sex. Then he continued trailing down, observing the V of her crotch. She was hairless. He hadn't expected that. Finally, at long last, he reached her feet, and the memories of how she had reacted when he cleaned her feet made his face burst with heat.

Alex was only aware of the danger he was in when Nyx released a choking amount of killing intent.

"Erm… Nyx, this isn't what it looks like," Alex said, backing away several steps. "T-the door wasn't locked, so I didn't know anyone was in here… um… can we talk this out, please?"

"I hate perverted things!" Nyx shouted before she stomped one of her tiny feet on the ground.

Alex squeaked when the floor suddenly came alive. A large chunk of the floor extended, shooting straight at him. Alex reacted on instinct. He called upon his Aura of Creation, created a sword that covered his right hand, sidestepped the floor, and cut straight through it with his ethereal weapon.

The floor crumbled.

Nyx stared at him as though she hadn't expected him to defend himself.

"L-look, Nyx. I know this looks bad, but I promise you that I didn't walk in on purpose." To emphasize his words, Alex turned around, presenting his back to her. "I had no idea anyone was in here."

"Oh…" Nyx trailed off. Alex had no idea what she was doing, but from the rustling of clothes, he guessed she was getting dressed. "I understand. I made a mistake. I thought you were coming in here to peep on me."

"I'd never peep on a girl," Alex said. "Especially not someone who is so precious to me."

The rustling stopped. "I am… precious to you?"

"Of course. I wouldn't have let you stay with me if you weren't."

The rustling started again. "I thought you were letting me live with you because you're too nice."

"W-well, I suppose." Alex coughed into his hand, hoping to hide his embarrassment. "But in the time we've started living together, you have become very precious to me."

"I see." Another pause. The rustling stopped again. "I'm dressed."

Alex turned around to find that, indeed, Nyx was dressed now. Her dark black outfit contrasted with her pale skin. The hem didn't reach the middle of her thigh, which allowed him to see the bands around her thighs. Likewise, her dress was sleeveless, and her arms were covered in armbands. Alex knew from experience that these were material that she used to transmute her primary weapons.

"I'm sorry for walking in on you." Alex rubbed the back of his head as he bowed in apology.

Nyx grabbed her left arm. "It's all right. Um…"

"Hm?"

"Do you… think I'm pretty?"

Huh?

"I think you're gorgeous," Alex answered honestly, mostly because he was too shocked by the question to answer it any other way.

"I-I see."

Nyx looked down, her hair covering her face, and walked past him. The door slid up, but he didn't hear footsteps. Alex turned. Nyx was standing in the door, her head still turned toward the ground. He couldn't see anything except her hair, which was long enough to reach her ankles.

Finally, she turned her head and pierced him with a glare. "If you tell anyone about what happened here, I'll hurt you."

Those were the last words she said before she left. Alex stared at the now closed door, trying to process what happened, only for his neuro processor otherwise known as a brain to come up with the words "cannot compute."

"I have no idea what just happened," he said to the now empty room.

2

Alex's destination after taking a shower was not his own bedroom, but was instead, the bedroom belonging to Ariel. He stood in front of the door. Unlike the shower, which anyone could open, bedroom doors could only be open by people keyed in. From his understanding, only Ariel and Gabrielle was keyed to this door.

He knocked once.

"Who is it?"

"It's Alex."

There was a pause.

"Hang on." Loud thumping reached his ears, followed a beep before the door opened with a slight hiss. Ariel stood on the other side, dressed in modest yellow pajamas. She frowned at him. "What do you want?"

"Remember when you said you could break the seal on my mind?" Alex asked.

Ariel's demeanor changed as she straightened her back. "I do. You want me to do it now?"

"Yes, please."

"All right. Let's go to your room. This is gonna knock you out, so you'll want to be on your bed or something."

"Okay."

They both entered his bedroom, and Alex walked over to the bed and laid down as the door slid shut. Ariel climbed onto the bed and straddled his waist. Alex suddenly became aware of the fact that Ariel was also a girl.

"W-wait! What are you doing?!"

"Don't move!" Ariel demanded, only to gasp when Alex tried to push her off and ended up brushing against her wings. She threw her head back and released a sound that Alex knew well. It made him wish he could bury his head in the sand. "I-idiot! I told you not to move—ahn!"

"I'm sorry, but what else do you expect me to do when a cute girl randomly straddles me?!"

"C-c-c-cute?!"

Alex couldn't be sure, but he could have sworn he'd just heard a *poof!* sound effect as Ariel's face burst with red. The girl swayed on top of him for a moment, and Alex realized that her thighs were really muscular for such a tiny girl. He could feel them flex even through the fabric of her pants.

"S-s-shut up! Just be quiet and let me work!" Ariel demanded.

"R-right."

Alex turned his head and tried to ignore Ariel as she straddled his stomach. She was warm and soft. It made ignoring her difficult, but he did the best he could as she leaned over, reached out, and placed her hands on his temples.

"The seals are located inside of you," she said softly, suddenly no longer embarrassed. She was totally focused. "In order to unlock them, I need to send my power into your mind and create a key to unlock it. It might feel a little weird at first. Also, I should mention this, but I can only unlock the first seal right now. I'm not sure what you'll see, but it won't be all of your memories."

"That's fine," Alex said. "Even if I only get a few of them back, it will be enough. Thank you, Ariel."

"I-idiot! Don't thank me for something like this! Anyway, here we go!"

Alex soon understood what Ariel meant when she said it would feel weird. It was like an electric shot racing through his brain, and while it didn't hurt, it did leave a strange, tingling numbness in its wake.

Not even a second later, his vision went dark.

3

I was walking with Dad. He was taking me to meet someone. He wouldn't tell me who we were meeting, only that it was a surprise.

"Are we there yet?"

"Not yet."

"... Are we there now?"

"No."

"How about now?"

"... No."

"What about—"

"We're almost there, Alex." Dad laughed and ruffled my hair. "Just be patient."

"I don't know what that word means," I lied. "I'm only four."

"A four-year-old who built a miniature robot." Dad gave me a look that all but said he didn't believe me. I ignored him.

The place where we were walking was really pretty. There was grass and trees and no walkways. I liked that—no walkways. I wasn't afraid of heights, but I didn't like them either. Back when we lived in Mars City's eastern district, I would always walk in the exact center of every walkway because I was afraid I would fall off.

I looked back at Dad. He was a lot taller than me... well, I guess that wasn't so surprising since he was an adult and I was just four. Bright silver hair sat on his head a mess of spikes. The fringe of his bangs hovered over his bright blue eyes. He had long, pointed ears and two wings, pinons that jutted from his back and were covered in pristine silver feathers. He looked down at me and grinned.

"Is something wrong, Alex?"

"No..." I shook my head. "I'm just surprised you're not using the illusionist."

"Haha! Well, the person we're going to meet is super important, and she already knows what I really look like."

"That so?"

"Just so."

"And you won't tell me who?"

"I said it was a surprise."

"Whatever. It's not like I care."

"Hmm... if you say so. Oh, look! We're here."

I looked at the house that we stopped in front of. It wasn't very large, just a regular, one-story house with several windows, door, and a fence. It was probably made from plasteel, but I couldn't tell for sure. I preferred using durasteel for my inventions. It was stronger and didn't break as easily.

We walked up to the front door. Dad knocked on it three times, and then waited. There was a muffled shout, followed by footsteps from beyond the door. I was tempted to put my ear against the door, but I knew my dad wouldn't like that.

The door opened and a woman stood in the doorway. She had brown hair and dark eyes that created a contrasted with her pale skin. The hem of her long, white dress fluttered as she moved. She *was wearing an apron as if she'd been cleaning when they arrived. Upon spotting Dad, the woman's pink lips curved into a wonderful smile.*

"Sandalphon!" the woman greeted, using Dad's real name. Huh, so she knew his real name. "I didn't expect to see you for another hour or so?"

"I thought we'd come early," Dad said.

Behind the woman was a little girl. She had long brown hair like the woman, her mother, I guess, and the same colored eyes. Her button nose made her look super cute. As she caught me staring at her, she hid behind the woman. I guess she was shy.

"Dad, who are these people?"

Dad smiled at me. "Alex, I'd like you to meet your new mom and little sister."

4

The next morning was a rush to get ready. While Alex had packed everything up, there were still a lot of last-minute things that he needed to do. He also had to make breakfast, lockdown his lab so no one would go in and accidentally activate one of his and Gabrielle's not-working inventions, and then he had to make sure Alice knew what she needed to do.

"I don't know how long we'll be gone, so I've made sure to prepare over two weeks' worth of food," Alex was telling Alice.

"I know."

"I also made sure you have enough soap and shampoo to make it through a month," Alex continued. "All of it is in the cupboard next to the clothing rack in the changing room."

"I know. You told me that last night."

"Also—"

"Don't go down to the lab." Alice rolled her eyes. "I know. You don't need to worry. Going down to your lab is too troublesome for me."

"Right..."

Alex reached out before Alice could say anything and pulled her into his chest.

"W-what are you doing?!"

"Please take care of yourself." Alex hugged Alice close. They may not have been related by blood, but he loved her as if they were. "I know it's troublesome, but make sure you do all your homework, don't talk to strangers, keep that stun gun I made on your persons at all times, and for the love of Mars, don't just watch Titan Girls all day!"

"I-idiot, brother," Alice mumbled into his chest as her arms wrapped around his middle. "No fair... hugging me so suddenly."

"I'm hugging you because I love you."

"T-troublesome."

Alex and Alice were standing in the hallway with Ariel, Gabrielle, Michelle, and Nyx.

Gabrielle and Nyx were dressed and ready to go. Gabrielle wore her brand-new translucent crisis suit, which blended so perfectly with her skin that Alex could only tell she was wearing it from the glossy sheen. Over her crisis suit, she wore a white unitard. It didn't cover her legs and about 50% of her butt cheeks, which were exposed until just below her knees, where a pair of white boots began. The unitard was short-sleeved, so most of her arms were bare as well.

Nyx wore the same outfit that she always did, a black dress that didn't even reach the middle of her thighs, sleeveless, and several bands that went around her arms and legs. Black boots covered her feet.

While Alex was hugging Alice, Gabrielle was giving her sister last minute instructions as well.

"Don't forget to call me if something comes up," she said.

"Of course." Michelle gave her sister a gentle smile. "If anything happens, we shall make sure to call you."

Gabrielle nodded. "Also, make sure you go to school every day. Try to make friends. You've been given a really unique opportunity. Don't waste it."

"Yes, I understand."

"And before I forgot, make sure not to touch any of the inventions inside of the lab. A lot of them aren't finished yet."

"Don't worry so much, Big Sis." Ariel gave her sister a grin and a thumbs up. "We've got this!"

"I do wish you would let us go." Michelle placed a hand on her cheek. "However, I do understand why we cannot. Please do not worry, Honorable Sister. I will keep Ariel and Alice out of trouble."

"Huh?!" Ariel gave Michelle the stink-eye. "What do you mean 'keep Ariel out of trouble'?! If anything, I'm the one who's going to be keeping you out of trouble."

"You say that, but…"

"Don't just leave your sentences half-finished! If you have something to say, then say it!"

"Hey, Ariel," Alex said as he let go of Alice.

"What is it?" Ariel asked, blushing when he came up to her and placed a hand on her head.

"I want to thank you for last night," Alex said.

"Oyo?" Michelle perked up. "What happened last night?"

"Shut up!" Ariel shouted at her sister.

"Thanks to you, I got back some of the memories about mine and Alice's parents." Alex ran his hand through Ariel's hair. It was really soft. "It means a lot to me. Thank you."

Ariel looked at the ground. "W-whatever. I only did it because I wanted to see if I could. I wasn't doing it for you."

They finished their goodbyes, Alex gave Alice, Ariel, and Michelle a few last-minute instructions, asked them to be careful, and then he, Gabrielle, and Nyx took a shuttle to the Mars Spaceport.

The Mars Spaceport was a building that had been built into the dome. It protruded out, a massive structure of durasteel and glasteel that extended for about one hundred meters in all directions. On the outside, it didn't look like much, but the inside was another story entirely.

"So many people…" Gabrielle murmured as she, Alex, and Nyx entered the spaceport.

"There are always people coming and going from Mars," Alex explained. "There's a lot of trade that goes on between planets, so a good deal of these people are either traders dealing with goods, or business men and women heading to another planet in order to broker a trade agreement."

"Uh huh…"

"And she's not listening."

Gabrielle's head turned this way and that, taking in the sights with eyes that sparkled like a child's on Mars Day. Alex could understand why. She had never been to the spaceport before, having used her teleportation device to transport herself inside of the dome.

Alex grabbed Gabrielle's and Nyx's hands and tugged on them. "Come on. Let's hurry up and stick together. We need to meet with Azazel and Prince Arthur."

Alex walked past several large pillars, massive cylinders of durasteel that acted as supports for the building. The sound of hundreds of feet pounding against the floor drowned out his own footsteps. Gabrielle and Nyx kept close to him, with Gabrielle even going so far as to hug his arm to her chest.

It was easy enough to spot Azazel. Really, Alex would have had to be blind to miss him.

Azazel was tall, easily standing at around 244 centimeters if not taller. Strapped to his chest was a large, segmented breastplate. Thick pauldrons covered his shoulders, and the grieves that he wore went up to his knees, glinting as sunlight reflected off of their polished surface. Hair the color of dirty snow drifted lazily in the breeze created by atmospheric generators. Dark purple eyes glowed brightly within their sockets. Two massive white wings jutted from his back, flapping like real wings, and long, pointy ears protruded from either side of his head.

The people were giving Azazel a wide berth. They stared at the giant angelisian with frightened eyes. Since there was basically this massive no-man's-land around him, it made spotting Prince Arthur, who stood next to Azazel, much easier.

"Ah! Princess Gabrielle! Groom-to-Be!... Nyx," Azazel's greeting of Nyx was much colder than when he greeted Alex and Gabrielle. "I see you have no luggage. I'm assuming everything is in your D-space?"

"That's right," Gabrielle chirped.

"Are you sure you wish to come with me?" asked Prince Arthur. "This has nothing to do with you. You've no obligation to help me."

Alex frowned. "And I told you that it does. I'm also not doing this for free. There are a few things I'd like in exchange for helping you."

"Ah ha!" Prince Arthur barked. "I see. I see. You are a shrewder man than I thought. Very well. Let us be off."

Prince Arthur's vessel was located within a private docking bay. Being the crown prince of another solar system apparently made him something of a VIP.

The docking bay that Prince Arthur's shuttle sat in was massive, which was funny because the shuttle itself was quite small.

Streamlined and elegant, the shuttle reminded Alex of an arrow. The front was tapered into a point. A viewport made of black glasteel, or a similar substance, created a vizier in the front and was undoubtedly the cockpit. The rest gleamed silver.

Several people were waiting for them.

"Karen, Yumi… Kazekiri?" Alex blinked. "What are you doing here?"

"I… I heard you were leaving, so I have decided to see you off," Kazekiri said.

"Really?"

"Yes, really! I wouldn't be here if it wasn't to see you off, you know!"

"Ah ha. Very true. Thank you, Kiri-Kiri. This really means a lot to me."

"I wish you would stop calling me that…"

Alex wouldn't lie and say that Kazekiri coming to see him off didn't warm his heart. They had only recently become friends, thanks to a few chance encounters, but Alex now considered her to be one of the most important people in his life. She had also really helped him out the other day when he'd been suffering from indecision on what to do about Gabrielle.

Kazekiri twirled a strand of long, flaxen hair between her fingers. Alex had always thought she had gorgeous hair. They contrasted with her dark eyes, but complimented her fair skin. She wore the blue unitard with purple edgings that marked her as a part-time employee of the Mars Police Department. Alex tried not to let his eyes be drawn to the way the unitard strained against her breasts, or how it conformed to her thin waist and hips… or how lovely her thighs looked in blue.

It was difficult.

At least I got a handle on keeping those voices out of my head.

The voices, which he had taken to calling Voice Number One and Voice Number Two, had been silent for a while now. Alex didn't actually know if this was his doing, or if there might have been another reason.

"Promise me you'll take care of yourself out there," Kazekiri said. "There's no telling what sort of trouble you'll run into."

Alex grinned. "I'll do my best."

Nodding, Kazekiri looked away, and Alex wondered if he'd said something wrong, but then Karen stepped in front of him. She was giving him a slightly amused look. Her lips were quirked into a grin.

"I had no idea you and Kazekiri got along so well."

"I-it's not that we get along!" Kazekiri shouted. "It's just… we're friends, so I…"

"Right. Right. Friends." Karen chuckled a bit, and Kazekiri quickly turned her head. "Anyway, Alex. I can't really stop you from going, but I want you to promise me that you'll try not to be as reckless as you usually are."

Alex wanted to tell her that he never acted recklessly, but that would be a lie. After having caused several hundred million credits worth of property damage during routine missions as a cadet, he knew this to be true.

"I promise."

"That's all I can ask for." Karen nodded, and then she surprised him by grabbing his head and pulling it into her chest. Alex was about to panic as his nose became buried in the valley of her breasts. Her next words stopped him. "Take care of yourself. I want you to come back safe and sound."

Alex couldn't speak, but the words served to calm him down. He looked up and nodded. Karen smiled before letting him go.

"I will." Alex turned to Gabrielle and Nyx. "You two ready?"

"Yes!" Gabrielle said, while Nyx merely nodded.

"Princess Gabrielle! Please be safe!" Azazel was crying as Alex, Gabrielle, and Nyx wandered up the small boarding ran in the back. "Please don't do anything reckless! And please don't take apart the prince's spaceships! A-and always brush your teeth!! Oh! Why do I feel like a parent watching his daughter go away on her honeymoon!! My wives don't even have kids!"

"Put a sock in it, Azazel!" Karen snapped. "Wait. Did you just say wives?"

The last thing Alex saw before the boarding ramp was sealed shut was Karen grabbing Azazel by the ear.

Turning to view the shuttle's interior, Alex wondered if maybe he had been expecting more, because he was honestly disappointed with how plane it looked. There were several seats located on either side of the shuttle, and there was a doorway that led into what he guessed was the cockpit. However, nothing really stood out. It looked like any number of small shuttles that he'd seen.

"Prince Arthur," Gwenn said as she stepped out from the cockpit. "We are ready to launch."

Gwenn was an older woman with light brown hair tied into a severe bun. The hem of her black and purple dress swished around her legs as stopped before them, hands clasped in front of her. Numerous frills outlined the dress. It made her look a lot like a classic maid. Meanwhile, the rimless glasses that she wore gave her a studious appearance.

"All right." Prince Arthur turned to them. "You three had better get yourselves strapped in."

"Okay!" Gabrielle grabbed Nyx's hand and pulled her to one of the chairs.

Alex looked dubious. "Can this thing really take us all the way to Camelot?"

"Of course not," Prince Arthur said with a grin. "This shuttle is just what we used to talk here. It's not fit for space travel. However, it will at least take us back to my flagship."

"Flagship?"

Prince Arthur said nothing more, and Alex, Gabrielle, and Nyx strapped into their seats, while the prince entered the cockpit with Gwenn. Minutes later, the shuttle rumbled. Alex felt his stomach drop and his throat tighten, but having already experienced this sensation once before, he was more prepared for it this time.

There were several viewports that they could look out of. Small bubbles that offered a little window to the outside world. Through it, Alex watched as the ship spun around, orienting itself toward the exit. Then the world outside moved by faster before, with a sudden start, the interior was gone and the barren landscape of Mars opened up before them. However, even that eventually disappeared to be replaced by the inky blackness of space.

"Are you nervous?" Nyx asked Alex.

He smiled at her. "I'm better now than I was during the rescue operation last week."

"Don't worry!" Gabrielle beamed at them both. "If you get space sickness, I can always use Mr. Healer to make you better!"

"Does it work?" asked Nyx before Alex could accept her offer.

"Well… there are still a few bugs that I need to work out."

"Then no thanks."

"Aw!"

A few minutes later, as the ship was sailing through the void of space, Alex finally saw something in one of the viewports. It was just a tiny speck at first. However, it became larger as time passed. Soon, Alex realized what it was. A ship. No, a massive ship.

At a glance, Alex could only judge it to be about maybe a kilometer in length. Silver. Gleaming in the darkness of space. Reminiscent to a sword, the ship seemed almost flat—relatively speaking. While one end converged into a point, the other became what looked almost like a hilt. The closer they got, the more details Alex could pick out. He could see no fuselage, but there were numerous blinking lights flashing across its surface. Several small potholes on the surface made him wonder if perhaps they were gun ports.

"What is that?" asked Alex.

"That's a blade-class battleship," Gabrielle said, squinting. "This one is bigger than the ones I've seen. I guess it's because this is Arty's flagship."

"Blade-class battleships are some of the largest in the galaxy," Nyx added.

"Hm!" Gabrielle nodded. "They combine a perfect balance of attack and defense. There are over one hundred and twenty-five laser batteries and seventy-five turrets. They also use the most recent angelisian energy shield, which is powered by a miniature pulse generator. One blade-class battleship is equal to about ten destroyer-class cruisers."

"You seem to know a lot about this ship," Alex said.

"I should," Gabrielle said. "After all, I'm the one who built the first prototype."

"What?"

Their shuttle soon reached a blue energy field, which is straight through. Alex had never seen anything like that.

It's probably a shield designed to keep the atmosphere from leaking out of the ship.

They didn't have anything like that on Mars, or in the rest of his solar system, but that didn't mean it was impossible. Most of the galaxy was light years ahead of them.

Alex's toes tingled when the shuttle set down in the docking bay. Prince Arthur and Gwenn came back into the cargo hold. While Gwenn lowered the boarding ramp, Prince Arthur clapped his hands as Alex, Gabrielle, and Nyx unhooked themselves from the crash webbing.

"Be sure to watch your step, especially you, Alexander Ryker," Prince Arthur said. "It's pretty obvious to me that you don't have much experience with being in space. Gravity is simulated on this ship, so it will probably feel a lot different than what you are used to."

"Don't worry about me," Alex said, standing up and frowning.

Prince Arthur grinned. "In that case, just follow us."

As they stepped out of the shuttle, the first thing Alex realized was that gravity really did feel different. It wasn't huge. He wasn't floating up to the ceiling. However, it was enough to affect his balance, and he almost stumbled before correcting himself.

The docking bay was huge, far bigger than the one on Mars. Alex couldn't judge its size at a mere glance, but there were nearly two hundred ships located inside of this. It was more of a hanger bay than a docking bay. Most of the ships looked like fighters, but there were a few shuttles like the one they'd flown on. Dock workers were moving around the hanger, connecting fuel lines or performing maintenance.

There were also a number of droids. Most of them were squat little things. They looked like barrels on wheels. However, walking among some of them were bipedal robots, though these, unlike Madison, actually looked like robots. Light reflected off their silver frames. They had green photoreceptors built inside of metal sockets. Spindly arms and legs. Thick carapaces. Alex was reminded of the droids he'd seen holopictures of from the late 2500s before the change of the new calendar.

Several people were present when Prince Arthur exited the shuttle, a group of men and women who were lined up on either side of a durasteel walkway. Black pants contrasted with white collared shirts. Everyone wore a shoulder cape that only covered one arm, and a strange black rifle was slung across their backs. They clacked a heel against the floor and saluted him.

"Welcome back, Prince Arthur!"

Prince Arthur grinned. "It's good to be back."

Alex followed behind Prince Arthur and Gwenn as they walked between the two lines of people. So, this was what being a prince was like, huh? Even nobles reveled in less pomp than this, though Alex supposed the ruler of a solar system, or soon-to-be ruler, would warrant more respect.

There was a person standing at the end of the line. Her hair descended from her back in dark girls, and eyes like obsidian gazed at Prince Arthur with a tenderness that made Alex pause. Her skin was an olive-color, lighter than Selene's but darker than Gabrielle's. A white gown covered her body, pleated and descending down to her ankles, though from the way she moved, it was clearly more functional than it looked. Unlike everyone else, who carried rifles, she had a sword strapped to her left hip and blasted on the right. Her ears were slightly pointed.

"Darling," the woman said. "I'm guessing you failed to win Princess Gabrielle over?"

Prince Arthur scratched the side of his head and sighed. "Well, it would seem as though I never stood a chance."

"I told you it wouldn't work out."

"You did."

"And now we've found ourselves in quite the predicament."

"Urk. I'm sorry."

As Prince Arthur was subtly brow-beaten by the woman, Alex sidled up to Gwenn and asked, "what's going on here?"

"Please do not concern yourself with this," Gwenn said. "They act like this all the time."

"Who is she?" asked Gabrielle, who had come up alongside him with Nyx. While Gabrielle had tilted her head, appearing curious, Nyx remained impassive.

Gwenn opened her mouth to respond, but Prince Arthur beat her to the punch.

"Please allow me to introduce her, Gwenn." He stood beside the beautiful woman, one arm around her shoulder as he smiled at Alex, Gabrielle, and Nyx. "This is Nimue, my fiancé."

"Oh…" Alex mumbled. "So, she's your fiancé. That makes… sen… se…?"

Alex trailed off as Prince Arthur's words finally penetrated his brain. He blinked several times, trying in vain to process the other boy's words. It took a while, longer than it should, but he eventually realized what the other boy had said.

He blinked once. Twice. Thrice. Alex took a deep breath. Held it and counted down from three, two, one…

"YOU MEAN TELL ME THAT YOU ARE ALREADY ENGAGED AND STILL TRIED TO MARRY GABRIELLE?!"

… and shouted in a voice so loud that everybody there had to cover their ears, lest they find themselves going def.

5

The blade-class battleship was called Excalibur. Alex's initial estimation of it being a kilometer in length was way off. At a grand total of 2.5 kilometers from aft to bow, Excalibur was one of the largest ships that he had ever seen. Were it not for the fact that it only had twenty levels, it would have been the same size as the space barge that hovered around Mars.

Alex and the others had not been given a grand tour of the facilities, but that was for a variety of reasons. First and foremost, it would take around a week to see everything. Second reason was that they had no time to a tour. The ship had already entered hyperspace. However, the biggest reason was because of Alex's anger at Prince Arthur.

"I can't believe him!" Alex ranted as he paced back and forth across the room, the soft carpet under his feet the only victim of his wrath. "That pig! That chauvinistic bastard! Who the hell does he think he is?!"

The room that he, Gabrielle, and Nyx found themselves in was beyond luxurious. Alex had visited Jasmine's house (Jameson was rarely there, so he wasn't worried about getting in an argument), so he was used to posh, but her home had absolutely nothing on this room.

Red walls covered in intricate designs, beautiful mosaics, and extravagant landscapes met his eyes no matter where he looked. Even the domed ceiling was covered in gorgeous art, revealing in the splendor of a clear blue sky that changed colors to depict morning, midday, evening, and night. A sitting room, a bar, and a lounge made up two-thirds of the room. Nyx was currently sitting on the couch as she watched a holographic monitor depicting a battle between two alien fighters. The rest of the room was made up by a bed, one covered in red velvet and large enough to fit at least six people.

Alex ignored all this as he continued to rant. "I can't believe he would try to marry Gabrielle when he's already engaged! What is his problem?!"

"I'm still not sure why you're so angry," Gabrielle said. "Is something wrong with what he did?!"

Alex whirled on her, his expression no doubt reflecting the shock that coursed through him. "What do you mean? He tried to marry you when he's already engaged!"

Gabrielle tilted her head. "Is that bad?"

"Is that…" Alex actually had to stop himself from yelling. Did this girl not understand? Prince Arthur was engaged to another woman, but he had tried to take Gabrielle as his bride! He had never heard of someone trying to do something so horrendous. "Of course it's bad! He tried to two-time!"

"I don't know what 'two-timed' means." Gabrielle shrugged, and then paused. "Oh! Does this have something to do with that polygamy thing?"

"Polygamy thing?" Alex blinked.

"Yeah!" Gabrielle nodded. "Kiri—Kazekiri and the others were saying something about how polygamy was about someone marrying more than one person."

"Yes, that is the definition of polygamy." Alex also nodded along with her.

"They said it was wrong."

"That's because it is."

"But it isn't."

Alex needed a moment to register her words. Even then, he still couldn't quite understand. "What do you mean?"

Before Gabrielle could answer, Nyx stood up from the couch and walked over to them. Her bare feet padded along the ground before she came to a standstill beside Alex, who had stopped pacing back and forth thanks to Gabrielle's words.

"Please allow me to answer this question, Princess Gabrielle," she said.

"Okay!" Gabrielle acquiesced easily enough.

Nyx nodded in acknowledgement of Gabrielle before turning her attention on Alex. She fixed him with a stare that he knew well. It was blank, seemingly dead, but Alex had gotten used to her impassive nature.

"In your solar system, monogamy is the only legally acceptable practice for marriage," she began. "However, that is not true for the rest of the galaxy. Polygamy is legally practiced across the entire galaxy. There are many men and women who have their own harems. Some, like Prince Arthur's father, have eleven wives. Even King Lucifer, Gabrielle's father, is married to three women." She paused and gave Alex a look. "You should already know this. You learned about it the other day."

Alex felt heat spring to his cheeks. "I think I became so angry when I found out Prince Arthur was already engaged that I forgot."

"I assumed as much."

"I'm sorry you two had to hear me rant like that," Alex said.

"It's okay." Gabrielle smiled at him. "You got angry on my behalf, right? That makes me really happy!"

Alex could do nothing but blush. Meanwhile, Nyx frowned at him and Gabrielle. It was just a slight one, but the fact that he could see it meant something was bothering her. He thought about asking if anything was wrong, but the door to their room slid open and Gwenn entered seconds before he could.

"Princess Gabrielle. Alexander. Nyx." The stern-looking woman nodded at each of them in turn. "It looked like you have unpacked. Would you like me to give you a quick tour of all the more important facilities on Excalibur?"

"Yes, please!" Gabrielle said before either he or Nyx could voice their own opinion.

Alex gave Nyx an amused smile. "I guess we're going on a tour."

"Indeed," Nyx said, nodding slightly.

Excalibur was not only a large vessel, but there were a number of recreational and otherwise nonstandard facilities within it. Alex didn't know what surprised him more: the fact that there was a bath within this ship, or the fact that it was unisex, meaning men and women bathed together. Gabrielle had wanted to try the baths. Fortunately, they were still on tour.

The mess hall was could hardly be considered such. It was more like an expensive restaurant that Alex normally only saw in the upper district. Crew members could eat there for free, apparently it was one of the perks for working on this ship, and all of the food was beyond divine. He, Gabrielle, and Nyx had been allowed to sample some of the food. He had no idea what they were eating, but it made him feel emasculated as a chef.

By this point in the tour, Alex would have been surprised if that was all this place had, but on top of a massively luxurious bath and restaurant, there was also a theme park, a gigantic training facility, an engineering room, and several shooting ranges. Not only did Gwenn show them the facilities, but she also let Alex see the engine room.

"This… what is this?" Alex asked as he looked through a see-through material that he did not recognize. It wasn't glassteel. It was something else. He had no idea what it was.

"That's a pulse generator," Gabrielle answered for him.

Alex looked at her. "This?"

"Yes."

"That thing?"

"Yes."

"Huh…"

What Gabrielle referred to as a pulse generator looked nothing at all like a generator—not from his perspective. To him it looked like a large floating ball that was spinning really fast inside of a room shaped like a sphere. A pulse of energy would be released every two seconds. It was a vibrant blue that washed over the room before being absorbed into what looked to Alex like cooling vents, though they were probably something else entirely.

Gabrielle had taught him about pulse generators, another one of her inventions. They were quasi-dimensional engines that generated energy by tapping into a power source not of this galaxy. According to what she told him, one pulse generator produced the same amount of energy as a star every .5 seconds. It was so ridiculous that if Alex didn't know Gabrielle, he would have never believed her.

"I give up." He pressed his forehead against the glassteel. "I have no idea how I can even compete with this kind of technology."

"Huh?"

"Never mind."

After the tour concluded, Gwenn led them back to their room, which was good because Alex didn't know where anything was. They had taken so many twists, turns, and lifts. He had gotten completely lost.

"I'll be back when it's time for dinner," Gwenn told them. "There are outfits in the drawers. Please use them to make yourselves presentable."

The door closed behind her. Alex frowned at the parting comment that Gwenn had made, but when he looked at his plain clothes and compared them with the clothing that Prince Arthur had been wearing, he could see where she was coming from. The prince had been decked to the nines. Meanwhile, he was wearing jeans, a white shirt, and a gray sweater with a hoodie. It didn't exactly mesh with the people around him.

"Hey! Look at this!" Gabrielle said as she held up an outfit, having, at some point, wandered over to the dresser. "It's an angelisian fishtail gown! I haven't seen one of these since Papa tried forcing me to wear one!"

Nyx was also next to Gabrielle. She stared at the dress like it was an enemy. "I have never seen something like this before."

"Wanna try it on?"

"Very well."

"If you two are gonna get dressed, then let me go outside," Alex called out.

"Huh? Why would you do that?" asked Gabrielle.

"Because Nyx hates perverted things," Alex said, giving Nyx an amused smile.

6

Alex did not feel comfortable in his white tuxedo, or rather, he supposed it would be more accurate to say that he felt too comfortable. The pants and undershirt were softer than velvet. They caressed his skin in ways that his normal clothing did not. It was soft—too soft. Added to it was the necktie. He'd never worn a necktie before. It felt like he was being choked.

Gabrielle and Nyx looked much more stunning than him. Gabrielle had chosen a green gown that matched her eyes and had no back, revealing her supple muscles and slender shoulder blades. Meanwhile, Nyx had chosen an all-black gown—with Gabrielle's help—which showed off her modest amount of cleavage. Oddly enough, when Alex had looked at her breasts, she had not tried to beat him for being a pervert.

Half an hour after they were dressed, Gwenn came back and escorted them to a private dining room. The carpet was dark red but inlaid with golden designs. Low lighting complimented the warm woods and lent the room a romantic atmosphere. Alex could see plenty of dinner dates happening there. That said, the room only had one table—a long table shaped like a rectangle that could seat about half a dozen people.

Prince Arthur and Nimue were already present. While the prince had changed into white silk pants, black boots, and a white, long-sleeved collared shirt with a purple doublet thrown over it, his fiancé, Nimue, was dressed in a much simpler evening gown made of shimmering purple. It complemented the slightly darker skin tone, which looked a lot more natural than those people who went to tanning salons only to come out orange.

The talking sword, Caliburn, was noticeably absent.

"I'm glad you three could make it for dinner," Nimue said as all three of them took a seat. Alex found himself sitting in between Gabrielle and Nyx. "And you, Alexander, have you calmed down?"

"Yes… erm, I apologize for my outburst." Alex could feel his face flush with shame as he looked down, unable to meet the calm gaze of this girl who couldn't be much older than him. "I was already aware that polygamy is legal in the rest of the galaxy, but when I heard that Prince Arthur was already engaged and tried to marry Gabrielle, I just sort of lost it."

"That is quite alright. Your feelings for Gabrielle must be strong indeed, and I've learned that your solar system does not allow polygamy, so I understand why you might be angry." Nimue smiled at him, and Alex's stiff shoulders involuntarily relaxed. "That said, if you insult or yell at my prince while in my presence again, I shall not hesitate to lop off your head."

Alex was nonplussed. "Erm. What?"

"Let us not be antagonistic now," Prince Arthur said. "It's dinner. That's a time for good food and pleasant conversation, not death threats."

"Yes, dear," Nimue said.

As the group all sat down, several waiters came out and presented the group with what Prince Arthur called their "first course." Alex had no idea what it was. It was definitely a type of soup, red, and slightly bubbly. When Alex tried a bite, it had a taste that he could not quantify. It wasn't bad, but it was so foreign to his taste buds that he couldn't decide whether or not he liked it. The second course consisted of crab legs from something called a Cameleon Crustacean.

"Tell me more about your situation," Nyx said as they finished eating appetizers. She had some crab on her left cheek, so Alex did what came naturally and wiped the food away with his finger.

Nyx looked away.

Huh? Did I do something wrong?

"Before we departed for hyperspace, I did manage to pick up more information about the situation in Camelot," Prince Arthur said.

Camelot was both the name of the solar system and the name of the planet that Prince Arthur ruled. Apparently, the planet was located closest to the sun, and thus was considered the "shining jewel" of the solar system, which was why they were given the same name.

"Lancelot has yet to launch an attack on Camelot, but it's only a matter of time," Prince Arthur began. "He has taken over Winchester, which is the closest planet to Camelot and is, or perhaps I should say was, controlled by Bedivere. The takeover happened quite swiftly. From my understanding, what happened couldn't even be called a battle. It happened so quick and so suddenly that even the regular citizens are unaware of what really happened."

"What about your half-brother?" Alex asked. "Is Bedivere imprisoned or…?" he trailed off because he didn't want to ask if Bedivere was dead.

Prince Arthur shook his head. "Doubtful. Bedivere is… well, I wouldn't call him a coward, but he's the type to retreat when outmatched. My guess is that he's lying low somewhere, though I've no clue where that might be. It matters not anyway. Once we get to Camelot, I'll have my men search for his whereabouts, but the more important matter is to decide what we should do about Lancelot."

"Lancelot is your brother, right?" Gabrielle tilted her head. "Couldn't you just try talking to him?"

Prince Arthur gave her a mirthless smile. "If Lancelot could be reasoned with, I doubt we'd be having this conversation."

"Your relationship with your siblings doesn't seem very good," Alex said.

"Our relationship is complicated." Prince Arthur shrugged. "At one point, all of us were rivals. Now that I'm crown prince, some of them would do anything to see me lose my place. Of course, then there are some, like Bedivere, who have never really cared and just do what they want."

"There are also some who have allied with Arthur," Nimue added. "Dinadan and Gawaiin are my husband-to-be's staunchest supporters, while Bedivere, Hectar, Percival, and Cador were firmly neutral in the matter. Bedivere will likely join us now that his planet has been taken over. However, Lancelot, Morrigan, Segwarides, and Tristan firmly opposed Arthur being named crown prince."

"What about your last sibling?" Alex asked. "Erm… what was his name again?"

"Urien," Prince Arthur said. "He's a bit of an odd one. I don't think he much cares for anything but his research. He's currently neutral, but he'll switch sides to whoever he feels can benefit him the most."

So, including Prince Arthur, there were four who would be on their side, four against them, four who were neutral, and one whose allegiance was unknown.

During their conversation, the waiters had brought out what Alex guessed was the main course. They came in pushing several silver carts with a large plate covered by a silver lid. When the plate was removed, an earthy yet mouth-watering scent wafted through the air, causing Gabrielle's stomach to gurgle. Once more, Alex didn't know what the food was, other than that it was a fish of some sort.

Each person received their own fish. It was a whole fish, too. Even the head was still attached.

"Let us shelve this discussion for another time," Arthur said. "Go ahead and dig in."

The sound of clinking plates and tableware filled the room as everyone began eating. Alex didn't want to admit that the main course was better than anything he could make, but he couldn't lie to himself. This good, unknown though it was, tasted better than any recipe in his repertoire.

I wonder if I could convince the chef who made this to part with the recipe... though I'm not sure it'd matter. I doubt any of these ingredients are available on Mars.

After the main course came desert. Well, Prince Arthur called it desert, but it was really just a cup of some type of cafa mix, or what tasted like really expensive cafa. Nimue called it 'käfē. It was basically Camelot's version of cafa, but the stuff they were drinking was modified with additives like cream, sugar, and other stuff. It tasted delicious, whatever it was.

One thing that struck Alex as they sipped 'käfē and conversed was how similar Prince Arthur and his people were to Alex's people. They came from different solar systems, were technically a different species (though they looked identical) and had many different beliefs and laws (not the least of which was polygamy, but for all that, the similarities between their two cultures was astounding. In some ways, Alex felt like he was looking at a slightly distorted reflection.

I wonder if all sentient species evolve similarly. Maybe being sentient means our thoughts are hardwired a certain way, regardless of species.

Alex had no answer to his own hypothesis. He was an inventor, not a biologist.

"Now that we've all been fed, perhaps it's time I told you what we're going to do first," Prince Arthur said. "We'll be heading to Camelot before anything else. I need to consult with my advisor, Merlin, before I make any rash decisions. I'd also like to try solving this matter through diplomacy first, so I'll send a representative to speak with Lancelot."

"What would you like us to do?" asked Alex.

"You'll remain on standby for now," Prince Arthur said. "With luck, we won't actually need you, but should the worst come, we can probably use the fact that you are engaged to Gabrielle to our advantage."

Since this was Prince Arthur's problem, Alex agreed to his proposition. His ultimate goal in all this was to help Camelot retain its peace, and also to broker a deal with Camelot so he could fulfill another promise.

Gwenn escorted him, Gabrielle, and Nyx back to their room, and the three of them got ready for bed. It wasn't until all of them were dressed in pajamas that Alex realized something he should have realized hours ago.

"Um… we're not all gonna sleep on the same bed, are we?" he asked.

"Of course we are!" Gabrielle, now decked out in cute pink pajamas, said. She had actually been going to sleep naked, but he and Nyx had put a stop to that. "You've accepted and returned my love, so that means we're engaged now! Why wouldn't we sleep together?"

Alex couldn't really argue her point. It was true, in a way, though he felt sleeping together was taking it way too fast. However, there was one life raft that he could cling to.

"But what about Nyx?" asked Alex. "I'm sure she's not comfortable sleeping in the same bed as us. I think it would be best if I take the couch. That way you two can have the bed."

"I do not mind sleeping in the same bed as you two," Nyx said suddenly.

"W-what?"

Alex gawked at Nyx, who refused to look at him. She stood with her head turned, left hand clutching her right arm, hips cocked at a very slight angle.

There was no way this could be happening. Nyx was telling him that she didn't mind sleeping in the same bed. This was a dream. It had to be a dream. Nyx always claimed that she didn't like perverted things, but sleeping with another individual, a member of the opposite sex at that, could lead to some pretty perverted things happening.

"See! Nyx agrees!" Gabrielle beamed at him as she grabbed his arm, then grabbed Nyx's arm. "Now, let's have some fun before going to bed!"

While the word "fun" invoked all kinds of erotic images, fortunately for Alex, Gabrielle was far too innocent to actually mean anything like that. It turned out that fun for her was staying up late and watching holomovies. Space, it seemed, had their own channels and forms of entertainment. Gambling was huge, so there were many shows that involved races and gladiator-style fighting.

Gabrielle's favorite show to watch was about whacky inventions that people tried to create. While Alex was actually interested in watching that with her, Nyx didn't seem to like it, so they ended up compromising by watching a holomovie about an inventor who traveled the galaxy solving mysteries.

Nyx was hooked. She seemed to enjoy the mystery aspect and kept trying to guess who the villain was. It was the first time Alex had seen her like that. Meanwhile, Gabrielle and he kept commenting on the inventions that the inventor used. Some of the stuff he had was impossible to build because it went against numerous scientific principles, but they both had fun thinking of different inventions that could accomplish the same task.

It wasn't until hours later that the three of them, beginning to feel tired, decided to crawl into bed. Alex was so exhausted his eyes barely remained open. Thinking on it, so much had happened today that Alex should have been tired long before now, but adrenaline had likely kept him from succumbing. Now that all of the

excitement had worn off, he felt like a corpse that had been reanimated through science.

He barely even felt it when his head hit the pillow. Even when Gabrielle nestled herself against him, he said nothing. He didn't even respond when Nyx curled up on his left. His eyes were drooping.

"Hey, Alex," Gabrielle said.

Darkness flooded his vision as he became unable to keep his eyes open even a second longer. Still, even though he was too tired to keep his eyes from closing, he was not so tired that he wouldn't respond to her.

"Yes, Gabby?"

"I'm really happy you told me you love me."

If he wasn't so tired, Alex was sure his face would have turned into a bonfire.

"I am, too."

"Hey, Alex?"

"Yeah?"

"I love you."

"I love you, too."

As silence descended upon the room, Alex contemplated those words and what they meant until, at long last, sleep claimed him.

CHAPTER 2

ARRIVAL

According to Gwenn, it would take a week to arrive at Camelot—the solar system, not the planet. Given that they were on a giant alien warship, one would think that Alex would be having a blast going around and looking at everything, but that was not the case.

He, Gabrielle, and Nyx were guests. However, being guests did not mean they could go wherever they pleased. Many areas were restricted to them on account of them not being personnel employed by Prince Arthur. Basically, because they were not part of the crew, they could not visit many of the places that Alex wanted to see.

The tour they had taken after boarding had apparently been the only time they were allowed to visit places like the engine room and such. Gwenn had informed them the morning after their first dinner with Prince Arthur and Nimue that they were only allowed within the theme park, the private cafeteria, and the unisex bath during certain hours of the day, which had apparently been done so they didn't mingle with the crew members.

Since there was nowhere else for them to go, he, Gabrielle, and Nyx had traveled to the theme park.

Dubbed Camelot Land—quite the original name, Alex thought sarcastically—the theme park was larger than Alex had expected. It contained numerous rides and attractions, including a number of roller coasters, a virtual reality shooting range, various food stalls, and even a haunted house. What's more, all of the buildings were designed similarly to those of a human theme park.

Once more, the similarities between their two species struck him has odd. It really did seem like every race he met had a culture similar to his own—in some aspects. In others, they were different. However, even with a race like the Jāhilīyahns, which didn't look even remotely human, there were still enough similarities that Alex felt comfortable engaging them in conversation and was able to reach an understanding.

Alex thought it was strange. Perhaps he was just being paranoid.

"Come on, Alex! Let's go! I wanna ride the roller coaster!"

Gabrielle dragged him and Nyx through the mostly deserted theme park. He only counted a handful of people. At least half of them were people who worked at the theme park. Alex remembered traveling to a theme park dome called Mars Land several years ago with his sister, and it was a lot more crowded than this, though he guessed the reason there wasn't that many people was because most of the crew was on duty.

It made having a theme park inside of a battleship seem really excessive.

Looking at Nyx, Alex gave the girl a helpless smile, which the pretty assassin returned with a mostly blank look.

Because there weren't any lines, they were able to board the roller coaster that Gabrielle wanted to ride without having to wait. They were strapped in with a locking mechanism. Then, with a low creak, the car moved.

Boy, did it move.

Having ridden roller coasters before, Alex had expected it to start off with a slow crawl as it moved up a large hill to the first peak. However, it seemed technology in these theme parks were also quite a bit more advanced than human technology. The coaster shot off without so much as a warning. Alex, finding himself completely unprepared for the sudden acceleration, screamed like a little girl.

Surprisingly enough, no one screamed more than Nyx did. Through the tears streaming from his eyes as they went through numerous stomach-turning twists, harrowing turns, and gravity defying loops, Alex could see Nyx, her mouth open wide and eyes bulging as she screamed her head off.

"WHAT IS THIS?! THIS IS TERRIBLE! I HATE THIS! I'M GETTING OFF!!"

It was probably a good thing that Nyx could not concentrate Because it looked like she was trying to transmute the car. Alex had no idea what she'd transmute it to, but really, transmuting anything would likely cause them to enter an even more precarious situation.

Unlike him and Nyx, Gabrielle's joyful laughter rang through the air. It was enough to almost make him resentful.

When the ride stopped, it was all Nyx could do to keep from vomiting. She stumbled out of the car, her face puke green, and then slumped onto the ground as though she was about to be sick. Alex didn't feel too hit himself, but he was faring much better.

"Come on." He grunted as he grabbed her arm, slung it over his shoulder, and pulled her up. Nyx leaned into him, knees wobbling. He grunted again as he took another step forward. "Let's get you somewhere you can rest."

Fortunately, this place was like any other theme park, so there were tons of benches to sit down and relax at. Alex found one such bench and placed Nyx on it. The pretty assassin, who wasn't looking quite as pretty right then, leaned her head back and closed her eyes. She shuddered every few seconds. Alex, wanting to help her somehow, stood in front of her and gently rubbed her shoulders.

"Are you okay, Nyx?" asked Gabrielle. "Did you not like the right?"

"No, Princess Gabrielle," Nyx's voice was slurred, "I did not like going on that... urp.. Ride!"

Nyx suddenly lurched forward and vomited... right onto Alex's shirt.

Alex stared in horror at the bits of food, liquid, and other stuff that was now splattered all over his shirt. The feel of Nyx's vomit was disgusting, sticky and gross. Worse, the scent invaded his nose and made him want to vomit now.

"Ohh…" Gabrielle watched on, eyes wide with surprise. "That looks bad."

Alex wanted to say something sarcastic, but he didn't want to hurt Gabrielle with his biting tongue.

"Gabby, got anything that can clean this off?" he asked.

"Yes!" Gabrielle swiped her finger through the air, opening a rift in front of her. It looked like the fabrics of reality were being torn apart. What she pulled out looked innocuous enough. It reminded Alex of a very small vacuum. "This is Mr. Clean! He'll clean that puke right away!"

Alex grimaced at the word puke, but Gabrielle didn't seem to pay attention as she pressed a button on the vacuum, which whirred to life with a slight rumble. She pressed the edge of Mr. Clean to his shirt. While doing that, she explained how this thing worked.

"This is doesn't just clean something; it removes stuff by erasing it at the molecular level, ensuring that it cleans something perfectly."

"I haven't seen this invention before," Alex muttered.

"That's because I never had a chance to use until—whoops!"

Alex would have wondered what Gabrielle meant when she said "whoops!", but a sudden breeziness caught him by surprise. He looked down. His pants, shirt, and shoes were now gone. It looked like Mr. Clean had erased more than merely the vomit.

He looked back up at Gabrielle and Nyx. They were staring at him, one with a blank face that was just a little red, and the other

with open curiosity. In fact, Gabrielle's eyes were staring at what was between his legs.

He looked down again. He was completely exposed. Alex took a deep breath, counted down to ten in his head, and then opened his mouth…

… and screamed so loud that it echoed across the entire theme park.

1

Alex ended up borrowing a spare uniform from one of the workers at the theme park, which had been an even more embarrassing situation than being naked. Because he was, well, not clothed, he'd been forced to rely on Gabrielle for aid. Unfortunately, this meant allowing Gabrielle to tell the worker what had happened to him, in detail, oh so excruciating detail.

By the end of it, Alex wasn't sure whose face as redder: His or the poor guy lending him a spare change of clothes?

His. Definitely his.

After getting back to their room, changing into both his crisis suit, which he hadn't worn to the theme park, pants, a shirt, and a gray jacket with a hood, Alex headed over to the baths. Even though Mr. Clean really had managed to erase every molecule of vomit, he still felt gross. He wanted to wash the feel away with a nice bath.

Fortunately, he was at one of the times where Gwenn had designated that he and the others could take a bath.

After getting changed in the massive changing room, Alex wandered into the even more massive baths. Grander than even Mars Homespring Resort, the baths consisted of not one but multiple truly opulent baths. Some of them were more like pools. They expanded for kilometers. A few were designed to look natural, reminiscent of a pond, or an ocean shore, or a lake. One even looked like a volcano, though fortunately the stuff in it was not actual lava. There were waterfalls interspersed at various pools. The shower stalls were to his left.

It was empty. There were apparently designated times when the baths were available. Gwenn told him they were making an exception and leaving these times open for them out of consideration for Gabrielle's position as princess of the Angelisian Empire.

Alex cleaned himself with the shower stalls and slowly waded into the nearest bath. It was just a regular hot spring bath, a tub about ten meters wide, circular, and with a large step around the edge for him to sit on. Sighing in content, Alex leaned his head back and closed his eyes.

The doors slid open. Alex blinked. Then a voice spoke up.

"Wow! Look at how big this place is!"

Alex froze on the outside, though on the inside, his mind was a riot of activity.

I know I shouldn't be surprised, but for the love of Mars, does she really have to follow me into the baths?!

"What do you think, Nyx? Isn't this incredible?!"

"… It is big," said another voice, one that made Alex's blood run cold.

"I wonder where Alex is?"

Two sets of footsteps came closer. Alex dared not turn his head in fear of what he would see.

"Hehe, it seems your concentration is slipping," Voice Number One said, sounding happy that it was now free.

"Please remain calm, Alexander," Voice Number Two popped into his head next. *"I know it is difficult to control your desires, but you should not let your fear control you. That will only make things worse."*

"What kind of advice is that?"

"It is sound advice."

"It's the dumbest advice I have ever heard, and I've heard lots of bad advice."

"Oh? And what kind of advice would you give him?"

"Listen up, brat! Those two babes are coming your way. The moment they spot you, jump them and fuck them like a dog in heat."

Alex sighed. *Do you two ever shut up?*

"Not unless you can make us."

Before Alex could respond to that, the sound of feet padding against tiles suddenly stopped. He froze. A shiver ran down his spin. He was sitting at the edge of the pool, and it was literally the one closest to the entrance, so there was no way they couldn't not have already seen him.

Sure enough, Gabrielle called out to him seconds later.

"Alex! I knew you'd be in here!"

Alex was contemplating whether or not he should turn around when, without warning, a dark shadow flashed overhead seconds before an object hit the water with a splash.

Water sprayed in Alex's face. He closed his eyes to avoid having water blasting them. When he opened them again, it was to find a naked Gabrielle standing in front of him, shaking water out of her hair like a dog.

"Hot damn! Look at those titties bouncing!"

"Gabrielle is quite the beauty. That said, you should be more respectful."

"You say that, buy you were also looking at her bazangas."

"…"

Alex wanted to sigh, but he couldn't, not because of the irritating voices, but because of Gabrielle—her breasts, to be more precise. Outside of just having a lot of volume, they were also quite, well, bouncy. Every time she moved, every time she shook her head, every time she did anything, they jiggled. It made thinking about anything besides how much he wanted to kiss those succulent —

"Hehehehe…"

Alex stopped himself before he could travel down that path. This was the whole reason he had been so reticent about dating Gabrielle in the first place. Now that he had committed to this path, now that he had confessed, there was no going back, so he would need to master himself if he wanted to make Gabrielle happy.

"Alex! Alex!"

Upon hearing Gabrielle's voice, Alex opened his eyes—

"Gya!"

—to find another pair of eyes right in his face! Bright green and vibrant like a pair of binary stars, Gabrielle's eyes were literally centimeters from him. Her nose was so close it was touching his.

He jerked his head back, but he was already leaning against the lip of the tub. Stars swam across his vision as pain wracked the back of his head. He blinked several times to rid himself of the dizziness, and when he did, Gabrielle was sitting right next to him, so close that he could feel her naked thigh touching his.

"Hee-hee! I knew you would be in the bath!"

Alex didn't dare look at Gabrielle as he tried to relax. It was okay. Gabrielle did this all the time. He just needed to calm down and take things in stride.

"Well, I did say I was going to the bath," he sighed. "I also told you not to follow me."

"You did, but taking a bath alone is boring, so I thought it would be better if we went in with you."

"We?" Alex asked before remembering that Gabrielle hadn't been alone. Nyx had entered the bath with her.

A sudden splash at his side made Alex instinctively turn his head. Nyx was sitting there. Unlike Gabrielle, who hadn't bothered to cover herself, Nyx held a towel in front of her. He could still see her side breasts, which were tantalizing in their own right, but he couldn't see anything else.

When he saw her looking at him, Alex realized that he had been staring and looked away.

"I'm sorry," he apologized.

"Don't be." A strange sound like several pebbles hitting the water resounded beside him. He assumed Nyx was shaking her head. "I came in here of my own volition. I… don't mind being in here with you."

"Uh… uh huh…"

Alex had no idea what to say.

"I know what you could say. Nice rac—doof!"

"You do realize that every time you speak crassly, I'm just going to hit you right?"

"Hmph!"

"Isn't this nice?" asked Gabrielle. Alex would have silently thanked her from taking his mind off the voices inside his head, but she was leaning against him, and her breasts were pressing against his chest. "Taking a bath with others is definitely more fun than taking one alone."

"I'm not sure why you two couldn't have just taken a bath after I was done," Alex said.

"Silly." Gabrielle giggled at him as though he'd said something inconceivably funny. "Then you wouldn't have anyone to take a bath with."

"What flawless logic."

"She does make a good point."

Since when did you two start agreeing?

"I guess that's true," he said.

Gabrielle broad, self-satisfied smile was quite possibly one of the cutest things in this galaxy. "Tee-hee!"

Alex eventually settled down. He wouldn't say he was comfortable, merely that it became easier to not lose himself with two naked girls in his presence.

Gabrielle eventually couldn't sit still and started swimming around the pool. Considering how comfortable she appeared doing so, he imagined the baths in her father's palace were a lot like this.

While Gabrielle swam about, Nyx remained sitting by his side, not saying a word. Their thighs were touching. Alex felt like he should have been nervous being so close to such a pretty girl, one who could kill him at the drop of a hat, but he was strangely placid. Perhaps all of his worry simply disappeared thanks to the absurdity of his situation.

Unfortunately, as the door slid open again, and another voice spoke up, Alex realized that the situation had just become a whole lot worse.

"I thought I'd find you three here," Prince Arthur said as the sound of feet padding into the room caused Caspian's ears to prickle. There wasn't just one set of footsteps. There were two. "Gwenn told me you three would be in here."

Alex still hadn't turned around, mostly because he wasn't sure what he would see. A naked Prince Arthur walking up to them? He was with someone. Prince Arthur and Nimue? Alex dreaded to think about what he might find.

Beside him, Nyx stiffened as though her body had been paralyzed.

Unlike him and Nyx, Gabrielle stopped swimming around and stood up, smiling that innocent smile as she waved at Prince Arthur.

"Arty! Nimue! I didn't know you were joining us!"

So the other person is Nimue.

"We were originally going to use the private hot spring until Gwenn informed us that the three of you were in here," Nimue said as two soft splashes echoed. Out of his peripheral vision, Alex saw both Prince Arthur and Nimue wading into the water. They both had a towel covering their naughty bits, thank Mars.

"Does everyone in space have no modesty?" Alex asked in a mumble so soft no one could hear it.

"Modesty is not something people are particularly bothered by." Except for Nyx, who sat right beside him.

"I should have guessed that." Alex rubbed his face. Meanwhile, Nimue was traveling over to Gabrielle, while Prince Arthur was heading in his direction. "What about you?"

"I… do not like people looking at me while I'm naked," Nyx said quietly.

"Then why the fuck did she get in the bath when she knew you were already taking one?"

While crass, Voice Number One made a good point, so Alex asked the question. Nyx, upon hearing it, turned her head. Alex thought he might have said the wrong thing, but then she spoke in a voice so soft he almost missed it.

"It's because… I don't mind if you see me."

Huh…

As Alex tried to process these words, Prince Arthur had finally reached them. He seemed completely at ease with everyone's nakedness. Alex wondered what kind of self-confidence it took to be that unbothered, but then, Nyx had informed him that most people across the galaxy didn't share his, or indeed the rest of his solar system's, hesitance with nudity. Maybe this was just how everyone was.

Perhaps if he had been just a little quicker on the uptake, he would have noticed Nyx's shoulders shaking as Prince Arthur spoke with him. Maybe if he hadn't been so busy trying to keep his own head, he would have seen Nyx lose hers. But he didn't.

"Don't… COME ANY CLOSER!"

And so, when Nyx slammed her hands into the water and transmuted it to create a massive hand that rose high above their heads, all he could do was gawk with everyone else.

"I hate… PERVERTED THINGS!!!"

Just like that, he, Prince Arthur, Gabrielle, and Nimue were crushed beneath several tons of water.

2

They came out of hyperspace several hours after the bathroom incident. Alex still felt a tad waterlogged, but he wasn't anywhere close to the shape Prince Arthur, who had been the recipient of Nyx's giant transmuted water hand, was in.

In either event, Alex was dressed once again in his jeans, a shirt, and hoody. His invisible crisis suit was underneath. Nyx was also back in her black dress, and Gabrielle wore a white skirt, blue shirt, and sandals. Like Alex, she was wearing a translucent crisis suit.

Coming out of hyperspace was apparently a big deal. As Caspian stood on the massive bridge to the Excalibur, he looked over the many people sitting at consoles, checking various systems and making sure everything was in working order. The bridge, which consisted of the command chair that Prince Arthur sat on, overlooked the workstations, so Caspian, who stood near the railing with Nyx and Gabrielle, had a perfect view of everything.

The viewport ahead of them revealed the splendors of hyperspace; Alex had never seen anything quite like it. Streaks of dazzling light passed by his eyes. According to Gabrielle, these were the many numerous stars that they were shooting by at speeds that exceeded light.

A sudden ping made Alex tilt his head. A voice spoke over a speaker seconds later.

"All hands! We are now exiting hyperspace. All hands! We are now exiting hyperspace in three. Two. One."

Alex didn't even feel when they exited from hyperspace. All he knew was that the lines before his eyes, dazzling streaks of red, blue, and yellow, suddenly blurred, slowed, and became pinpoint pricks within the viewport. Stars. A sea of stars scattered across a canvas of velvet took up more than one-fourth of the viewport, and down below, just barely visible, was a small dot colored blue, green, and white. A planet.

That must be Camelot.

There were flashes of light surrounding the planet.

"Prince Arthur!" Someone at a station called from down below. "We've emerged safely from hyperspace! However, we're picking up short bursts of energy around Camelot!"

"It's laser fire!" Another aide, this one sitting at a communication station. "Camelot is under being attacked by our own forces!"

Prince Arthur frowned as he commanded. "Show me what's happening outside! Zoom into quadrant six!"

A holographic display suddenly appeared over the viewport. It showed Camelot, a planet that didn't look too dissimilar to Earth. Flashes and streaks of light surrounded one section of the planet. It was those flashes that the display suddenly zoomed in on.

Alex narrowed his eyes. "Those are…"

"The ones that look like arrows are our fighters," Prince Arthur said. "They're arrow-class fighters, used for hit and run battles. Very agile. They're great for attacking large targets and chipping away at their shields. The big frigates that look like giant ovals are Pendragon-class battleships. They're our solar system's heavy hitters."

Just as Prince Arthur described, there were numerous small craft darting to and fro, attacking the larger ships, the Pendragon-class battleships, in squadrons of six. Meanwhile, the larger Pendragon-class ships were battering each other from a distance. It was a chaotic throng. Since all of the ships looked the same, he had no idea who was on whose side. Far away from the battle proper, another ship sat. Shaped like a sword, it could only be a blade-class battleship.

"I want a status report!" Prince Arthur barked.

One of the aides down below answered him. "It looks like Tristan is attack Camelot, sir! All attempts at communication have been denied!"

"I see." Prince Arthur narrowed his eyes. "Then it's just as we feared."

He looked at Nimue, standing on his left. She caught his gaze and nodded. Alex had no idea what was going on between them, but as Prince Arthur stood up and left, Nimue sat down and began barking commands like an experienced commander.

"All hands, to your battle stations! Switch our targeting information! Change all vessels with an ISS transponder attached to the Clarent into hostiles! Charge ion cannons! Target sector alpha-zeta-six-six-nine! Aim to scatter their formation!"

All of the men and women below dutifully continued to work, some calling off readiness, others giving status updates. Everyone had a purpose, and they diligently worked to fulfill that purpose. There was not an ounce of confusion.

Alex felt differently.

He stood on the bridge, gazing at everyone with his two companions, looking at all of the people as they worked without an ounce of fear, and he wondered if he could even do anything in this situation. This was not a situation that he'd ever been in. He was in completely over his head, with not a single idea of what should do, or even what he could do.

Could he really help Prince Arthur?

The holographic display changed, with some of the vessels being displayed getting highlighted and red, while the rest became blue. That must have been their system to designate friendlies from hostiles.

"Weapons at the ready! They're on target!"

As the announcement came over them, Nimue gave a grim smile. "Fire!"

Curving around the ship as if gravity was somehow pulling them in, nearly three dozen beams of condensed energy flew forward. Alex realized that his own vision was skewed. The beams weren't curving. He was simply seeing it that way.

All of the beams, condensed discharges of ion energy, sailed into the attacking fleets formation. Several of the Pendragon-class warships were struck. From the holographic display, Alex could see the energy splash against the shields, and then skitter across the shields, which flickered blue for several seconds.

"The enemy is aware of our presence," an aide announced. "One contingent of arrow-class fighters is breaking off and heading our way."

"Leave them to Arthur and his contingent," Nimue said. "Prepare to fire again. This time, target sector Alpha nine-nine-six-D."

The orders were given once again, calm and focused, and Alex found himself admiring Nimue's poise. They had just exited hyperspace to discover that Tristan, one of Prince Arthur's half-siblings, was attacking Camelot, but rather than panic and let her fiancé do all the thing, she had taken command of the ship and was issuing orders with a calm that Alex didn't think he could imitate. It was impressive, to say the least.

"Hmm… it looks like a hole has opened in the enemy formation."

"A hole? Where is… oh, near the tip of their formation on the upper-left quadrant."

"Yep. Hey, brat! Have that olive-skinned bitch fire her ion cannons there!"

Alex resented being called a brat, but he really wasn't in the mood to get into an argument. He waited for a moment to see if Nimue would realize the hole. However, she kept giving commands, ignoring the small gap that had opened in the enemy formation, which either meant she hadn't seen it, or she had and was ignoring it.

"Excuse me," Alex said, walking up to Nimue. Gabrielle and Nyx trailed behind him.

"I apologize for being gruff, but I am quite busy right now," Nimue said. "If you do not shut up, I'll toss all of you back into your room. So, if you'd please—"

"There's a gap in their formation," Alex said, silencing Nimue. "Sector four-four-beta-omega."

Nimue frowned at him, then frowned at the screen, eyes narrowing as she studied the holographic display. The expression cleared. She looked back at him, her eyes suddenly appraising. Alex wasn't sure he appreciated that look.

She pressed a button on the command chair and said, "Arthur, dear, there's a gap in their formation at sector four-four-beta-omega."

"Got it," Prince Arthur's voice said. "We're launching now. I'll take some of my men and we'll drive straight through their formation!"

Even as he spoke, several arrow-shaped ships streaked through the viewport. The holographic display zoomed in on the contingent of arrow-class fighters. Alex watched as around three dozen of the fighter's broke formation and traveled for the two battling fleets, while the rest of the contingent clashed with the other arrow-class fighters.

Alex wished he knew more about ship-to-ship warfare. He had studied it during his time at the academy, but studying up on tactics was one thing, while actually seeing a battle unfold before his eyes was quite another.

"Nimy," Gabrielle said suddenly. "If you wait until Arty widens the gap in the enemy's defense, then fire your ion at alpha-zeta-four-three-nine-nine in exactly ten seconds, you'll be able to break apart the enemy formation."

Alex blinked. Nyx blinked. Nimue studied Gabrielle with uncanny interest.

"What makes you think that will happen?"

"Look at how their formation is moving." Gabrielle pointed to several spots where the movements of their ships were out of sync with the rest of the fleet. It looked like they were splintering. "If you look closely, you'll see that their formation isn't actually breaking apart. They're converging on a new location to reclaim the initiative."

"And that new location will be alpha-zeta-four-three-nine-nine?" Nimue asked.

Gabrielle shook her head. "No, it will be omega-omega-six-BB-six. However…" Here, Gabrielle pointed at the enemy blade-class battleship, no doubt the enemy flagship. "… The flagship will move to that location once Arty hits the hole in their defense. It will have to if they want to compensate for the new problem."

"I see," Nimue murmured as she cupped her chin. "Yes, they would definitely have to do that." She pressed a button on her command chair. "On my command, fire ion cannons at alpha-zeta-four-three-nine-nine!"

Nimue received a chorus of affirmatives. Alex watched what was happening on the screen. Prince Arthur's group had flown into the gap and let loose with a payload of some form of explosive. It wasn't one of flames. Alex noticed the tell-tale signs of ion discharges.

Ion was short for ionized particles, a form of electronic discharges that disrupted the energy fields used to power many forms of technology. Ion storms were a huge problem on Mars because they could even short out the lightwave barriers. It looked like the ion cannon operated under the same principles, taking the ionized particles, condensing it into a beam, and firing it off.

Alex realized something as he watched the blade-class battleship begin to move exactly where Gabrielle had said it would.

If our solar system was attacked by anyone else in this galaxy, we wouldn't stand a chance.

It was a hard truth to accept, but in light of the evidence staring him in the face, he couldn't accept anything else.

He had already known that they were technologically behind the rest of the galaxy. Gabrielle's inventions proved that. However, a part of him had believed that Gabrielle, and Angelisia, were an exception. He had assumed the technological advantage that other solar systems had would be small.

Alex had been wrong.

While he had been standing stock-still in shock, the blade-class battleship was reaching the quadrant of space that Gabrielle had predicted. Nimue, staring intently at the holographic display, counted under her breath. Then…

"Fire all ion cannons!"

Alex had no idea how many ion cannons this ship had, but it must have been many, for the number of streaking beams that tore through space were so numerous it formed a tunnel around their battleship.

The ion cannons slammed into the enemy blade-class battleship. Come to think of it, what exactly was that battleship's name? As the beams of energy crashed into the shield, they splashed against it like water before skittering across the surface.

Those ion cannons must have been powerful. That, or there had been so many that the shields couldn't withstand the barrage. The blue outline surrounding the battleship flickered several times. Sparks skittered across the surface. Then, almost like an android shutting down to recharge, the shield and even the ship itself became silent.

"The Clarent has gone silent," an aide said. "All systems have been shut down."

"Excellent," Nimue said. "Prepare a boarding party to storm their Clarent and take everyone there into custody."

Alex remained standing alongside Nyx and Gabrielle, the three of them now forgotten, as Nimue issued commands to her crew. Outside of the viewport, the battle continued. However, it was clear from how the enemy ships were dispersing that the battle was already over.

"Hmm… how intriguing…"

What is?

"That angel bitch is a talented commander. She was able to look at the entire battle and accurately predict exactly what would happen as though she were clairvoyant."

"She must have gone through intensive training to be capable of predicting what would happen in a battle almost a full minute in advance."

Alex glanced at Gabrielle, who was studying the holographic display with the same pouty face she used when inventing. There was nothing different about her now. Her countenance was the same she always had.

And that's when it hit him.

They were in the middle of a battle, and Gabrielle was just as calm now as she always was. Thinking on it, she had always been like this. When Shii-rya had kidnapped Selene, when the

Jāhilīyahns had attacked them, and even more recently when MacArt had kidnapped her, Gabrielle had never displayed even an ounce of fear. No, it was more than that. It was like she had no sense of danger.

Alex was beginning to realize that he knew very little about Gabrielle.

3

It took about an hour for everything to settle down. With Prince Arthur back in command, they hooked up with the fleet protecting Camelot, and then began rounding up all of the forces that had attacked. While many of the forces were able to flee, there were quite a few that had been grounded thanks to the ion cannons. The enemy flagship, the Clarent, was one such vessel that had to be thoroughly searched with a boarding party.

Alex and Nyx were part of that boarding party; Nyx was a well-known assassin, so it was obvious they would ask her, and she had vouched for Alex's skills, so they were allowing him to go as well.

He was grateful to Nyx. Really. Were it not for her, he would have been left with nothing but his own thoughts and the voices inside of his head.

The boarding party consisted of a dozen individuals, a mixture of men and women wearing skintight military uniforms with armor. They looked like a variation of Gabrielle's crisis suits. The color scheme of white and black supposedly signified their status as a special forces' unit.

As Alex sat beside Nyx in the boarding shuttle that would take them to the Clarent, he glanced at the individuals around them. Silver breastplates shone in the light as if freshly polished. Greaves of the same color clicked together as the soldiers tapped their boots against the ground. Everyone was carrying rifles, silver ones that vaguely reminded him of assault rifles, but were shorter and more streamlined. Only the captain, a tall woman with russet hair and a scar running across her left eye, had something different—a blaster pistol, she had called it.

The ship was already traveling toward the Clarent. There were no viewports in this boarding shuttle, so he couldn't see the outside. However, according to the pilot, the Clarent was still unresponsive.

"Alex," Nyx said suddenly.

"Hm? Yes?"

"I've been thinking about your powers," Nyx began, "and I've noticed that it takes a while for you to change weapons. What's more, you can't use your Aura of Creation for anything other than weapons and shields."

Alex nodded. Had this been anyone else, he would have cried at how she pointed out his deficiencies, but this was Nyx. If she was telling him something, there was a point to it.

"I think you should try calling out the name of your attacks."

"Excuse me?"

Nyx turned her head. Half-lidded eyes the color of blood stared at him from beneath a dark fringe of hair. "Using the Aura of Creation takes a lot of focus. You have to visualize what you're using it for, and then make it happen. However, visualizing something in the middle of battle is hard. That's why I think if you call out the name of your attacks, it will make you faster at creating them."

There was some manner of truth to her words. Calling out the name of an attack would make it easier to picture in his mind. At the same time, as Alex imagined himself calling out an attack name like Titan Girl did in her holodrama, he couldn't help but blush. The idea was embarrassing.

"I… I'll think about it," Alex replied diplomatically.

"You should seriously consider it," Nyx added. "It will help."

Alex knew she was right, but still…

"Captain Tanner, we're approaching the Clarent," a voice called out over the speaker.

The fabric of Captain Tanner's unitard creaked as she shifted in her seat and pressed a button on the wall next to her. "Very good. Board through the aft cargo haul. If it's blocked by debris, blow it sky high."

"Yes, ma'am."

"You heard the man," Captain Tanner addressed the soldiers. "We're about to begin boarding the Clarent. It's time to get ready. Set weapons to stun. We're not here to kill anyone. We're splitting up into two groups. Markus Antonio, your squadron will go aft, while mine heads to the bridge. Round up everyone you see. You two…" she pointed at Alex and Nyx. "You're coming with me. I'd like to see those skills you've boasted about."

Alex and Nyx were left with no choice but to follow Captain Tanner's instructions. A slight rumble was followed by a soft hiss as the boarding ramp lowered. Everyone stood up and rushed down, moving in formation. He and Nyx followed behind the group at the captain's orders.

The docking bay they were in was smaller than the one aboard the Excalibur. According to Captain Tanner, the Clarent was an earlier model of the blade-class battleship, and thus it was about two-thirds smaller. That was still a lot of ship to search, though.

As booted feet hit the durasteel grating, Alex realized something.

There was nowhere there.

The place was empty.

"Creepy."

"Do you think they left?"

"Maybe they were never there to begin with."

Could you two please stop talking?

At the end of the docking bay was a large sliding door that led into a well-lit hallway. Their boots made soft clangs against the metal floor as the two squadrons split up. Alex and Nyx followed Captain Tanner's squad as they moved around a corner.

Click.

Alex froze. That sound... it made him think of something metallic tapping against the wall.

Click-click. Click-click-click-click.

The sound was coming from above him, so Alex looked up, and then blinked in shock as almost a dozen small robots that looked like spiders crawled toward them along the ceiling.

Alex screamed out a warning, but he couldn't really tell what he had said. He was too busy calling upon his Aura of Creation. It came to him, an ethereal blue flame that enveloped his body—until he transformed it into a pair of whips that he held in each hand.

By this point, the spiders were dropping from the ceiling on top of him and the others. Alex didn't hesitate. He lashed out with his whips. Left hand. Right hand. Each time he swung a whip, one of the spider robots blew apart. However, it seemed as though the more he destroyed, the more that appeared.

The soldiers were quick to get in on the action. They moved with a smooth precision, lining up their shots and taking the spider robots down one by one. Captain Tanner was particularly impressive as she dual wielded a pair of blaster pistols, firing simultaneously at different targets with pinpoint accuracy.

It wasn't just the soldiers who fought alongside him; Nyx was also there. She stood by Alex, a pair of armbands transmuted into two curved swords, which she swung with an elegance that was as beautiful as it was deadly.

Unlike Alex, who remained in one place, Nyx danced around the hall, her blades singing a hymn of death. Every attack sliced through a spider robot. Her blades cleaved through the metal bodies as though they were made of butter. As more spider robots descended from the ceiling and crawled along the walls, Nyx transmuted her hair, and several strands that suddenly transformed into blades joined her dance.

"Keep moving as you fight!" Captain Tanner commanded as she moved backward, firing at the swarm of tiny robots. "Don't stop! We have to make it to the bridge!"

Alex would have proposed they split up, with one group staying here to keep these spider robots at bay, while the rest moving toward the bridge. However, Captain Tanner seemed to have other ideas. She kept them together. He guessed she was wary of splitting them up in case these were a ploy to do just that.

The blade-class destroyer consisted of many halls. These halls had numerous halls perpendicular to it, creating a network that branched off in several directions. Some of the hallways had doors that led somewhere, but most of them seemed to just connect one section to another. The design also seemed much different from Prince Arthur's flagship. Alex didn't know if it was because the Excalibur was a newer model, or if it was thanks to the crown prince's personal taste.

It probably didn't matter, since, either way, Alex had no idea where they were going. All he could do was continue to fight, using his whips to cut through spider robots alongside Nyx, whose multiple swords were but mere flashes of light as she killed almost a dozen for every two that he destroyed.

Even with him and Nyx taking the rear to fight, their progress was slow. It felt like they were crawling to their destination at a snail's pace. If they didn't find some way to get rid of all these in one fell swoop, this would continue until they were overrun.

"Nyx!" Alex called out as he cut through one of the spider robots as it leapt at him. "Can you transmute the wall to block these from coming after us?"

Nyx didn't say anything, but he could see her face scrunch up in concentration. She spun around, all eight of her blades flashing out to create helicopters that diced numerous spider robots into pieces. As she came out of her spin, she nodded, cut through six more robots, and then her hair was transmuted from swords into fists. Kneeling, Nyx slammed her hands on the ground, while her hair slammed into the walls and ceiling.

It happened in less than a second. The walls, floor, and ceiling enclosed in front of Nyx like a blast door. Several spider robots made it past the transmuted doorway before it fully closed, but Alex took care of those with his whips.

Captain Tanner and the others looked at Nyx with something resembling awe. Alex understood the looks. Apparently, a transmutation on this scale was impossible for a regular person to do.

"We should keep going, right?" Alex asked Captain Tanner, snapping the woman out of her stupor.

"Right. Let's move!"

The bridge was located on the sixth floor. They were on the first. Blade-class battleships were apparently divided into positive and negative floors. The first floor was literally the one in the middle. Below that were floors -1 through -10, and above that were floors 2 through 11. It was an odd system, but Alex didn't bother telling anyone what he thought about it.

A pair of elevators stood at the end of a hallway they turned into, but, sadly, they were being guarded by another pair of robots. These were much bigger. They had four legs that were squad and had tri-pronged claws. Instead of arms, a pair of blaster rifles were attached to their shoulder joints. Heads shaped like bullets. Bright silver. Red vizored eyes. These were clearly a type of battle droid.

Several of the soldiers opened fire. However, before the bolts could reach them, a shield flared into existence around the droids. The blaster bolts splashed against the shield and were harmlessly reflected off them.

"Shit! Everyone take cover!" Captain Tanner ordered as the droids returned fire.

While the soldiers all dove back behind the wall, Alex did not. He raised his hands and projected a flat shield. The blue shield covered the entire corridor. Alex grunted as the blaster bolts slammed into the shield and dissipated harmlessly. They were a lot more powerful than weapons used by the Mars Police Force.

His arms shaking as he struggled to maintain the shield, Alex understood that he wouldn't be able to keep this up for very long. He needed to take these things out quick.

He judged the distance between him and the droids. Sixteen meters. He could make it—no, he would make it.

Releasing a loud battle cry, Alex rushed down the corridor as the droids continued to bombard his shield with a ceaseless hailstorm of blaster fire. His arms strained as he pumped more energy into the shield. Cracks appeared and were regenerated. Just a little further. He was only ten meters away more. Eight meters.

Alex stumbled, but he quickly righted himself and kept running. Five meters. Once he got closer, it felt like the blaster fire hit his shield more frequently. More and more cracks started running through it, to the point where Alex couldn't continue regenerating them and simple shoved as much energy into his shield as he could for one, final push.

One meter.

Alex released a battle cry as he covered that last meter of distance. Then he slammed into the two droids, which were shoved against the wall before being crushed between his shield and the wall.

Normally, since his shield was made of energy, it wouldn't have done anything since the shields surrounding the droids deflected energy, but Alex had used it as a purely physical attack. The shields didn't protect against that. Thus, the two droids were quickly crushed thanks to a combination of the wall and the Alex's overwhelming strength, bolstered by the Angelisian crisis suit that he wore.

Unable to maintain the shield, Alex let it shatter like so much glass as he stumbled backward. His shoulders heaved as he took several deep breaths. While his ability to create small weapons had improved, creating a shield still took way too much effort. The problem was that he had to continuously pump energy to maintain it, and then he had to feed it even more energy every time it received damage. He wondered if there was a more efficient method of projecting a shield.

"That was quite impressive," Captain Tanner said, studying Alex as he wiped sweat from his forehead. "I had not realized you were half-angelisian."

"It's not something I go around advertising," Alex said.

"Indeed." Captain Tanner addressed her men. "Let's continue moving!"

Everyone clambered into one of the elevators, which slowly ascended. Alex was in the back with Nyx. Sweat covered his forehead. He had plenty of energy left over, but the problem was dealing with the mental exhaustion that came from creating and maintaining a barrier.

"Are you okay?" asked Nyx.

Alex smiled at her. "I'll be fine."

They continued on, and while they did run into a few more battle droids, Alex was put on edge when he noticed that they hadn't run into any people. There should have been soldiers on top of droids. Where were they? How come they were only being faced with minimal opposition? Something was definitely suspicious about this. It caused the hairs on the back of Alex's neck to prickle.

The group came upon another door. It was locked. Captain Tanner gestured toward one of her men, who came up and inspected the door before pulling a plug from his vambrace and hooking it into an outlet beside the door. Alex realized that the man's vambrace had a console built into it. As some type of code flashed across the screen, the soldier began typing, until there was a soft ping and the door slid open.

Everyone hustled into the bridge, sweeping their guns across the area as they moved. Alex and Nyx followed after everyone else.

The bridge was smaller than the one on the Excalibur. It had the same general scheme, a command station overlooking the rest of the crew from above. There weren't as many stations, perhaps signifying that this ship didn't have as many guns, or maybe it was because of the smaller size. Consoles beeped and booped. In the center of the bridge was the command chair.

It was empty.

So was the rest of the bridge.

"What is going on here?" asked one of the soldiers.

"This is spooky. It's like a ghost ship," another said.

"Pipe down," Captain Tanner barked. "Keep your eyes peeled. There's no telling what's going to happen."

Alex looked at the many empty consoles as the soldiers spread out. Not all of them were empty, but the ones that weren't were being operated by droids instead of people.

The hairs on his arms prickled as well.

"Captain!" one of the soldiers called. "I've just hacked into the logbooks. It seems the Clarent was being manned by a skeleton crew that made use of the escape pods half an hour before we arrived."

Skeleton crew was a term used to describe when a vessel was operated by the barest minimum necessary to maintain its primary functions. If this had been operated on such a crew, it would explain why no one was around to oppose them. However, the fact that everyone had escaped suggested something else.

"Ma'am!" Another soldier spoke up, her voice high-pitched with fright. "This ship is set to self-destruct in several seconds!"

"WHAT?!"

Alex barely had time to grasp the situation, but the moment he heard the word "self-destruct", he reaction on instinct. He grabbed the Nyx and Captain Tanner, who were the only people next to him, and pulled them into him. His Aura of Creation activated as he called upon it. Then a large dome of blue energy surrounded him. He pumped as much energy into the dome as he could, hardening it until he could see nothing outside.

And then it happened.

To Alex, it felt like an intense pressure was pushing down on him from all sides, like he was slowly being crushed into a tiny cube by a trash compactor. As if in response to this sensation, the barrier he'd put up shrank. Alex gritted his teeth and spread his arms as he shoved more energy into the shield, as he concentrated harder on maintaining the barrier.

It hurt. This was nothing like creating that single panel shield to crush the battle droids. Every fiber in his body was screaming at him. Having his nerves boiled in lava would have hurt less than this. He wanted to cry, to scream, to curl up in a ball, but he didn't. He couldn't. Nyx and Captain Tanner were with him, and if he didn't maintain the barrier, they would all die.

"Dragon's breath," Captain Tanner murmured as the explosion surrounding their dome died down. Alex thought it was a term used by her people to describe their shock.

He understood what she was feeling.

The dome that he was keeping up was partially translucent, so they had a clear view of the outside, and what they saw was ruin. Destruction. The bridge they had been standing on was gone. Of course, it wasn't fully destroyed, but what remained were chunks and warped durasteel. About 3/4ths of the bridge had been destroyed, while the part they were still next to spun around them in lazy circles.

No one else had survived.

As he turned his head, Alex saw that none of the people who came with them were alive. A few burnt out corpses drifted by them. However, there weren't enough bodies to account for the five others. Some had probably been vaporized, or maybe they were blasted off into space.

"This is… terrible," Captain Tanner muttered as she floated within Alex's left arm.

"It looks like this ship was rigged." Nyx cocked her head to the side. "It seems like a waste to blow up a ship to get rid of a single squadron."

Captain Tanner shook her head. "I'm sure they were expecting Prince Arthur to come on board. He generally likes doing these things himself, but he deferred this position to Alexander and you. Were it not for that, Prince Arthur would have died and Lancelot could have easily claimed the throne."

"Alex," Nyx said when she realized that he wasn't speaking, "how are you holding up?"

"N-not good," he admitted with a grunt and a smile. "I… I've trapped all the oxygen I can inside with us… but maintaining an energy barrier dense enough that it doesn't escape is... more difficult than I thought..."

Alex was honestly surprised he could even speak. It was taking everything he had to maintain the barrier.

Nyx nodded and reached up, cupping his face with her soft hands. Alex wondered what she was doing. However, when she began wiping off the fluid dripping from his mouth and nose, he finally recognized the damage that erecting and maintaining this barrier was causing him.

"It looks like the mental strain is beginning to cause you damage."

Sh... shut up. I'm trying to concentrate...

"I am sorry. A task like this would have been easy if you and I weren't separated by the seal."

"You'd still have to contend with me. Even if you became one, your powers wouldn't work properly unless you subdued me."

"Yes... I suppose that is true."

"Of course, I don't expect that to ever happen. Angels like you don't have what it takes to turn me into a sub."

Can you two... shut up!

Alex was already struggling to keep the barrier up, and these voices were breaking his already fragile concentration.

"Can you contact the Excalibur?" asked Nyx.

Captain Tanner shook her head. "I have a communicator capable of doing that, but all of the wrecked equipment is interfering with it. I've turned on the transmitter, which should be sending an SOS. We'll see if that will do anything."

"Alex, how long can you maintain the barrier?" asked Nyx.

Alex shook his head. Not only did he not know, but he could no longer afford to speak. Sweat was beading along his forehead, soaking into his crisis suit, and his body was beginning to shiver from a combination of physical exhaustion and mental stress.

"You are reaching your limit," Nyx observed.

Still unable to speak, Alex could do nothing but offer her a pained smile.

"I understand. Please allow me to help."

Alex would have wondered what she meant, but he wasn't even given time to ponder the words, for barely a second had passed before Nyx leaned up and pressed her lips to his.

It took Alex several seconds to understand that Nyx was kissing him. On any other occasion, he probably would have panicked. He couldn't right then. It wasn't just because he didn't have the strength.

As Nyx kissed him, Alex felt something flow from her into him. It wasn't just her tongue, which had pushed its way inside of his mouth, but something else. Power. Energy. It rushed through his body, sending his fatigue away. The infusion of energy allowed him to concentrate harder, to increase the strength of his barrier.

All the while, Nyx's mouth never left his.

4

Help did eventually arrive in the form of an emergency shuttle, which picked the three of them up about fifteen minutes after the Clarent exploded. As the shuttle ferried them back to the Excalibur, Alex noticed that Nyx kept leaning against him. Whatever she had done to him must have exhausted her. He tried to hold her hand, but he couldn't find it for some reason.

The shuttle soon entered the Excalibur's docking bay. It set down, the systems were shut off, and he, Nyx, and Captain Tanner were allowed to exit.

"ALEX!"

"Gabrie—oof!"

Almost before he could even speak, Gabrielle slammed into him like a speeding shuttle. Alex's feet tingled as he felt a moment of weightlessness. Then he nearly swallowed his tongue when he hit the floor back first.

Groaning, he tried to regain his senses. It his head hurt. His nose had also began bleeding again. He was about to tell Gabrielle to get off him… but he didn't.

"I'm so glad… you're okay…" Gabrielle cried into his shirt. "When that ship exploded, I thought my heart was going to stop."

Alex closed his eyes, reached up, and placed a hand on the back of Gabrielle's head. Thanks to the symbiotic relationship between him and the crisis suit, he could feel Gabrielle's silky hair against his fingers, a sensation that was softer than velvet. He would have enjoyed stroking her hair were it not for the tears staining his clothes.

"I'm sorry for worrying you," he muttered.

Gabrielle shook her head. "Don't be sorry. I'm just glad you're okay."

"As am I," Prince Arthur said, making his presence known.

As a reluctant Gabrielle climbed off Alex, he stood to his feet and, ignoring the water on his shirt, looked at Prince Arthur. The crown prince bore a regretful expression. He inclined his head toward Alex.

"I apologize," he said. "I should have never let you go on this mission. Had I known that you and Nyx would incur injury, I would have gone myself."

Alex shook his head. "If you had gone instead of me, I doubt you'd be alive."

While Prince Arthur furrowed his brow at that, Captain Tanner stepped forward and saluted. "I believe Alexander is correct, Your Grace. It was only thanks to Alex that myself and Nyx survived that explosion."

"Is that so?" Prince Arthur closed his eyes, sighed, and then opened them again. "In that case, I am grateful you were here, Alexander. Without you, things could have been much worse."

Alex shrugged. "You're welcome."

Even though the battle was over, there was little time for them to loiter around. Everyone went back to the bridge as the Excalibur linked up with the fleet.

Prince Arthur took command of everything, asking for status reports on vessel conditions to a detailed oral report on how this battle started. Alex, Nyx, and Gabrielle were present. They had a first-hand accounting of what happened.

It seemed the attack came without warning. Tristan's fleet, which consisted of ten pendragon-class ships, two contingents of arrow-class fighters, and the blade-class battleship Clarent, had come in from an asteroid belt located on the opposite side of Winchester. The fleet had attacked them, taking them by surprise. It had been impossible to mount of defense at first because their transponders were all marked as friendly. This had allowed the enemy fleet to take out more than a third of their ships before they were able to change transponder codes.

Orders were given for the ships that were damaged to dock at a repair station, which apparently orbited Camelot. Rescue ships would be sent out to render aid to any ships that got destroyed and bring back survivors. Meanwhile, Prince Arthur had the Excalibur settle into orbit above Camelot. He planned to disembark, leaving Nimue in charge of maintaining the fleet.

Alex, Gabrielle, and Nyx were naturally going with him.

They used the same shuttle that had ferried them from Mars to reach Camelot. As the ship lifted off the docking bay doors and entered space, Alex stared out the viewport.

The blackness of space contrasted with the blue-green world that was their destination.

INTERLUDE

TROUBLE ON THE HOMEFRONT - PART I

Kazekiri's day started the same way it always did. She woke up, got ready for school, lectured her brother, hopped onto a shuttle, and went to Atreyu Academy. It wasn't until she arrived at the academy that the differences between her normal days and today became prominent.

Alex and Gabrielle haven't returned...

Most days, Kazekiri would always see Alex, Alice, Ariel, Gabrielle, Jasmine, Nyx, and Michelle standing by the front gate, saying their goodbyes. She would always get dragged into their conversation by Gabrielle, who would welcome her with a smile and a hug.

That didn't happen today. Alex, Gabrielle, and Nyx were gone. They were off to a solar system called Camelot, to help the crown prince of that solar system defend his title from his half-siblings… something like that. Commander Karen had told her some of what they were doing, but she had only filled her in enough so she knew that they were leaving.

Kazekiri walked past the school gate with a frown, entered the school building, and began walking toward her classroom.

Atreyu Academy was a massive building with a streamlined design. While it was shaped like a rectangle, there were numerous moving walkways trailing around the outer walls, along with elevators and jump points. Since the academy was so large, nearly 2.65 square kilometers, these transportation methods were necessary for students to reach their classes on time.

If one were to look at the academy from a bird's eye view, they would've also noticed the many gardens that dotted the interior. They were marked by sunroofs. Kazekiri used to love traveling up to the roofs and peering down at the gardens through the sunroofs from behind the fence.

It was quiet up there. No one would disturb her. She used to think peace and quiet were great.

Now she wasn't so sure.

The classroom was mostly empty when she entered; Kazekiri liked to arrive early. Only five of the thirty-seven people were present.

Walking up the first flight of steps in the tertiary seating, Kazekiri set down the bag holding all of her books and was about to sit down herself—when a pair of hands snaked around her torso and cupped her breasts.

"KYA!!!"

Kazekiri tore away from the hands and spun around. As she expected, the person standing behind her, grinning from ear to ear, was none other than Ryoko.

A dark-skinned woman that even Kazekiri would admit was alluring, Ryoko was the kind of unrepentant pervert who enjoyed groping people for kicks. Vibrant yellow eyes reminded Kazekiri of a very amused cat. The cat-like smile on the other girl's face didn't do anything to disabuse her of this notion.

"Ryoko." Kazekiri scowled. "How many times have I told you not to grab people like that?"

"Don't know." Ryoko's lips split to reveal white teeth. "I lost count."

Kazekiri resisted the desire to rub her face.

For as long as they had known each other, she and Ryoko had never gotten along. Ryoko would always cause trouble, either with her flagrant groping of both men and women, or her crass language. Kazekiri would always lecture her on why she should follow the rules and how not following the rules caused the moral backbone of their society to degrade.

Naturally, Ryoko would disagree and this caused them to fight. She and Ryoko had fought over this numerous times. Back when they were younger, Ryoko had the backing of her friends, and they had taken to harassing Kazekiri whenever they had the chance. That stopped after she became a part-time employee for the Mars Police

Force, but the damage had already been done. The two of them hated each other.

Until recently.

Over two weeks ago, Gabrielle had used one of her inventions that stuck hers and Ryoko's hands together for a full day. They had been forced to stay together at school, go home together, take a bath together, eat dinner together, and even sleep together. During this time, she and Ryoko had talked and come to something of an understanding.

Kazekiri still disapproved of what Ryoko did, but she no longer harangued her as she once had. Likewise, Ryoko didn't insult her for following the rules.

More people soon flowed into the room. Kazekiri and Ryoko conversed quietly, not really talking about any one subject, and not going near any subject that would cause either of them to start arguing. As more and more people arrived, including Selene and Serah, it became obvious that something was missing.

"So..." Ryoko looked at the seat next to Kazekiri. "... Gabrielle still isn't back yet?"

"It seems that way," Kazekiri said.

"You know where she is, don't you?"

At the looks Ryoko, Selene, and Serah gave her, Kazekiri turned her head. "I... I do, but I can't tell you. I'm sorry."

Last week, Gabrielle had stopped coming to school. She wasn't on Mars anymore, having gone into space with Alex, so of course she wouldn't be there. Kazekiri had been sworn to secrecy on the matter by Commander Karen, so she could not tell anyone about their friend's whereabouts.

"It's fine." Ryoko shrugged. "I think we get it."

"It definitely has something to do with Alex," Selene added with a nod. "I'm sure something important has happened, and like an idiot, he rushed off with Gabrielle to save the day."

It was a testament to how well Selene knew Alex that she could pretty much guess what he was doing without knowing the details. Kazekiri wasn't jealous. Of course not. Far be it for her to be jealous of how well Selene knew Alex. She was merely curious to know how well those two knew each other. That was all. There were no exterior motives or anything.

Classes that day went by slowly. Granted, they had been going by slowly ever since Alex and Gabrielle left. Kazekiri's mind had, much to her chagrin, been filled with thoughts of those two. She was worried.

No one in their solar system knew what awaited them outside of this solar system. There could be millions of unknown dangers, and those two were walking right into the heat of a civil war for the throne of another solar system. Kazekiri couldn't help but feel worry.

She had actually protested letting them go when Commander Karen had told her about what they were doing, but she had said they had no right to hold them. Alex was engaged to Gabrielle. Gabrielle was the daughter of King Lucifer, ruler of the galaxy. If they wanted, they only needed to get in contact with King Lucifer and any laws they created would become meaningless. It galled her, but there was nothing she could do.

The only class that Kazekiri enjoyed that day was hand to hand combat instructions.

At her request, Alex had made her a training regimen and even gave her a few private instructions on how to fight. She'd been incorporating what she learned into her fighting. Whatever she had to say about Alex's talent as an officer, she couldn't deny that he knew how to fight.

Her opponent that day was Tifa. The girl was nearly two times larger than Kazekiri, and her burly arms shot out more quickly than she would have imagined such a big girl capable of. At the same time, while they were fast, they moved in a straight line. Tifa's punches were predictable and easy to avoid.

"H-hold still!" the girl growled.

Kazekiri did not hold still. She continued to dance around the attacks like a butterfly flitting away from a net. Left. Right. Back. Duck. Spin. Sidestep. Kazekiri constantly moved, doing her best to remember what Alex had taught her, to recall his words.

"Because of the way your body is proportioned, you don't want to make any large, unnecessary movements. That will simply cause your bust to get in the way of your fighting. Instead, move as little as possible. If you have to dodge, do so by taking one step to the either side or one step back. This will keep you from jostling yourself, which should allow for a wider range of motion. Once you

get dodging down, observe your opponent to learn their attack patterns, and then hit them with a strong counterattack."

Alex had not only taught her this basic tactic, but he had mentioned that because she was a woman with a larger than average chest, she'd do better practicing judo, a type of martial arts that relied on using other people's strength against them. She didn't know much, but she had taken his words to heart and begun learning.

Tifa's punches were getting sloppier. This made them easier to dodge. Kazekiri had been doing exactly as Alex had taught her, watching her opponent to predict t for any opening that might present itself.

One such opening came when Tifa over-extended her latest punch. Kazekiri moved in quicker than a blaster bolt. She took two steps forward, grabbed Tifa's arm, spun around, and used her leverage plus Tifa's momentum to lift the much larger girl into the air and toss her. Tifa screamed as she flew through the air, but that scream was silenced when the girl slammed back first into the mat.

"This match goes to Kazekiri," Instructor Monica announced.

"I won?" Kazekiri blinked. She raised her hands and looked at them, as though unable to believe that these hands had just defeated Tifa. "I can't believe I won."

"Don't get a big head," Tifa muttered as she clambered to her feet. "It was just one round. It won't happen again."

Despite what Tifa said, Kazekiri was so happy that as classes came to an end, she still hadn't been able to get rid of the smile on her face. She was smiling all the way home. It wasn't until she entered the house and saw the extra pair of shoes that the smile faded.

Loud stomping and several curses echoed from the kitchen. It was not Keichii's voice. It was a voice that sounded vaguely familiar. She felt she should recognize this voice, but at the same time, she didn't want to know.

Slowly, Kazekiri wandered into the kitchen.

She paused. Her eyes widened in shock. Her heart tried to beat its way out of her throat. Her mind froze in terror.

A man stood in the kitchen, a plate of food in one hand as he rummaged through the cabinet. His off-white shirt was covered in stains and stretched over his large gut. Scraggly brown hair fell about his face, clean but filthy, as though it was covered in oil. His skin was a kind of pasty white. As he turned to face her, no doubt responding to the door opening, she caught sight of brown eyes.

"Kazekiri. Hurry up and get started on dinner. I'm hungry."

The words jolted her. "F-father?!"

Her father, the man who she and Keiichi had run from, the man who she feared more than anyone else, was standing in her kitchen and demanding she make him dinner. The situation was so surreal that Kazekiri didn't know whether to laugh, cry, or hide in her bed.

"What? Did you not hear me?" her father demanded. "I said hurry up and make dinner!"

Kazekiri needed a moment to think of what she should do. After a few seconds, Kazekiri concluded that she didn't have to do what he said. She was no longer the little girl who cowered before her parents.

She squared her shoulders and glared at him. "What are you doing here? You should be rotting away in a prison back on Earth."

The look on her father's face, the rage in his now narrowed eyes, brought back all of the terrible memories from her past. Despite wanting to put up a brace front, Kazekiri's face paled and her knees shook.

"Are you talking back to me?" he asked. Kazekiri wanted to stand up to him, but once again, her head shook against her will. Her father grinned as he walked toward her, cracking his knuckles. "It seems you need to remember what happens to bad little girls who disrespect their fathers."

Kazekiri tried to run away, to get out of the house and to the police station, but her father was faster than he looked. He kicked at her legs. Tumbling to the ground with a cry, Kazekiri became disoriented when her chin slammed into the fake wooden floor. She tasted blood in her mouth. However, the sharp sensation on her chin and taste of liquid iron became secondary to the feeling of rough hands grabbing her hair and yanking on it.

"I didn't put up with your mother's cheek, and I certainly won't put up with yours." Her father's acrid breath washed over Kazekiri's ear. She smelled alcohol on his breath. He had already been drinking. "It's time to make sure you understand your place."

Kazekiri considered herself to be many things. Strong. Proud. A good citizen who followed the rules. However, in that moment, as her father began to beat her with his fists and feet, she went back to being the little girl who kept getting abused by her mother and father.

As tears streamed down her face, Kazekiri realized that despite all her efforts to the contrary, she hadn't changed from her past self at all.

CHAPTER 3

MERLIN AND PERVERSION

Camelot was nothing like Mars. Of course, that went without saying. Mars was a desolate planet where people lived inside of domed cities that protected them from the basically non-existent atmosphere, while Camelot was a blue and green planet filled with vast oceans and ardent forests.

Looking at the planet from the viewport of the shuttle, Alex could see that they were traveling toward a city—a massive city that looked similar but different to Mars City. The architecture held a strange style that was like a mix of old and new. Gleaming skyscrapers sat next to squat buildings made of limestone. Powerful archways connected numerous large buildings together without blocking the view for those down below. Unlike Mars City, which eventually became so congested with walkways and hubs that the further down you went, the less you could see above you, everywhere he looked offered a crystal-clear view of the bright, blue sky.

"What do you think?" asked Prince Arthur, and despite being stuck in crash webbing like the rest of them, he looked rather regal —not to mention smug.

"It's an amazing city," Alex admitted, though he was a bit annoyed by the smug look the prince wore. "I've never seen anything this amazing before."

"It's okay," Gabrielle said, leaning over Alex's shoulder to look out the window.

"I've seen better," Nyx added.

Alex couldn't be sure, but he could have sworn that several spears had appeared to pierce Prince Arthur's chest. The crown prince certainly looked like someone who'd been shot in the chest with a blaster bolt.

"W-well, I imagine that the princess of the Angelisian Empire and the galaxy's most notorious assassin have been to many planets," Prince Arthur said.

"Not really," Gabrielle rebutted. "I barely left the palace when I was younger. I just think Angelisia is more impressive."

"O-oh..." The stunned look on Prince Arthur's face almost made Alex snicker. However, the crown prince recovered with admirable swiftness. Coughing into his hand, he said, "in either event, we'll be arriving at my palace in just a few moments."

It wasn't long before the palace came into view, spreading out before them as they passed through a large archway. Glistening in the afternoon sun, five towers jutted into the sky, the light reflecting off their gleaming surfaces, which appeared to be made from a material that Alex didn't recognize. It wasn't metal, but it wasn't stone either. Surrounding the towers was a large wall. The towers themselves were connected via a series of archways. Meanwhile, nestled beneath them was a large structure that spread out across the land. The tallest tower among the group was spearing straight through the building, which must have been the palace.

They set down on a landing pad not far from the palace. As they stepped out, the group, or rather, Prince Arthur, was greeted by several guards decked in dazzling silver armor. With swords strapped to their waists and rifles in their hands, the group of warriors saluted.

Prince Arthur waved them down as he and Gwenn walked past the group. While Gabrielle seemed right at home and Nyx uncaring, Alex could not help but the nerves that settled in his gut as he followed the two. He still wasn't used to all this pomp.

The procession of guards trailed after them, marching in two perfect lines, and the sound of their stamping feet nearly made Alex cringe.

Passing under an archway, Alex soon realized that they had entered the palace proper. It was not defined by any doors. The palace was very open, with no walls and only massive columns to mark their entrance, allowing anyone who pleased to walk in. While he questioned how secure such a thing would be, he didn't deny the aesthetic appeal, though Alex soon discovered that there were, in fact, doors that led deeper into the palace. They came upon one soon enough. The outside must have just been decoration.

It was gigantic. The door easily towered over him and the others, a double door made of a dark wood and inlaid with golden designs of a dragon. Two guards stood on either side of the door. When their procession appeared, they saluted, swiped a card through a slot behind them, and then, with a precious groan, the doors slowly opened.

As Prince Arthur led the group into what a wide hallway, he began giving orders.

"I want a status hourly status reports on any suspicious activity happening around the planet. You. Make it happen."

"Yes, sir!"

"Put our military on high alert. Code Omega. Also, change our transponder codes. I don't want an incident like what happened today occurring."

"Yes, Your Grace!"

One by one, the people in his procession were given orders and hurried off to accomplish those orders. While this was happening, Gwenn typed in her tablet, probably taking down notations of the orders for future reference.

"Also, bring Merlin to the war council room."

The procession halted. Alex only noticed the strange tension in the air after nearly tripping over Gabrielle's feet when she suddenly stopped.

He looked at the faces of those around him, wondering about the uncertainty in them. Who was this Merlin character? Why did he evoke such a strange reaction from everyone?

Prince Arthur also paused. His face, which had been blazing determination like a wildfire, suddenly shifted into one of consternated exhaustion.

"Let me guess… he's not peeping again, is he?"

Peeping?

The guards still present looked at each other, their faces reflecting the uncertainty they felt. Alex thought he felt the tension in the hallway rise. It seemed this Merlin, whoever he was, caused a lot of problems.

"We're… not sure," another guard said. "See, the thing is, we don't actually know where he is."

"So I see." Prince Arthur sighed, placed his hand in his face, and appeared to think about what he'd learned for a moment. Several seconds passed. The crown prince straightened and said, "Merlin will show up when he feels like it. For now, let's focus on the matter at hand."

And with that, Prince Arthur began giving orders once again.

It wasn't long before they reached another doorway, this one just as big, and passed through to find themselves standing in a large room made of shining tiles. Several columns decorated with motifs and the like lined either side of the room. In between these columns, large stained-glass windows revealed figures. It wasn't until Alex saw several of the windows, which showed a figure pulling a sword from a stone, that it told the story of how Prince Arthur became crown prince. Rather, it was the legend that had been told since before he was crown prince.

They walked down the red carpet in the center of the room, which led to a dais. A gilded throne sat atop it. A pair of steps led to it. Made from a material that glittered like gold, with a soft red cushion for Prince Arthur to sit on, and an armrest that curved around the entire thing, Alex didn't think he'd ever seen a more opulent chair. It was ridiculous.

As the crown prince sat down, he gestured for Alex, Gabrielle, and Nyx to stand beside him. When they did, he looked at one of the few remaining guards who hadn't run off to follow one of his orders.

"Have you located Bedivere yet?" he asked.

"I am afraid we have not uncovered his exact location," the guard said. "All we know is that he's still somewhere on Winchester."

"Hmm…"

"You mentioned that Bedivere was good at hiding," Alex said.

"That he is." Prince Arthur paused. "Back when we were children, Bedivere would always know of the greatest hiding spots in the palace. It wouldn't surprise me if he kept this talent for hiding even after gaining his own planet."

"Then he probably has a lot of hideouts on Winchester," Gabrielle said. "If it was me, I would have at least twenty different hideouts, and I would move between them every few days to keep my bodyguards—I mean, to keep any pursuers from locating me."

Alex snorted at how Gabrielle specifically mentioned her bodyguards. Knowing her as he did, he would not have been surprised if she'd created several hideouts that she used when running away from her bodyguards, which she had done frequently before meeting him. According to what he'd learned from Ariel, Gabrielle had run away dozens of times every year.

And the last time she ran away, she actually escaped. The girl is more cunning than people give her credit for.

"You bring up a good point." Prince Arthur raised a hand to his mouth, biting on his index finger as he furrowed his brows. After another moment, he sighed. "All right. I'll come up with a method of locating Bedivere. In the meantime, Gwenn, why don't you show these three around? They've traveled all this way. It would be a shame not to let them see the sights."

"If that is your wish, Your Majesty." Gwenn bowed to Prince Arthur, straightened, adjusted her glasses, and then looked at them. Her every movement was completely meticulous. "If you three would follow me, I shall escort you around the city."

"Really?" Gabrielle brightened. "That sounds so fun! Come on, Alex, Nyx! Let's go!"

"All right. All right. There's no need to drag us behind you," Alex laughed as Gabrielle, in her enthusiasm, had grabbed both him and Nyx and was now pulling them behind her.

The two quickly started walking faster to keep up with Gabrielle's strides as they all followed Gwenn out of the throne room. The place where she led them to was a massive room that Alex soon realized was a garage. There were several shuttles sitting inside. Most of them looked like the kind of crafts that flew through the air, but there were a few that had the distinct appearance of something that hovered. A speeder, Gabrielle called them.

"Ahhh!" Gabrielle's excited squeal precluded her actions as she rushed toward one particular shuttle. "This is an XG3! They stopped making this speeder around a year after I was born! Look at what great shape it's in!"

"Would you like to ride in that shuttle?" asked Gwenn.

"Can I?"

Gwenn nodded. Gabrielle squealed again.

Since it appeared they were using that shuttle, Gwenn had everyone else climb aboard as well.

The shuttle had a tapered end, while the cockpit was situated near the front. It was an open cockpit with only a small glassteel panel to protect them from the wind. The cockpit was large enough to seat five people, two in front and three in back. Widening out behind the cockpit, the XG3 featured a strange fishtail appearance.

Gwenn started up the shuttle as Alex found himself sitting between Gabrielle and Nyx. He was startled when the shuttle started hovering. There had been no sound to announce the engine turning on, but then he realized that this probably used repulsor technology, which did not make any noise.

I need to build my own shuttle with that technology.

"So cool! So cool!" Gabrielle turned to him. Her eyes were like a pair of bright emeralds sparkling as the sunlight hit them. "Isn't this amazing, Alex? We're riding an XG3! This vehicle is a classic!"

"You certainly know your shuttles, Princess," Nyx said.

"I've always liked studying old technology." Gabrielle rubbed the back of her head and grinned. "Antique speeders like this use an older form of anti-gravity technology, which was the basis for some of the shuttles I invented."

Nyx nodded. "I heard that you were the one who pioneered anti-gravity technology and incorporated it into actually spaceships."

"Tee-hee!"

"I heard the same thing," Gwenn said from the front as she smoothly drove the speeder out of the garage. "You were hailed as the first person to ever be capable of incorporating anti-gravity nodes into a spacefaring vessel. It was your invention that helped revolutionize space travel."

It always amazed Alex to hear about Gabrielle's achievements. Alex had often been hailed a genius inventor who had won several prizes on Mars for his ingenuity, but when he got right down to it, he had nothing on Gabrielle. She was the true genius.

And now she's my... my fiancé.

The thought made his heart skip a beat.

They hovered over a cobblestone road that led them out a set of gates and down the hill that the palace was located on. From his position, Alex could make out the city below. They were closing in on it quickly.

Entering the city of Caerleon through a massive archway, Alex realized that down below the towering skyscrapers was another world entirely.

Street vendors selling their wares called out to potential customers passing by. They were selling all kinds of product: produce, clothing, jewels, and trinkets. The stalls were packed together on either side of the wide street, which several shuttles aside from theirs traveled down. Pedestrians walked along either side of the road, carefully minding the traffic. Most of them were adults, but there were also a few kids running through the streets.

Alex thought the architectural wonders that were the skyscrapers created a strong juxtaposition with the almost olden feel of the street vendors.

"Carleon was founded over fifteen thousand years ago," Gwenn informed them as she expertly drove through the traffic of cars and people. "This was actually the planet where Prince Arthur's family originated from. The first king of Camelot, who bore the same name as the prince, hailed from here and spread his influence across the world, eventually creating what many consider to be a utopian. While a lot of the architecture has changed since then, street vendors like this have been around since ancient times."

"That's pretty amazing," Alex admitted. He couldn't even imagine fifteen thousand years' worth of history.

"Isn't it?"

After parking the XG3 in a side street, Gwenn had them all disembark and began taking them around to the various sites.

Carleon had a rich history. Much of the architecture extolled that historical background. Some of the buildings that were standing had been there for thousands of years. Of course, they had been refurbished so much of the original structure was gone, but Gwenn told them that all of the refurbished buildings were one hundred percent historically accurate recreations, right down to how they were built.

The group walked along many different roads, bought trinkets and whatnot from the street vendors, and traveled to several parks that were interspersed across the city.

As they were walking down one particular street, loud laughter erupted from a nearby building. Everyone stopped. However, while he, Gabrielle, and Nyx all remained curious, most of the people only paid the building a cursory glance before moving on.

Gwenn sighed.

"If you'll excuse me for a moment," she said before entering the building.

Alex looked at Gabrielle and Nyx. "What do you think that was about?"

"I don't know," Gabrielle said as Nyx shrugged. "Should we go in?"

"Well, I am kinda curious," he admitted. "Gwenn looked pretty annoyed."

As one, the group began walking to the door, but they stopped when several voices echoed from inside.

"Gwenn? Tch! What are you doing here? I thought you and that blasted prince had left for some backwater planet."

"We did. We came back. And now here I find you flirting with girls in a brothel. You have some nerve."

"Hmph! You say that like there is something wrong with me flirting with girls in a brothel."

"There is something wrong with it. Try acting your age for once."

"Maybe I will when you try getting laid!"

"What was that?!"

Looking at each other, the three of them finally pushed open and the door and walked into the room. None of them were sure of what they would find. However, Alex would wager that an old man surrounded by half-naked women glaring at the "daggers in her eyes irate" Gwenn was not necessarily it.

The old man looked… well… not quite as old as Alex expected. He had a few wrinkles lining his face, mostly around the eyes and mouth, pure gray hair that had been neatly combed back, and a trimmed goatee. His outfit consisted of… pants. Alex looked down and realized that the rest of his clothing had been cast off. Judging from the women with their hands all over his chest, things had been seconds away from getting heated. What's more, his chest, stomach, and shoulders were fairly defined. Alex wouldn't say he was in great shape, but it was clear that this old man kept himself in decent health.

"Who's the old guy?" asked Gabrielle, her voice loud enough to carry across the entire interior.

The "old guy" perked up at the sound of her voice. His head turned toward her, and then his eyes lit up when they landed on her. Giving a grin that seeped with lecherous intentions, the old man pried himself from the women's grip, stood up, and made his way to them.

"Greetings, my name is—WAAA!!"

Alex and Gabrielle winced when Gwenn stuck out her foot and tripped the old man. The wince came from how they could hear the loud *crunch!* of the old man's nose smashing into the floorboards.

"… Ouch."

The old man groaned as he pushed himself onto his hands and knees. Wincing as he sat down, he muttered something under his breath, and the wound on his nose healed. Even the blood had disappeared.

"What the hell was that for?" the old man asked, giving Gwenn a nasty look.

Gwenn adjusted her glasses. "I just felt this irresistible urge to see you fall flat on your face. That's all."

"That's a terrible reason!"

"Anyway," Gwenn addressed him, Gabrielle, and Nyx, "this sorry excuse for a man is none other than Prince Arthur's adviser, Merlin Ambrosius."

"Huh?" was all Alex could say.

2

Merlin, Alex discovered very quickly, was an unrepentant lecher. It was no exaggeration to say that his salaciousness knew no bounds. Almost immediately after the initial introduction was made did he try to hit on both Gabrielle and Nyx.

Tried was the keyword, of course.

After all, Nyx didn't like perverts.

"Man… I cannot believe that girl." Merlin rubbed his bruised and battered face. "Who the hell attacks a helpless old man like myself with alchemy."

"You deserved it," Alex said.

"I hate perverts," Nyx added.

"Tch!"

They were once again in the throne room, and Prince Arthur was once again on the throne. Either he'd left and came back before them, or the more likely answer, he'd never left in the first place. Alex wondered if that was what it meant to be a ruler. When he became the Emperor of the Galaxy, would he have to sit on a throne all day?

Heh. I'm already thinking about what will happen once Gabrielle and I are married.

"Merlin." Prince Arthur sighed. "I don't mind your predisposition for propositioning the farer sex, but please do that on your own time."

"I was doing it on my own time." Merlin tapped his staff against the ground. "You're the one who called me when it was my free time."

Merlin was fully dressed now. His black shirt and pants were covered by an equally black shoulder cape. However, the inside of the cape was crimson. It was the only color on his outfit, which caused all eyes to be drawn toward it. Alex wondered if perhaps that was the point.

"Your Majesty," Gwenn addressed Prince Arthur. Standing on his left, she adjusted her glasses and glared down at Merlin, the vitriol in her eyes matching the tone in her voice. "I believe we should ask another court mage to be your adviser. It is clear that this one does not believe in being responsible, nor does he have any moral scruples to speak of. It's simply unfathomable to keep him."

"What's unfathomable is your general stupidity," Merlin snarked. "I knew you were a dumb broad from the moment I laid eyes on you, but it seems I still overestimated your intelligence. This is what happens when you focus on training only the muscles you move instead of the one in your head."

"So says the man who can only get laid when he pays for it."

"So says the woman who couldn't get laid even if she paid for it."

"That is quite enough," Prince Arthur spoke with quiet confidence. Despite the softness of his voice, it carried to everyone present. Gwenn and Merlin stopped talking. "I'd normally let you to fight because it's funny, but we don't have time to argue. Merlin, I'm sure you know what is going on. I would like your opinion on the matter."

Merlin tapped his staff on the ground again. Did that thing have a function, or was it merely ornamental? Alex didn't know. However, it seemed pointless to have a staff that didn't serve some kind of purpose, and that thing didn't seem like a walking stick or something like that. The old court adviser didn't seem to need one anyway.

"Lancelot is an idiot, and Morrigan might be a hot mess with enough power to blow up a planet, but she isn't much smarter than her brother."

"Then you agree that Igraine is most likely responsible for what's happening?" Prince Arthur deduced.

"Probably." Merlin nodded and tapped his staff against the ground. That was going to get annoying. "Igraine has always been an ambitious one. She's also cunning enough and immoral enough to use her own children as a distraction to achieve whatever goal she has set."

Alex leaned over to Gabrielle and Nyx. "Do either of you know anything about Igraine?"

"No." Gabrielle shook her head. "I don't know anything about her."

"I know of her," Nyx said. "Before marrying Uther Pendragon, she was a bounty hunter who had a reputation for always capturing her mark in the criminal underworld, dead or alive. She's supposed to be really talented at ergokinesis. There's a never confirmed rumor that she can manipulate every form of energy available."

"That isn't just a rumor." Merlin tapped his staff on the ground. Gwenn twitched. "Igraine is a skillful energy manipulator, though being able to manipulate all forms of energy comes with its drawbacks. She doesn't have much power. Naturally, this means the amount of energy she can manipulate at will is quite weak. Some of the abilities that come from energy manipulation are unavailable to her thanks to this. For example, she can't create shields—at least, not very well—and her aura is quite weak, too."

"Her mind is more dangerous than her ability," Gwenn said. "She's a dangerous individual who has killed many through cunning and deceit. Her powers are merely used to augment her intelligence."

"What do you think she is after?" asked Alex.

"Who knows." Merlin shrugged. "I can't think of anything that she might want outside of the throne, but it's not like controlling Camelot will guarantee her a spot."

"Thinking about what Igraine might be planning probably won't help us," Prince Arthur said. "If she is behind this, she'll reveal her plan in time. Right now, I think we should focus on Lancelot and Morrigan."

"In that case, the first thing we should do is send a diplomatic envoy to question their motives," Gwenn said.

"Their motives don't matter," Merlin rebutted. "What matters is that they attacked us. Instead of sending an envoy, we should send an armada."

"Attacking right now is pointless," Gwenn argued. "If we attack Winchester, they can just abandon it. They might even be using Winchester as a feint to make us send our army there, so they can attack us from the flank." She turned to Prince Arthur. "I believe two things are necessary for us to do right now. We need to send an envoy to Lancelot and Morrigan, and we need to send a missive to Dinadan and Gawain. We should let them know what's going on and ask them to aid us."

"Merlin?" Prince Arthur said. "What do you think?"

"If you are going to bother sending an envoy, then you should at least make it a ploy to search for Bedivere," Merlin grumbled. "Not only does he have numerous hideouts throughout the solar system, but he knows many navigation routes that could help us reach each planet in half the time normal routes do."

"Fair point," Prince Arthur said.

The conversation lasted awhile longer. It was ultimately decided that Nimue would travel to Winchester alongside the royal guard, Prince Arthur's most elite unit of protectors. Her job would be to convene with Lancelot and Morrigan. The premise was that she wanted to know why they attacked Camelot and what they hoped to accomplish.

Meanwhile, another force would be sent with her. They would infiltrate the city and search for Bedivere, who was unlikely to have left the planet since Lancelot was tracking all incoming and outgoing traffic. Alex offered himself for the task.

"Are you sure?" asked Prince Arthur. "I know you said you wanted to help, but traveling incognito to a planet you've never visited even once might be asking for too much."

"Nyx will be going with me, so I'll be fine," Alex said.

"I'm going, too!" Gabrielle said, but Alex shook his head.

"No, I've actually got a different task for you," Alex said with a wide grin.

3

After the conversation on what to do about Lancelot concluded, Gabrielle and Nyx were offered the chance of taking a bath. They accepted. Sadly, they were not able to take a bath with Alex, which depressed Gabrielle, who had been hoping to spend some quality time washing his back.

Still, it was fun taking a bath with Nyx. The much smaller girl was sitting on an ornate stool as Gabrielle used a loofah to scrub her back. As she did, Nyx's back muscles flexed.

"You have such smooth skin," Gabrielle complimented.

"That's only because of the nanomachines," Nyx replied. "They give me a form of regeneration through transmutation."

"Is that so? Hm. Well, I guess if your body was made entirely of nanomachines, they would be able to regenerate any damage done."

Nanomachines were one of the most advanced forms of bioscience. Sentient, microscopic machines that could perform any number of biological functions, from repairing damaged muscles to enhancing the body to even allowing a person with no abilities to gain one like pyrokinesis. They were arguably the most versatile creation in regard to any technology dealing with biomatter.

Gabrielle knew nothing about bioscience save for the basics, so she didn't know how nanomachines worked. Sadly, that required knowledge on biology. She found biology boring.

After they had both washed each other's backs, Gabrielle and Nyx waded into the tub. It was very big. It was shaped like a donut. There was even an island in the center. Traveling along the tub's circumference was a bench for people to sit on.

"Ah… this is nice," Gabrielle said. Nyx didn't say anything, but that was okay. Her friend was quiet. "It's too bad Alex isn't allowed to join us."

While there was no designated men's or women's bath, Arty had forbade the men from entering while she and Nyx bathed. Gabrielle wasn't sure why. She had asked, but all Arty said was that it would help keep perverts from trying to sneak a peek.

Nyx, again, said nothing, though she did nod.

As they relaxed in the bath, the door several meters away, which led into the changing room, opened. Gabrielle turned her head. A woman was entering. Olive skin, black hair, and obsidian eyes. It was Nimue, Arty's fiancé. She smiled at the two as she entered the room.

"Do you mind if I join you?" Nimue asked.

"Sure!" Gabrielle beamed at the other girl. "The more the merrier!"

"Thank you."

Nimue climbed into the bathtub and sat down beside her and Nyx. Her hair had been wrapped in a towel. She leaned back and sighed in content.

"I always love taking baths."

"Yeah, baths are nice," Gabrielle agreed.

"Prince Arthur told me about his plan." Nimue suddenly looked at her. "You and I are going to Winchester as envoys to request an explanation from Lancelot."

"Yep. That's what's happening." Gabrielle nodded as she tried to make water squirt out of her hands. "It was pretty smart of Alex to suggest I go with you."

Nimue tilted her head. "Why is that?"

"Because if you go there on your own, there's nothing to stop Lancer from kidnapping you and using you as a hostage to force Arty from renouncing his claim to the throne." Gabrielle poked out her tongue as she clasped her hands together and made her fingers form the shape of a gun. "But if I go with you, then he can't do anything unless he's willing to invite war to this solar system. Not only would he be breaking the treaty, but Papa wouldn't take kindly to me being kidnapped, hurt, or used as a bargaining chip. Oh! I did it!"

Gabrielle cheered as she finally managed to squirt water from her fingers. Unfortunately, she had squirted water right in Nyx's face. The dark-haired assassin stared at her for several seconds, and then transmuted her hair into hands, which she used to squirt Gabrielle with water.

"Brrbbllgggrrgglllee!!"

Gabrielle was assaulted on all sides by Nyx's water gun attack, which was completely unfair since she was using alchemy. But Gabrielle had no intention of giving up. Oh, no. Two could play at this game.

Opening the gateway that kept her power sealed just a crack, Gabrielle planned on creating a giant water gun to shoot Nyx with. Sadly, the moment Gabrielle released the constraints on her power, the water around her exploded. It flew in all directions. Nyx was sent flying. Nimue was sent flying. The only reason Gabrielle didn't fly off herself was because she was at the epicenter. When the massive wave died down and calm returned, the bath was almost empty and Gabrielle was alone.

She rubbed the back of her head. "Whoops."

It was a good thing the bath water was recycled. The bath soon filled up again, and Nimue and Nyx rejoined her, though both of them were sporting a large lump on their heads.

"Well… that was… interesting," Nimue said.

"Yeah, sorry about that." Gabrielle rubbed the back of her head. "I've been training to control my power, but it's a slow-going process."

Nimue slowly shook her head. "You are most certainly Emperor Lucifer's daughter."

"You're too powerful, Princess Gabrielle," Nyx added.

"Tee-hee!"

"Going back to our earlier discussion," Nimue began again. "I am impressed that Alexander was able to come up with such a scheme. I know that he is your fiancé, but considering what I know of his background, I didn't think he understood politics well enough to conceive such a plan."

"Alex is amazing," Gabrielle said. "He knows lots of stuff. I'm sure he understood what Papa would do if something happened to me. He also knows that Papa isn't above destroying a solar system or two."

"Right…" Nimue shook her head. "Well, anyway, I—"

She stopped talking, and for a moment, Gabrielle wondered why.

"Huhuhuhu…"

Until she heard it. The sound of giggling.

"Huehuehuehue…"

It was unlike anything she had ever heard, but it was unmistakably a giggle. That said, it sounded weird… perverse somehow. If someone asked her to describe the sound, Gabrielle would have told them that it sounded like an old man giggling about something that made him really happy.

Nimue twitched. The twice lasted only for a moment, and then, she smiled.

"Gabrielle?"

"Yes?"

"Could you release your power one more time? This time, aim for that wall over there."

Gabrielle looked at where Nimue was pointing. The bathhouse was pretty big. While the floor was made entirely of tiles, the walls were half-tile and half-argonite. A few columns lined the wall, a fact that made Gabrielle somewhat amused. These Arthurians sure loved their columns. Nimue was pointing at the wall closest to the tub.

"So… you want me to release my power against that wall?"

"Yes."

"Okay."

Gabrielle shrugged and did as she was told. Her wings flapped, her ears wiggled, and her body was coated in a bright blue energy as she released her powers on the wall. The end result was a massive beam of energy so large it had a circumference five times larger than her blasting out of her hand. It slammed into the wall, blew straight through it, and continued on.

The earth shook, rumbling as though it had been struck by one of Papa's fists. Cracks appeared in the other walls and the ceiling, spreading out, multiplying, and causing several chunks of argonite to flake off and fall to the floor with a crash.

Wincing only slightly, Gabrielle carefully sealed away her power again. It was harder to seal away than it was to keep it locked up. Gabrielle likened it to a dam. Once the dam was unblocked, it took a lot of effort to block it back off, but keeping it blocked was easy.

Alex isn't the only one who's been training.

While she didn't train like Alex did, Gabrielle had been using Mr. Simulator as a practice ground for her own powers. She wanted to learn how to control her power. She wanted to help Alex by being able to look after him when one of her marriage candidates bothered them. Papa might have said that the police couldn't help, but at no time had he said that she couldn't help.

It was a wife's duty to watch her husband's back.

"So how was that?" Gabrielle asked, turning to Nimue.

Nimue gave her a thumbs up and smiled. "Perfect. Thank you."

"Tee-hee! You're welcome!"

Still sitting where she had been since getting back in the bath, Nyx sighed and shook her head.

4

Alex stood in the communication room, a smaller interior enclosed by walls on only three sides. The fourth side was dedicated entirely to a massive screen. It was currently blank, but Alex had used a device that he had made for the specific purpose of contacting his sister while traveling across the galaxy.

Gabrielle called it Mr. Caller, but Alex just referred to it as The Intergalactic Communicator. Of course, it wasn't a communicator. It was a device that allowed alien communication devices to sync with the communication devices from home, thereby letting him contact people. This would be his first test run.

The connection had already been established. Lighting up with a bright flash, the screen showed the call was going through via an old-fashioned ringing phone. He thought it was the best indicator to let him know the call was going through. Alex tapped his feet against the floor as the phone shook. He wondered how long it would take for Alice to answer.

Finally, after several minutes, the screen suddenly flashed again, this time to an image. It was Alice. His little sister was in her pajamas and rubbing her eyes as she yawned. She didn't seem to realize it was him.

"H-hello?"

"Alice?"

Alice froze. She lowered her hands and looked at the screen, blinking several times as she stared at him.

"Big bro?"

"Hey." Alex raised a hand in greeting. "It's been awhile since I've seen your face. I wanted to let you know that Gabrielle, Nyx, and I arrived on Camelot today."

"How am I seeing you?" asked Alice. "Your IDband can't reach me from across the galaxy now, can it?"

"No, nothing like that." Alex chuckled at his sister's words. "I'm using a device I made to connect your console to an alien communication device. It works under the principles of—"

"I don't need to know your techno-jargon." Alice waved him off before settling in her chair. The sleepiness in her eyes was gone. "Wow. So I'm really talking to you from across the galaxy."

"That's right."

"And how is it on Camelot?"

"It's a lot prettier here than Mars, that's for sure." Alex shrugged. "Other than that, I don't know what to tell you. We haven't been able to do too much site seeing."

"That so…"

"How are your grades holding up?"

"Hurk!"

Alex narrowed his eyes when Alice broke out into a cold sweat. She looked away from the screen, which only caused his frown to deepen.

"Alice…"

"W-well, I'm not… failing."

Not failing meant she was barely passing in Alice speak, and that, of course, meant that she was using her intelligence to its full potential. Alex hated it when she did this. His sister was so smart. In terms of intelligence, she might even be smarter than him. However, she didn't care enough to use it, preferring to laze on the couch and watch Titan Girls all day.

I wish there was something I could do to make her realize how important her studies are.

"When I get back, I am banning strawberry cheesecake parfaits for the rest of the year."

"What? NO!" Alice suddenly shouted, bringing her face so close to the screen that Alex could only see her nose, eyes, and the numerous freckles that were normally invisible. "Don't do that! You can take away anything but that!"

"If you don't want me taking away your cheesecake parfaits, then you had better get your grades up."

"I will! I'll bring them back up!"

"And they need to stay up," Alex warned. "I'm going to speak with your teachers and have them give me a report of your grades for every day that I'm kind. If I find that you decided to slack off until the very last second, no cheesecake parfaits for a year."

Alice's shoulders drooped as though the weight of an entire world was resting on them. She had never seemed more depressed than she was right then.

"You're cruel, Big Bro. Very cruel."

Alex shrugged. "Is it wrong for a big brother to want to see his little sister succeed? I know that you're so much more capable than you try to make yourself out to be."

To his response, Alice could only sigh.

"How is Jasmine doing?" he asked.

"Hm… she seems to be doing fine," Alice said. "She misses you, though, of course, she always says so in a grandiose way that makes it hard to tell if she's joking or not."

Truth be told, Alex missed her as well. Years ago, Alex had saved Jasmine from being kidnapped, and ever since then, she had become an irreplaceable part of his life. She always made time to see him, spent time with his sister on weekends, and came over for dinner several times a week. She was good for Alice. Also, he really liked spending time with her.

Of course, his feelings for Jasmine were mixed. After she turned fourteen, he hadn't been able to see her as a little girl anymore. Her body had matured, her thoughts had become less childish, and his desire for her had become a tangible thing. She had starred in more than just a few of his wet dreams.

Should I talk to Gabrielle about her?

Alex pondered that thought for a second. He had learned thanks to Prince Arthur that polygamy was an accepted practice in the rest of the galaxy. Part of him wouldn't deny that appeal of being able to create a harem with Jasmine, Gabrielle, Nyx, and Kazekiri… but it didn't really seem right. If a woman wanted to create a harem with him in it, he wasn't sure he'd be up for that, so how could he ask them to join him in such a thing?

He shook his head, promising himself to speak with Gabrielle about this matter at a later date. If nothing else, her opinion would be invaluable.

Alex spoke with Alice some more, but sometime during their conversation, a loud rumbling made Alex nearly lose his balance.

"What is that?!" asked Alice.

"I don't know!" Alex shouted.

As the planet continued to shake, cracks formed on the walls and ceiling. Several chunks of rubble fell from the ceiling. Alex watched in horror as one particularly large chunk fell on top of his Intergalactic Communicator. His eyes widened as, as though everything was happening in slow motion, he saw the pieces of his invention, now broken into tiny pieces, scatter across the floor.

"!!!!!"

Alex's scream was so loud that it echoed across the entire palace. Years from now, his scream would still be spoken of by the maids, who would propagate a rumor that the palace was cursed, in hushed tones of horror.

6

Alex was still in tears when Prince Arthur ran into him as he was ambling down the hall, his gait that of a man who'd lost everything.

"Ah! There you are!" Prince Arthur walked up to him. As usual, Gwenn walked behind him carrying a tablet.

"Prince Arthur," Alex mumbled, looking up through the eyes of a dead man.

The crown prince stumbled. "Um… are you feeling well?"

"I'm fine," Alex mumbled. "Did you need something?"

"I did." The prince's expression became serious. "The mission you are going on is likely going to be dangerous. I was hoping you'd fight me, so that I might see your skills for myself."

"A test, huh?"

Prince Arthur probably wanted to make sure he was capable of carrying out the mission. Alex didn't know how things were done in this solar system, but on Mars, the kind of task he was being given would normally be something for the special forces.

"Sure," Alex said. "I'll fight you."

"Excellent! Follow me."

The place that Prince Arthur led him to was a large room. They walked past numerous robots that were currently deactivated, their bodies slumped over as though they'd fallen asleep standing up. There was also gym equipment. Alex recognized some of it because it looked similar to the stuff used by the Mars Police Force. So, even the types of exercise these people did was similar to their own workouts? How strange.

In the center of this room was a ring, an elevated platform that was blocked off by a gate. Prince Arthur unlocked the gate and climbed onto the ring. Alex followed him.

As he looked around, Alex realized that there was more to this room than he first thought. To his left sat what appeared to be a large obstacle course. Over on the right, a shooting range sat against the wall. Behind him was a weapons rack filled with more weapons than he could count, each one of them esoteric, each one so alien he didn't know what they were called. Even further back was a pool. He had no idea what the pool was for, but it stood out for the sole reason that he couldn't think of a use for it here.

"Do you have a weapon?" asked Prince Arthur.

"I do, but I don't need one."

Alex took a deep breath, held it, and then thought about the people he loved, the people he wanted to protect. Power flowed through him. Were he to look at himself in the mirror, Alex knew he would be surrounded by the Aura of Creation.

"So, it's true," Prince Arthur murmured. "I didn't believe it when Captain Tanner informed me that you were half-angelisian, but now I see that she wasn't mistaken. The Aura of Creation is something only they can use."

Alex created a whip with his power. He swung it a few times, listening to the loud *crack!* it made as it struck the floor. Several slash marks were left where he swung. Frowning, he eased back on the amount of power he was pumping into it. He didn't want to cut up the crown prince of Camelot's flesh.

Prince Arthur blinked. "You use the Aura of Creation to make weapons?"

"Yes." Alex frowned at the stunned tone in the prince's voice. "Isn't that what it's supposed to be used for?"

The flabbergasted look that Prince Arthur sent him, an expression that all but screamed, *"are you an idiot?!"* to him, made Alex shuffle his feet.

"The Aura of Creation is literally the power to control the cosmos! It's also called Omni-Energy Manipulation by most of the galaxy. It is the ability to create, shape, and manipulate all feasible and imaginable forms of energy. There's literally no limit on the amount or type of energy you can absorb, project, or manipulate. That's why Angelisians call it the Aura of Creation!"

"Oh..." Alex blinked several times as he processed this information. "I had no idea it was that amazing."

"You..." Prince Arthur scrunched up his face to an almost painful degree before, with the biggest sigh Alex had ever seen, his shoulders slumped. "You have the most powerful ability in the entire universe, but all you do is make weapons with it. What the hell, man?"

"I also make shields," Alex defended himself.

Prince Arthur said nothing.

"Is this guy an idiot, or what?"

Sadly, while Prince Arthur had nothing to say, his sword had plenty to say.

"I've been meaning to ask…" Alex began, "but what is up with that sword?"

"Let's start sparring first," Prince Arthur said. "I'll tell you while we fight."

"Fine with me."

Alex and Prince Arthur moved to opposite sides of the ring. Since Alex was using his Aura of Creation to create a whip, Prince Arthur unsheathed Caliburn, the sword strapped to his waist. It was a beautiful sword. The blade was perfect, a bright silver that reflected everything like a mirror. Sigils of some sort were etched into the blade. A blue guard made of quillons shaped like a cross moved into a long handle that was meant to be held with two hands. Prince Arthur only held it with one hand.

Gwenn stood in between them, off to the side, her expression resigned.

"Are both fighters ready?"

They nodded.

"Then… start!"

While Prince Arthur rushed forward, Alex leapt back and tried to attack with his whip. It was no good. The crown prince slashed it apart with his sword. Alex blinked when the energy tethering his whip together was severed.

"Huh… you can cut through energy with that thing."

"Of course!"

Prince Arthur lunged forward and thrust out Caliburn, but Alex sidestepped, avoiding the attack, though he still felt the air pushing him away. This prince was no slouch. He had some power to him.

"Caliburn is a sentient blade forged long ago!"

Spinning on the balls of his feet, the prince made a horizontal slash with his sword. A crescent blade of energy was released. No, it wasn't energy. It was a wind blade. Alex held up his hand and created a shield with his Aura of Creation. The wind blade splashed harmlessly against it and dispersed, and then Alex created another whip that he used to attack Prince Arthur with.

"Because it's a sentient blade, Caliburn has the ability to manipulate the energy of the person wielding it, transforming the energy found within a living being into a weapon!"

I see…

Alex leapt backward as Prince Arthur thrust out Caliburn once more. A burst of wind appeared on the tip of the blade and shot at him. Alex didn't have time to dodge, so he created another shield. The condensed ball of wind slammed into the shield. Alex skidded backward along the floor, and thought the wind sphere eventually dispersed, it took more effort to block than Alex thought it would.

That first attack of his wasn't because he's strong. It was the sword projecting his energy into a powerful gale force.

"You manipulate the wind," Alex said out loud as Prince Arthur rushed forward and attacked him again.

"That's right!" Thrust. Alex dodged. "My ability to wind manipulation." Prince Arthur swung Caliburn from right to left. Alex leapt over it. "With Caliburn, that ability is amplified and the power can be increased up to ten-fold!"

As if to prove his point, Prince Arthur raised the blade over his head and swung it down. A powerful wind blade was unleashed. It gouged into the floor as it flew forward. Alex dodged to the left, then looked behind him, watching as the blade cut straight through the metal fence that kept them from leaving. The blade continued on, and Alex realized that it was far larger than he'd originally assumed. It tore apart the stone floor, splitting it open like an overripe fruit, and continued on to strike the wall.

It tore through that as well.

Whoa...

"Hmph! That's not very impressive."

What do you mean? He just tore through a wall with nothing but wind!

"With your Aura of Creation, you can do that as well."

I can?

"Yes."

"Who cares about energy manipulation? Listen, brat, with my Body Supremacy, you can make yourself so strong that even the destruction of a planet wouldn't be enough to hurt you."

Prince Arthur was now getting up close and personal. Alex's lips became a thin line as he moved left and right, doing his best to avoid the prince's swings, which were coming in faster than they were before. Alex could feel the wind being sliced. Several small nicks stung his skin, and small traces of blood trailed down his face.

Body Supremacy?

"It's the ability to amplify your own physical attributes of your own biology. You can take any physical attribute of your own anatomy, biology, or physiology, and enhance them. Not only can you strengthen your body to the point where even being crushed by a planet is survivable, but you can also create drastic changes to your body, like enhancing the density of your skin or shifting the malleability of your skeletal structure. The sky is the limit."

As Voice Number One spoke, Prince Arthur continued to attack with increasing speed and Ferocity. Alex continued avoiding his strikes. While he was powerful, the crown prince had a very linear attack pattern, which made avoiding his attacks easier. What attacks couldn't be avoided he blocked with a shield created from his Aura of Creation.

Alex couldn't believe he was listening to Voice Number One. For the longest time, he had been trying to block out both voices, but here he was, in the middle of combat, paying attention to what the voice said. It felt surreal.

"However, there is a downside to using Asmodeus' power."

Asmodeus… Alex had heard Voice Number Two call Voice Number One that many times, but he'd always been so busy trying to block them out that he hadn't really thought about it. So, Voice Number One was called Asmodeus. He wondered why that name struck a chord within him.

"Tch! Don't go airing my weaknesses, damn angel!"

Alex leapt backward as Prince Arthur tried to slash him from shoulder to groin. The attack extended thanks to a wind blade, but Alex created an energy blade and sliced through it.

What's the downside to Asmodeus' power?

"The downside is that unless you've subdued her, you'll lose control of your ability to think. You become a mindless beast. And even if you do subdue her, Asmodeus will always seek to manipulate your thoughts."

Prince Arthur released a battle cry as he leapt into the air and slashed downward. Alex coated his forearms in the Aura of Creation, creating thick vambraces as he raised them and blocked the swing. A loud sonic boom echoed from the point of impact. Fierce winds pushed the two away from each other.

"I think I've seen enough," Prince Arthur said, finally sheathing his sword. "You have talent. Your strong, fast, and you've got great reflexes. I think you'll be fine on this mission."

"I'm glad to hear that you're so confident in me," Alex said.

"Sarcasm doesn't suit you." Prince Arthur walked up to him and slung an arm around Alex's shoulder. "Now come! Let us do some male bonding in the bath."

"Yeah… okay. Sure."

Alex didn't have anything better to do, and he was sweaty, and honestly, it was probably okay since they were both guys. He didn't much care for "male bonding through skinship", but it didn't bother him. The idea of bonding by getting naked in the baths was big on Mars as well.

As Prince Arthur led him to the baths, the two voices inside of his head continued to speak.

"You're right on all accounts except one. I don't manipulate thoughts. I merely make people more honest with themselves."

"You turning them into raging beasts filled with nothing but lust."

"Like I said. I make them more honest."

Alex frowned as the conversation continued. There was something about those words that made him curious.

Is the reason I always feel so, um…

"Sexually frustrated?"

"Alexander?"

I was gonna say aroused, but whatever. Alex felt a vein bulge on his forehead. *Anyway, is the reason I always feel that way because of you?*

A snort echoed throughout his mind as he and Prince Arthur turned a corner. **"What? Are you stupid?"** Alex would have shouted at her, but she continued before he could, her voice dripping with condescension. **"It is true that thanks to my presence inside of you, you feel more lust than the average person, but it's not as if my presence can completely change your physiology. I have no control over what you feel so long as that seal remains in place."**

"Camelot to Alexander."

So that seal keeps you from influencing me?

"Yes, to my displeasure."

"Sadly, it doesn't just keep her locked away. It also sealed me away with it. I believe the seal was designed to make you appear human."

Appear human…

There was something about those words that made him pause. Appear human. The way Voice Number Two said that made it sound like he wasn't human at all.

"Hey, Alexander! Are you listening to me?" Prince Arthur asked suddenly. Alex stopped conversing with the voices in his head and looked at the crown prince, a question in his eyes.

"Excuse me?"

Prince Arthur sighed. "I was saying that we've arrived at the changing room. Honestly… you and Princess Gabrielle never listen when other people are talking."

"Uh huh…"

Since he was there, Alex looked around the large room, walked over to the nearest changing bin, removed his clothes, and put them in one of several available cubby holes. There were towels hanging from a rack. Alex grabbed one and wrapped it around his waist. Several meters away, Prince Arthur did the same.

"I think you'll appreciate this bathhouse," the prince bragged as they walked up to the sliding door on the other side of the room. "While it isn't as impressive as the one on the Excalibur, I take great pride in this one's construction."

"That so?"

"Indeed so." Prince Arthur grabbed the door, a manual sliding door, and slowly opened it. "I created it two years ago, back when I was still learning the ins and outs of being… crown… prince…?"

As Prince Arthur trailed off, face slowly paling and eyes growing wide, Alex peered past him to see why. The entire room was a mess. Cracks spread along the tiled ground, some of them so wide they looked like chasms. Parts of the roof had crumbled. Debris from the broken roof littered the floor. The bath, which looked like it had once been a magnificent bath indeed, was fractured and broken. Several meters from the bath, one of the walls had been completely destroyed.

"W-what the hell happened to my bath?!" Prince Arthur screamed, dropping to his knees as he stared at the scene with a look of utter despair.

"There, there." Alex patted Prince Arthur's head.

"Don't patronize me."

"Fuck damn. This place looks like a hurricane ran through it."

"Quiet, Cal."

Since there was no longer anyway for them to take a bath, Alex quietly left the bathhouse, leaving Prince Arthur to his depression. He went back to the room that he, Gabrielle, and Nyx had been given. After taking a shower in the comparatively small— meaning not the size of a house—bath, Alex emerged from the restroom refreshed.

Gabrielle and Nyx had arrived sometime during his shower. It was a good thing he'd gotten dressed before leaving. Gabrielle was sitting on the bed, tinkering with one of her inventions using the

All-Purpose Tool. Nyx sat on the couch and was reading a book. Huh. Alex didn't know she liked reading.

"Alex!" Gabrielle greeted with a smile, though she didn't get up. Alex looked at what she was working on. It was… a hand? No, a prosthetic. "I didn't realize you had come back already. You should have said something."

"I was the in shower," Alex said.

"I would have gone in with you!"

"Didn't you already take a shower?"

"I can always take another one!"

Alex could only shake his head at Gabrielle's words. He didn't doubt that she would have gone in with him if she knew. That was the kind of girl she was.

Gwenn came by around an hour later to fetch them for dinner, which they had with Prince Arthur and Nimue again. It was a grand feast. Alex didn't know if Prince Arthur always ate so much, or if he was trying to show off, but Alex though a six-course meal was a little too much food. He felt bloated from eating too much.

Night time soon rolled around. Alex, Gabrielle, and Nyx didn't get back to their room until the sun had already gone down.

Before they had left the dinner, Prince Arthur did inform them that they would be getting up early tomorrow for their missions, and to make sure they got plenty of rest.

Alex had already come to understand that he would be sleeping in the same bed as Gabrielle and Nyx. It filled him with dread, but at the same time, he was strangely calm as they all crawled into bed together. Gabrielle was, fortunately, dressed. She only wore pink panties and a large white T-shirt, but it was better than nothing. Nyx had a full set of black pajamas, a long-sleeved button-up shirt and pants.

As they all crawled under the covers together, Gabrielle immediately sought his warmth. She snuggled against him. Alex took several deep breaths to keep from letting himself feel lust. They were just sleeping together. It didn't mean they were doing anything, so the lust was unwarranted. He blamed Asmodeus for this feeling, though he knew doing so was illogical.

Nyx didn't snuggle against him. He was grateful.

"Tomorrow we're going to Winchester," he said softly, so as not to wake Gabrielle.

"That's right."

"I'm nervous. A lot can go wrong."

"Don't worry. I'll protect you."

"That so? Thank you, Nyx. It's good to know you'll be watching my back."

"You're welcome. I would even die for you, if you needed me to."

"Don't say things like that." Having been staring at the canopy, Alex finally turned just his head to look at Nyx. Like him, she was lying on her back. Her head was also turned. Red, half-lidded eyes stared back at him. "I don't want you to ever say you'll die for me."

"Why not?"

"Because..." He paused before coming up with a suitable answer. "Rather than die for me, I'd prefer you lived for me."

"I see."

As Alex lay there on his back, Gabrielle nestled against his left side and drooling on his chest, a small hand sought out his underneath the cover. He recognized the unique softness. Nyx was the only person who had hands that were this soft, a consequence of being a person created out of nanomachines.

"If that is what you want, then I'll do my best to live for you," Nyx said, her voice quite serious.

Alex didn't respond with words, but he did squeeze her hand back.

"Alex… the photosynthesizer doesn't go there!" Gabrielle muttered in her sleep, smacked her lips several times, and then slowly drifted off again.

Alex and Nyx looked at each other, smiled, and then closed their eyes and drifted off.

INTERLUDE

TROUBLE ON THE HOME FRONT - PART II

"Mistress. It's time to get up."

Jasmine woke up to the gentle voice of her maid. Slowly opening her eyes, she fluttered her eyelashes several times as Madison's face swam into view. Brown eyes. Brown braided hair. A pretty face with fair skin, a small nose, and pink lips, placid and soothing.

"Madison," Jasmine mumbled as she sat up in bed. Yawning, she stretched her hands high above her head, luxuriating in the simple pleasure of feeling her muscles stretch.

She had been exercising a lot more recently, ever since Alex had left for parts of the galaxy unknown. It was mostly a way to kill time… no, that was a lie. She missed Alexander and by exercising, she felt like she was still close to him, felt like he was still nearby. After all, those exercises that she did were tailor made for her by Alexander.

"Good morning, Mistress." Madison inclined her head. "I have prepared the bath for you. Please refresh yourself while I finishing cooking breakfast."

"Thank you."

Madison really was the best maid she could have asked for. No one would have even suspected that she wasn't human, that hidden underneath her flesh was metal and circuits.

Alex had made Madison for her, created her after learning about her circumstances at home. He had said it was so she wouldn't be lonely. Even to this day, the memory of that time remained within her, a slow, pleasant but at the same time painful burning that caused her heart to beat faster. She would never forget what Alexander had done for her, what he continued to do for her.

Gracefully climbing out of bed, for the Queen of Grace never did things ungracefully, Jasmine padded barefoot into the bathroom. She stripped off her pajamas and placed them in a hamper. Then she journeyed across the marble floor. After taking a sonic shower that cleaned her body in seconds, she slowly entered the large tub and leaned back, sighing as several petals caressed her skin.

The water was the perfect temperature. Not too hot. Not too cold.

I wonder what Alexander is doing? Is he safe?

Jasmine did not know where Alexander had gone, what he was doing, or when he would be back. She only knew what Alice had told her. Alexander had left the solar system for a place called Camelot. He was going to help someone. He had gone with Gabrielle and Nyx.

She bit her thumbnail.

Why did he not ask me to come with him?

It was a foolish question; she knew exactly why Alexander had not requested she come with him, why he hadn't even told her. It was obvious. He wanted to protect her.

For as long as she had known him, Alex had always done his best to protect others. He saved people from bullies, fought off criminals, and always jumped headfirst into trouble for others. It was how he'd been long before becoming a cadet in the Mars Police Force.

Climbing out of the bathtub, Jasmine allowed water to cascade off her body as she stepped out and walked over to the large sink, with its porcelain surface gleaming brightly. She placed her hands on either surface. Fingers splayed, she looked at herself, frowning.

Her blonde hair wasn't in its traditional drill-like curls. It descended along her back. Several strands framed her face. Soft skin. Small nose. Pink lips. Blue eyes. Many people at school often said she looked like a princess, though if one asked her, she would have told them she was the Queen of Princesses.

Taking a strand of hair and twirling it between her fingers, Jasmine wondered…

Would Alexander like it if I greeted him with my hair done? He has complimented me on it.

Several droplets of water flew from her hair as she shook her head, dispelling the thought. Alexander was not there now. Regardless of what she wanted, she would have to wait. Patience. She would become the Queen of Patience.

After drying off and getting dressed, Jasmine wandered into the massive and empty dining room. A long table sat in the center, unused by anyone but her. She sat down. Seconds later, Madison exited the kitchen as though she had sensed her and placed a tray of her favorite breakfast on the table.

Waffles. Blueberries. Maple syrup.

Her parents would have thrown a fit if they found out her favorite breakfast was so mundane, but this had been the same breakfast that Alex had made the day after rescuing her from those kidnappers. It was a meal that brought her warmth. She normally didn't eat it, but today, she had requested that Madison make it for her.

While she ate, Madison fixed her hair into her signature drills. When she finished breakfast, Jasmine walked to the door with Madison trailing behind her.

"I'm off," she said.

Madison smiled as she clasped her hands together. "Be safe. I'll see you when you get back."

"Oh ho ho ho! Do not worry! I am the Queen of Safe!"

It took only five minutes to reach Atreyu Academy. Her mansion had a personal warp pad. It transported her directly to a connected warp pad in the school.

Upon arriving, she did the same thing she always did: Travel to the front gate and wait. Alexander wouldn't be there. Even so, Alice, Ariel, and Michelle would be coming.

As expected, the three arrived five minutes after she reached the gate. Jasmine greeted them with a smile.

"Oh ho ho ho! Alice, Ariel, Michelle! A grand day, is it not? Oh ho ho ho!"

While Ariel looked at her like she was weird—how rude!—Michelle smiled at her.

"Good morning, Jasmine. You look lovely as always."

"And you, Michelle. You cut your hair."

Michelle twirled a strand between her fingers. "I thought it was time for a change."

"It looks great!"

"Thank you!"

Jasmine liked Michelle, who always greeted her with a smile and spoke with respect. She didn't even care that this girl was the younger sister of the trollop who was trying to steal her Alexander. In class, after school, talking to this girl was very fun. They could chat for hours.

"Ha… you two are so troublesome," Alice sighed.

"I agree." Ariel crossed her arms and frowned at them. "The way you two get along so well makes me sick."

Jasmine raised a hand to her mouth and laughed. "Oh ho ho ho ho! There is no need to be so crass. Jealousy is unbecoming!"

"Jealousy?!" Ariel growled. "You think I'm jealous?!"

"I cannot fathom as to why else you would be so angry at us," Jasmine reasoned. "Do not worry. I do not blame you, nor do I dislike you. Indeed, I, the Queen of Magnanimity, would like nothing more than to be your friend."

"Fat chance of that happening!"

"Do not worry about her." Michelle sighed and gestured sadly to her sister. "She is merely envious of your, shall we say, assets."

"I am not!"

Jasmine had no idea what Michelle meant by assets, but she didn't let it bother her. With a laugh, she journeyed back into the school building with the other three.

School that day went by slowly. Homeroom was self-study, and Jasmine was already finished with everything she needed to work on. She had a strong desire to succeed, and when she wasn't enough to motivate herself, Madison was always there to push her.

Lunch was probably the most pleasant time for her. She, Ariel, Alice, Michelle, Neela, and Reenie gathered together and spoke while eating. Neela and Reenie were friends she had been her groupies at one point, but they changed to friends after she befriended Alexander. They weren't "in the know" about Ariel and Michelle, who they were and why they were there, but they were better off not knowing.

"Ugh." Ariel grimaced as she looked at her food—left overs, it looked like. "Ever since Alex left, all we've had to eat are left overs. I wish one of us could cook."

"It is a bit depressing," Michelle added as she popped a fishcake in her mouth. "Alex is a great chef. I guess that's what happens when you cook for yourself and sister for several years."

"Yeah…" Alice stared at her lunchbox; eyes crinkled in disgust. "Big Bro makes some of the best food. I miss his curry."

"You've all been talking about Alex an awful lot," Reenie said. "More than usual. Is something going on? Where did he go?"

"He left the planet," Michelle said.

"Wait." Neela blinked. "Alex left the planet. Why?"

"There is something important that he must do." Jasmine did not know what that important something was, but Alex wouldn't leave Alice for something nonsensical. "He will be back soon, I am sure. Oh ho ho ho ho! He would not leave his queen behind! Oh ho ho ho!"

"That laugh seriously creeps me out," Ariel muttered.

Atreyu Academy was an institution that allowed those attending to take specialized courses that would best help them be successful in the future. That was the reason so many people sought to attend. However, while Atreyu Academy had the highest number of students, it was also the hardest to gain entrance.

Jasmine was taking courses designed to help her become a successful business woman and maid. Business Science. Marketing. Maid/Butler Psychology. Customer Service. Her goal was to make the maid café, the one that her mother had owned, successful. After that, she would turn that one café into a chain of cafés, and they would become the most successful maid cafés on all of Mars before spreading to the rest of this solar system.

Of course, she was taking one other course. Maternal Basics. It taught her all she needed to know about being a wife, a mother, and a family member. This course she was taking for the day when she and Alexander finally became wed in holy matrimony.

After school, Jasmine said goodbye to her friends and headed home. She appeared on the family warp pad, which sat on a platform outside of the mansion. As she turned around, she caught sight at something out of the corner of her eye. It was a shuttle, a sleek craft that resembled a bird of prey. She recognized it. That was the shuttle her father used!

Her eyes widened.

Trying to do her best not to appear nervous, Jasmine walked into the mansion, stepping inside as the door slid open and closed.

Madison was standing there. Her expression was… surprisingly expressive. As a robot, one would not think Madison capable of such an openly emotional face, but Jasmine had seen this expression once before. It was the last time her father had shown up.

"Father is waiting for me, I take it?" Jasmine asked as she slipped off her shoes and set them inside of a rack built into the wall.

"It's… not just your father, Mistress," Madison said. "Your mother and brother are both here."

Jasmine felt her spine stiffen. Her brother didn't concern her, but her mother was great cause for concern.

She took several deep, calming breaths. It had been years since she had seen that woman. When she was younger, her mere presence brought Jasmine fear, but she'd become a lot stronger now. She could do this. She was the Queen of Fearlessness!

Squaring her shoulders, Jasmine stepped into the room where her… family… awaited.

CHAPTER 4

BEDIVERE THE NOT SO BRAVE

Alex woke up in a very interesting position the next morning. He'd already expected to find Gabrielle holding him like he was an overgrown teddy pair, but he had not expected Nyx to also be snuggling with him.

The pretty assassin was on the opposite side as Gabrielle, resting her head on his shoulder. Both of her legs were wrapped around his left leg. He was fortunate that she was fully clothed, or this situation would have been even more awkward.

However, as Alex was trying to figure out how to get out of this situation, something caused his entire spine to stiffen… and also another part to stiff. Soft, delicate fingers were wrapped around him, stroking him. He nearly screamed when the hand traveled up to his head, and then back down.

He was about to yell at Gabrielle for grabbing him, but not only was she asleep, both of her hands were visible.

That means…

He glanced down at Nyx. She was also asleep. Her eyes were closed, breathing even, but her hands were nowhere in sight.

Alex almost squealed and his toes nearly curled as the hand rubbed him again. Was Nyx really asleep? She must have been. He didn't think she could fake sleep like this, and she always said she hated perverted things, so he didn't think she would do this if she was awake.

I-I should wake her up…

"Why not just let this take its course."

"That would be wrong."

"You're the one who's wrong."

No statements from the committee.

"Nyx." Alex shook Nyx's shoulder to wake her up. "Nyx, come on. Wake up. Wake up, Nyyyyxxxx!!!" he ended his sentence at a higher-pitch than he wanted. Nyx had just tightened her hold on him, and it was painful!

Twitching in her sleep, Nyx stirred away, blinking several times as she stared at his bare chest. Alex had front row seats to the way her eyes widened as she realized their positions. What's more, her face, which almost always remained neutral, suddenly became bright red. She must have noticed where her hand was.

"EEEKK!!!"

Alex winced, both at the volume of Nyx's voice and at how she ripped her hand off him. It felt like his skin had been rubbed raw! Were he to look underneath the covers, he was sure that he would find the skin had turned red!

Nyx scrambled off the bed. Her movements were a lot more awkward and clumsy than usual. Alex had the pleasure of watching her feet get tangled in the bedsheets, listening as she squawked like a bird and windmilled her arms as she tried to regain her balance to no avail.

As she began to fall, Alex slipped out of Gabrielle's grip, stood up, grabbed Nyx's outstretched hand, and pulled her back to him. He fell back onto the bed with a bounce. Nyx was cradled to his chest. Her eyes were wide as she looked up at him, but he merely gave her a relieved grin.

"That was close, huh?"

"Um… yeah."

This was probably the first time he'd ever seen such an expression on her face before. Her shocked eyes combined with her delicately parted lips were beyond attractive. It made him want to lean down and kiss those lips, though he resisted. Either way, Alex promised to save this expression in his memory.

"Are you okay?"

Nyx said nothing. She looked down and nodded once.

"I'm glad."

They stayed that way for a while, with Nyx on his lap and in his arms. Alex had to marvel at how she felt. She was so small, seemed so fragile, and yet he knew that she was anything but. This girl was a deadly assassin. The juxtaposition between her appearance and her deadliness not only made her endearing to him, but it made him want to make her happy even more.

"Nnnggg…"

A loud yawn broke the sudden silence. Nyx leapt out of his lap, and Alex turned his head.

Gabrielle woke up, pushing herself into a sitting position before opening her mouth in a wide yawn as she stretched her arms above her head. She smacked her lips. As she lowered her arms, Gabrielle smiled.

"I slept really well last night!" she exclaimed. "Sleeping with you is definitely the best, Alex…?" She blinked and tilted her head, an inquiring look on her face as she stared at him and Nyx. "Is something wrong?"

"No," Nyx said.

"It's nothing," Alex murmured.

"Hmm…"

Before anything else could be said, a knock came to the door, and Alex decided to answer it. The person on the other side was Gwenn. She studied him for a moment, eyes trailing down and back up. Alex felt like a machine whose inner circuits had been exposed to a mechanic.

"Nimue is traveling to Winchester soon." Gwenn looked back at his face and adjusted her glasses. "You, Nyx, and Princess Gabrielle should get ready. I'll wait out here and escort you to the shuttle you'll be taking."

"Erm… thank you," Alex muttered before shutting the door. He turned around. Nyx and Gabrielle were staring at him, which caused him to shrug. "You heard her. It looks like we're starting this mission early. Let's get dressed."

Getting dressed was an awkward affair. Alex ended up changing in the bathroom. He grimaced and shivered as the invisible crises suit crawled up his body, inserting microscopic needles into his pores as it synced up to his body. Painful. Painful. Painful. It was like, well, like needles being stuck into his skin!

Sadly, the crisis suit still hadn't been properly calibrated for him, the reason being the seals on his body. He was at least half-angelisian. However, because that part of him was sealed, Gabrielle could only use a generalized calibration. Without the suit being perfectly calibrated, it would always be painful to take on and off, and it would never feel like a second skin, which she said it should feel like.

The suit finished syncing with him. Alex sighed in relief as he put on the rest of his clothes. He pulled his jeans up his legs, threw a gray shirt over his head, put on his jacket hoody, boots, and then placed black gloves on his hands. Looking at himself in the mirror, Alex smiled. No one would even know that his body was being enhanced tenfold by Gabrielle's crisis suit.

Gabrielle and Nyx were dressed when he arrived, though he had to pause. Nyx's outfit was the same. Gabrielle's was not.

Alex could tell from the slight sheen of her skin that she was wearing a crisis suit. However, a dress had been thrown over it.

Because it had no straps, her slender shoulders were laid bare, and the area around her bust was tight enough that he could make out the wrinkles along the front. While the upper half wrapped around her torso, the lower half flowed like a waterfall. There was a slit running along the left side. It was a gorgeous dress, and on Gabrielle, a girl who epitomized beauty to him, it looked enchanting.

However, Alex almost snorted when he noticed that Gabrielle was wearing spacer boots instead of heels.

I guess not even dressing up can change some things.

"You amazing," Alex complimented.

"Tee-hee!" Gabrielle's brilliant smile told Alex that he said the right thing. "Thank you! I don't normally wear stuff like this, but if you like it, maybe I can wear this sort of dress more often."

"You don't have to. I think you're beautiful no matter what you wear."

Alex was only being honest, but when his words caused Gabrielle to blush bright red, he wondered if perhaps he hadn't been too honest.

"T-thank you." Gabrielle sounded unusually demure. "Anyway, let's get going!"

"Right."

With Alex leading them, he, Gabrielle, and Nyx left the bedroom. Just as she had said, Gwenn was still waiting outside when they exited the room. The woman adjusted her glasses and looked at them.

"I see you three are dressed. Come. Let's meet with Nimue."

Nimue was already waiting at the hangar when they arrived, and she wasn't alone. Outside of her guards, six soldiers decked from head to toe in glimmering silver armor, Prince Arthur was also there.

Both the prince and his fiancé were decked in resplendent clothing. Chestplate and shoulder pauldrons over white clothing. Greaves and vambraces covering legs and forearms. Nimue's armor was smaller to fit her frame—smaller and more streamlined. Meanwhile, Prince Arthur's armor seemed a bit bulky. It wasn't like Azazel's ridiculous armor. Alex imagined Prince Arthur would still be quite swift while wearing it, but it was still a lot larger than his fiancé's.

"I've come to wish you all well on your respective tasks," Prince Arthur said as they arrived.

"Thank you," Alex said.

"Thanks, Arty!"

Prince Arthur gave Gabrielle a long-suffering sigh; Alex understood. That nickname was the one Gabrielle had given him years ago, back when they were kids, and it probably didn't feel pleasant to hear that used, especially since Prince Arthur had tried to convince Gabrielle to marry him.

And Prince Arthur already has a fiancé...

Alex shook his head. He would think about that later.

"I have my own task to attend to," Prince Arthur added, "so depending on how long it takes, I might not be here when you return."

Alex raised an eyebrow. "You aren't staying here?"

The crown prince shook his head. "I am heading to Glastonbury. I would like to check up on my mother and stepmothers. What's more, I need to confirm whether or not Lancelot's actions are truly something that Igraine put him up to."

"You will be careful, won't you?" asked Nimue.

"Of course." Prince Arthur's eyes softened as he gazed into Nimue's obsidian irises. "You know I will always be careful. I have to return back to you."

"Oh, Arthur."

"Nimue."

"Arthur!"

"Nimue!"

Alex looked away as Prince Arthur and Nimue began kissing… it was a very sloppy kiss, complete with smacking sounds and everything. Even with his head turned, Alex couldn't stop from visualizing it thanks to the noise. It sounded like there was some tongue action going on there.

Gabrielle had no such compunctions. Alex placed his hands over her eyes to keep her from watching this private moment, despite her protests.

After Prince Arthur and Nimue shared a kiss passionate enough that Alex thought his face had exploded, the four of them were seen off by Prince Arthur and Gwenn. Of course, he called it "the four of them", but that was because he wasn't including the six bodyguards who also boarded the sleek craft with them.

Unlike the previous vessels that Alex had been flown in, this one made him think of a luxury passenger yacht. The seats were arranged like booths. As he, Gabrielle, and Nyx sat on one side, Alex almost jerked because of how he sank into the soft cushion.

Nimue chuckled at him as she sat down, as though amused by his reaction.

"You are not used to opulence, are you?"

Alex shook his head. "Not really."

"It shows. You'll have to become used to this sort of thing, if you want to because Emperor of the Galaxy, that is."

"Ugh…" Alex looked away.

Nimue raised a hand to her mouth and giggled. It was very demure and lady-like. Nothing at all like the commanding presence she had displayed when commanding the Excalibur.

As the shuttle lifted off the ground and began flying, Alex looked out the window, watching as Prince Arthur and Gwenn vanished from his sight.

1

It took eight hours to get from Camelot to Winchester—a surprisingly short time considering they were traveling between planets. The distance between the two planets was about the same distance between Mars and Earth. It would have taken about two weeks to travel that distance using the shuttles from Alex's solar system.

The marvels of alien technology.

Winchester was a much smaller planet. However, its composition was more or less the same as Camelot's. From a distance, it looked like a sphere of blue, green, and white. Most of the planet was made up of green, which Nimue told them was because the majority of Winchester was forest, and the land to ocean ratio was about 3:1. Case in point, the planet only had one ocean, and it was surrounded by land.

Entering the atmosphere was smooth. Alex barely noticed it, save for when he looked out the window and saw the flames that had enveloped their shuttle due to atmospheric reentry.

"Where are we heading?" asked Gabrielle as the shuttle leveled off and began traveling horizontally instead of vertically.

"We're going to West Haven," Nimue said. "That's the capital of Winchester."

West Haven was called such because it was in what people generally considered the west. Found within a large plane, the city did not have the grandeur of Camelot's capital, but it was still a large city. Even from this distance, Alex could make out several gleaming skyscrapers. Even the castle, which was much more modest than Prince Arthur's, was a sight to behold.

The castle was apparently their destination.

"Lancelot is cautious, so he'll probably have the vessel inspected at some point," Nimue said. "There's a hidden cargo hold underneath the floor. It's protected from sensors and no one knows about it. Hide in there until night falls. The passcode to the boarding ramp is 96ruthrA."

Alex nodded. "We understand. Good luck, you two."

"Thank you."

While Nimue stood up and moved toward the entrance, which had descended to allow the honor guard the chance to walk off first. Gabrielle did not move. She stayed where she was, staring Alex as though she expected something.

"Um, aren't you getting off?" asked Alex.

Gabrielle continued staring at her. It was a surprisingly penetrating stare.

"I want a kiss," she said suddenly.

"Um… what?" he asked, dumbfounded.

"A kiss. I want a kiss, like what Arty and Nim did."

"Uh…"

Alex was at a loss.

"You… know what a kiss is?"

"It's when two people who love each other press their lips together." Gabrielle grinned, her chest swelling. "Michelle told me about them!"

"I'm not sure that's something to be proud of…"

This was a dilemma. He and Gabrielle would end up kissing now that he'd finally agreed to become her husband for real, but, well, he wanted the kiss to be something romantic. Alex didn't want their first kiss to be in the middle of a mission where everyone was watching.

Still, Gabrielle was looking at him like she expected a kiss, and Nimue was now staring back at them, having stopped when she realized that Gabrielle wasn't following her.

"Okay." He sighed. "Close your eyes."

"Yay!"

Gabrielle pumped her fist into the air before settling down and closing her eyes. Alex withheld a sigh as he leaned over… and placed a kiss on her cheek.

Gabrielle opened her eyes again.

"That's gonna have to hold you over for now." Alex did his best not to blush as he added, "I'd rather our first kiss be special."

Still staring at him, Alex had the pleasure of seeing Gabrielle's face go from confused to embarrassed awfully quickly. Her cheeks became red. She looked down, hair falling in front of her face as though to hide her blush. Beyond her parted bangs, with her head tilted down, she looked up at him.

Alex thought he would die from adorable.

"Er… t-that—I'll see you later, Alex!" Gabrielle stuttered as she stood up and rushed over to Nimue. The other young woman smiled at her, as if amused by Gabrielle's embarrassment. The two left soon after, and the boarding ramp behind them shut.

Finally, Alex released the sigh that he had been holding in. "Well, that was awkward. Don't you think so, Nyx?" No answer. "Nyx?"

Nyx was staring at him, not saying anything, just staring. Alex wanted to say something. However, for whatever reason, he couldn't. A tension filled the air, and it seemed to block his throat. It was as if he was being strangled by an invisible force.

Despite this, Alex pushed through the unknown fear that kept his mouth closed and forced himself to talk.

"Are you okay?"

Nyx turned her head. "I'm head."

You don't seem fine.

Alex didn't say what he wanted to, but that was because he was sure Nyx would either deny it, or she would hurt him. Well, she might just huff and ignore him. Still, it was better to just pretend he hadn't heard anything and move on.

"Let's get that cargo hold open," Alex said.

"Okay."

And thus, Alex felt like he had dodged the blaster bolt.

Barely.

2

Gabrielle tried her best to stop her face from growing hot, but she wasn't very successful. She didn't know why her face felt so hot. Her cheek still tingled from where Alex had kissed it, and the warmth seemed to have spread through the rest of her. She felt unusually self-conscious. Was this what being kissed felt like? What would happen if Alex kissed her lips?

The thought almost frightened her.

She and Nimue were walking down a wide corridor. The rug beneath their feet was a royal purple. Artwork lined one side and windows the other. Gabrielle looked out the windows. There was a garden outside, filled with an array of really pretty flowers.

Michelle would love it here.

She and Nimue were not alone, of course, as the royal guard, Nimue's bodyguards, walked around them on all sides. There was also Morrigan. She was the girl who had greeted them when they existed the shuttle.

"I had no idea the Princess of Angelisia would be with you," Morrigan said with a big smile. It was so wide that her eyes were forced to squint. Gabrielle normally liked it when people smiled, but this smile reminded her of something unpleasant. "I've always wanted to meet you?"

"Really?" Gabrielle was surprised. She had no idea there were people outside of her marriage candidates who wanted to meet her.

"Oh, yes." Morrigan's grin was still in place. "I've longed to speak with the creator of the pulse cannon."

"Blegh."

The bit of excitement Gabrielle felt at someone wanting to meet her disappeared. Now she remembered where she had seen this smile. It was the same smile that Papa's generals gave her when they asked her to create weapons for them, the same smile they wore when they made her create the pulse cannon.

I don't like her...

Gabrielle knew right then that she would not get along with this girl.

"Is something wrong?" asked Morrigan.

Had Gabrielle been someone else, she probably would have answered with diplomacy, the same diplomacy that her instructors had tried to shove into her brain. Her response would have been both sharp and soothing. It would have not given this girl any information she could use in the future. Commanding yet gentle. That would have been a diplomat's response.

Gabrielle was not a diplomat.

"I hate building weapons."

"Oh?" Morrigan tilted her head. "Why is that?"

"Because weapons do nothing but hurt people. I'd rather build inventions that help people."

"I rather like weapons." Morrigan giggled. She had a nice laugh, but it sent a chill up Gabrielle's spine. "Weapons are the keys required to control the masses, and they make a glorious sound when they're fired. Brother likes his close-combat weapons, but I like the ones that explode. The bigger the better. That's why I like your pulse cannon. Did you know that I even have the weapon test stored in my database?"

Gabrielle did not like politics, but she knew how to act when in the company of another royal. She maintained her calm facade. Even though she wanted to scream, even though she wanted to tell this girl she was an idiot, she didn't. She took a deep breath and smiled.

"I did not know that."

"Oh, yes," Morrigan continued, waving a hand through the air as if to emphasize her excitement. "I loved watching it! Seeing that planet explode was one of the greatest events I have ever witnessed! Better than anything else! It awed me! It astounded me! I had no idea that there were people out there who could create weapons of such incredible power!" Gabrielle's fingers twitched as Morrigan stared at her, eyes shining. "And to think the person who created it is the same age as me. Why, I'm beside myself with respect."

Slow breaths. Slow, steady, regular breathing. Deep breath in. Slow breath out.

It took a lot of effort to maintain her calm, but while Gabrielle did not like politics, she knew how to act like a politician when the situation called for it. A princess of Angelisia could not afford to act like a child in front of others. So even though Gabrielle wanted to shout at this call, to cry at the words that were like a high intensity laser to her heart, she remained calm.

And smiled.

"I'm pleased that you like my invention," Gabrielle said. "I would show it to you in person, but Angelisia has a policy against showing the pulse cannon to others."

Morrigan smiled. "Well, it is your ace in the hole, is it not? I'm disappointed, but that's only natural."

The conversation ceased as Morrigan continued leading them through several corridors, taking twists and turns seemingly at random. Gabrielle tried to keep track of where they had gone but couldn't. Still walking beside her was Nimue, a silent paragon of austerity.

It wasn't long before the reached a door.

"Here are your quarters," Morrigan said as she opened it. "I hope you don't mind that I put you two together. We were only expecting Princess Nimue, so we had not prepared a second accommodation for Princess Gabrielle. Of course, we have prepared a room for your bodyguards just across the hall."

Nim frowned. "Are you telling me Lancelot is not in?"

"Sadly, brother away on business right now, but he should be back sometime tomorrow. Please use this room to rest and refresh yourselves."

"Very well," Nim replied with poise. "We shall make use of these rooms. I appreciate your forethought."

Morrigan giggled as she held the ends of her skirt and curtsied. "You're welcome. If possible, would you both do me the honor of having dinner with me later this evening?"

"We would love to." Nim smiled at Gabrielle. "Is that not so?"

"Yes," Gabrielle said with a smile that she didn't feel.

"Very good. I'll have one of the butlers fetch you when it's time."

As Morrigan left, the royal guard stationed themselves alongside the corridor, with two taking the door to their room and the others stationing themselves at key junctions. They were quite efficient.

The room that Morrigan led them to was nice, though nothing like the one she, Alex, and Nyx had slept in on Camelot. There was only one bed. It was large and covered with satin sheets. Despite their situation, Gabrielle was kind of excited by the idea of a sleepover-like scenario with Nim. She wondered if they could have a pillow fight in here.

As she walked across the carpet and sat down on the bed with a bounce, Nim went over to the window on the opposite side of the room. She searched for something. Gabrielle didn't know what, but her fellow princess looked satisfied. Nim turned back to her.

She was smiling.

"You did awfully well back there. Morrigan is well-versed in learning where people's trigger points are and pressing them. Most people would not have kept so calm when faced with a subject they find disheartening."

Gabrielle weakly returned Nim's smile. "I might not like diplomacy and politics, but I'm still Papa's daughter. I know how to keep a smile."

"I saw."

Nim moved over and sat on the bed with her. Gabrielle looked at the ceiling. It was ribbed.

"Still, it was hard. I don't like talking about that particular invention."

The pulse cannon was often considered Gabrielle's most impressive invention to date. The Angelisian army had shown it off several times on unused planets, recording the planet's destruction and spreading the video to all corners of the galaxy. It was basically a deterrent. They were saying that this was what would happen if people opposed them.

Papa never approved of its creation…

While the people who had forced Gabrielle to create the pulse cannon were incarcerated, that didn't mean the weapon itself was no more. It was too powerful to simply dispose of. Papa had installed it on the flagships of his most powerful generals. Of course, their orders were to never use it unless the situation looked futile without it.

"I'll bet," Nim said.

Silence entered the room. It wasn't stifling, but Gabrielle wasn't fond of it either. She didn't like silence. Silence reminded her of the times when she was alone.

"I wonder if Alex and Nyx escaped the shuttle safely," Gabrielle murmured to herself.

"Oh, I'm sure they're fine," Nim said, giggling to herself.

<h1 style="text-align:center">3</h1>

As Alex sat inside of the hidden cargo hold with Nyx on his lap, her head pressed into his chest, he couldn't help but feel like someone was playing a very cruel prank on him. He was going to have words with Nimue when this was all over. Honestly, she should have mentioned that it could barely fit one person, never mind two.

"You're poking me," Nyx muttered.

It didn't take a genius to realize what Nyx meant by that. Alex felt the heat of shame creep on his cheeks as he resisted the urge to readjust himself. That wouldn't help. Actually, it would probably make things worse.

"I'm sorry," he whispered.

Nyx had her face buried in his chest because there was no space, so he couldn't see her expression, but he somehow felt she might be just as red as him. The heat he felt from her face burned hot enough that he could feel it through his clothes, or maybe that was his imagination. Crisis suits were heat resistant, after all.

"Do you…" Nyx began and trailed off.

"Do I?" Alex asked.

"Do you like me?"

Alex froze. It was only through force of will that he was able to make his mouth move. "Erm… are you talking about as a friend?"

"I meant… in a sexual way."

"Oho! Oho ho ho! What an interesting development."

"I'm surprised an assassin would bring this subject up while on a mission."

"It must be the close proximity and new situation! I bet she's never felt this way before."

"That might be it."

Since when did you two start getting along?

Alex sighed when he received no answer from either voice, but there were a lot of more important things to consider right then. namely, he needed to think about what he should say to Nyx.

"I thought you didn't like perverted things."

"I don't," Nyx said, and then paused. "At least… I don't with other people. I don't think I would mind… if you were the one who did perverted things to me."

"I like this girl more and more!"

"She's very honest with herself!"

Shut up!

Alex did his best not to look down, for if he did, then he would sure see Nyx's backside barely hidden by her black skirt.

"Can I ask what brought this on?"

"It's your fault." Nyx's words were partially muffled because her face was buried in his chest still. "It's because perverted situations like this keep happening that I'm thinking about it."

"I wish I could deny that, but…"

Looking at their situation, Alex did realize that stuff like this happened to him a lot. Strangely perverse scenarios had been happening ever since Gabrielle arrived on Mars.

Of course, a lot of that was Gabrielle's fault. The girl had no modesty. She tried to take baths with him, tried to sleep with him, and didn't care about walking around naked. Dealing with her was tough.

But it wasn't just Gabrielle who he kept getting into scenarios like that with; Nyx was also an unfortunate victim of circumstance. In the time she'd been living with him, he had walked in on her changing, walked in on her showering, and, well, stuff like what was happening at that very moment happened quite often as well.

"But I don't mind," Nyx added, gripping his shirt. "I, um, when you look at me with lewd eyes, I don't feel disgusted. Rather, I don't mind when you look at me like that, so…"

We are so not having this discussion right now.

"Why not?"

"Would it not be better to get this conversation out of the way now?"

Alex ignored the two voices, who seemed to have reached an accord of some kind, and focused on Nyx. He still couldn't see anything beyond her hair and backside. It made this conversation even more awkward.

"Let's talk about this after the situation here on Camelot is over," Alex said. Now probably isn't the best time. Besides, if we do have this conversation, I think Gabrielle should be present for it."

"Y-yes, I see. Princess Gabrielle is your fiancé, so it would be best to talk this over in front of her."

"Right."

"Very well. We'll shelve this discussion for another time."

"Thank you."

Alex could have sighed in relief. He had dodged another blaster bolt.

"Now, I think it's about time for us to get out of here."

The people with the scanner to check for hidden passengers and compartments had already come and gone. He and Nyx had heard them stomping over the floor.

Getting out was difficult. The exit had to be released manually via a handle lock, which required him and Nyx to shift around to reach it. However, open the exit hatch they did, and the two were soon climbing back into the main interior.

No one was present, and when Alex looked out the viewport, the dark evening sky was what greeted him.

"Let's go," Alex said.

"Hm."

Alex typed the passcode into the 96ruthrA. It was a weird passcode. The ramp slowly lowered, and he and Nyx peered down it. There was no one guarding the shuttle, which seemed kind of dumb, but Alex supposed the people here didn't see the point. They existed the shuttle. Alex closed the ramp. Then he and Nyx began making their way out of the castle grounds.

The castle reminded Alex of a pentagon. There were five buildings arrayed around one larger building. Having seen it from a bird's eye view, Alex knew that it was shaped like a pentagon, which Nimue had explained was inspired by the five primary elements of earth, fire, wind, water, and lightning.

The grounds around the castle were fenced off by a large wall, and there was only one gate in or out. Of course, with flight technology, a simple gate wasn't enough to stop people from entering. However, located at each of the four cardinal points was a tower. There was a generator in each tower, which created an energy shield that could be erected at a moment's notice.

Fortunately, the shield was not on right now.

Sneaking out of the palace was not difficult, though it would have been without his inventions. He and Gabrielle had created many devices. Some didn't work like they should, but there were a few that worked just fine.

Mr. Invisible was one such device.

It didn't make those who used it truly invisible, but so long as no one looked right at them when they were walking, it was unlikely they'd be caught.

The device worked on light bending principles. Mr. Invisible created a thin film of energy around the user, which bent the light around them, making it look like they weren't there. While this camouflaged them quite well, it did create a distortion in the air when they moved. With this device, they were able to walk past the guards, though there was one close call.

West Haven, the city that surrounded the castle, was located about half a kilometer outside of the castle walls.

Few people wandered the streets as they entered the city under the moon's soft glow. That did not mean there were no people wandering the streets, however, as several guards patrolled the town. He and Nyx used the alleys to sneak past the guards. It wasn't tough. The combination of the darkness, Mr. Invisible, and Nyx's know-how when it came to using alleys, allowed them to slip past everyone unscathed.

"Prince Arthur said that Bedivere was likely hiding somewhere in this city," Alex said as they stood behind a building. The alley they were in was empty save for a few portable trash compactors.

"We should probably find a tavern to sleep in and begin our search tomorrow," Nyx said.

"Right…"

Alex wanted to get started on their search right away, but they wouldn't find Bedivere unless they had some clue as to where they should look.

Since Nyx seemed more at home than him, Alex followed her as she led him down a series of side streets, alleys, and over several walkways. He didn't know where she was leading him. However, they eventually made it to a tiny corner of the city.

Dirtier than the rest of West Haven, the place immediately made him think of a red-light district. A few signs composed of gaudy lights lit the area. Alex read the signs and felt like cringing. *Love Town. Motel Sex Machine. The Pachinko Parlor.* This was definitely a red-light district.

I guess even space has places like this…

"Follow me," Nyx said… and then paused before adding, "and please don't say anything."

"Er… right."

Alex felt really out of his element as he and Nyx entered one particular building, which looked indistinguishable to all the other buildings on the outside. The only difference was the amount of noise coming from inside.

No one paid attention to them as they entered. Alex thought it was probably because everyone there already looked drunker than a lecherous old man being poured booze by several beautiful ladies. They walked past a group of people singing carols, dodged a man stumbling through the tables, and Alex barely avoided having some women who slurred her words attempt to hit on him. If it wasn't for Nyx punching the gal with a transmuted strand of hair, Alex might have had it far worse.

A bar sat in the center, and Nyx walked up to it and sat down. Alex followed her example.

This bar reminded him a lot of the one that he had been sitting in during the incident that got him expelled from the Mars Police Academy. Tables were situated around the room. There were booths lining the walls. The bar was longer than it was wide, and the reason for that was because of the platform above the bar, where several women in skimpy outfits danced around a series of poles.

Alex did not look at them. He did his best to avoid looking at them.

"What'll ya be havin'?" asked the bartender, a big man with a bald head and no eyebrows.

"Information."

"Information's gonna cost ya."

"That's fine."

"Hmph." The Bartender grabbed two glasses, filled them with glowing amber liquid, and set them in front of Alex and Nyx. "Drink."

While Alex hesitated, Nyx grabbed the drink, threw her head back, and downed it in a single gulp. Alex was impressed. He tried to do the same.

He failed.

The bartender guffawed as Alex coughed and sputtered. He hitched a thumb at Alex while grinning at Nyx.

"Newbie?"

"Never drank before, from what I've seen."

"I can tell."

"Go ahead. Keep laughing." Alex scowled. "Get me another drink and I'll show you who's a newbie!"

"Sure, kid."

The bartender made him the same drink, and this time, Alex downed it all without choking. However, the way it burned down his throat was nearly unbearable. He shivered from head to toe in disgust.

"Not bad." The bartender appraised him as he leaned against the table. "So, what kind of information are you looking for?"

"The kind that can help us locate a missing person." Nyx pulled something out of her dress and slipped it to the bartender, whose eyes widened.

"This is…!"

"The royal seal of Camelot," Nyx said. "Crown Prince Arthur has asked us to locate Bedivere for him. I don't think I need to tell you that he's been missing."

"No, you don't." The bartender sighed and eyed the seal with a grimace. "Unfortunately, I don't know where Bedivere is."

"But you know someone who does."

The bartender glanced around for a second, as though checking to make sure no one was listening. He did this while filling Alex's glass with more of that amber stuff. Now that he was thinking about it, that drink wasn't bad. It was making him feel all warm and cozy.

Alex downed another glass. It was really good. The bartender looked like he was saying something, but Alex couldn't hear for some reason. No. He could hear. He just couldn't hear well. Blinking, he realized that he also couldn't see very well. Everything was all blurry and out of focus. It reminded him of when he was looking… looking… looking at what?

Squinting, Alex looked to his left. Nyx was too his left. She was talking. He really loved Nyx. She was great, and she looked so pretty in her black dress… oh! He had another drink in front of him. He downed it.

"Hey, Nyx…" Alex leaned over and placed his head on Nyx's shoulder. He fell off the seat, but that was okay. Nyx could catch him. "Nyx… I love you."

"W-what?!" Nyx asked.

He grinned and pulled her into a hug. "You mean… so much to me… like, for reals. I really… I love you."

Everything was getting really garbled. It sounded like people were talking, but he couldn't understand them. Were they talking to him?

Alex felt his weight sag suddenly, and then his feet were being dragged across the ground. What was… oh, someone was carrying him. That must be it. Strange blurred figures were moving by him, and there were a lot of lights—at least, until it became dark.

"Nyx?" Alex asked. She was the person dragging him.

"How much did you drink?"

"Don't know. I just… drank what was put in front of me."

Nyx mumbled something under her breath, but he didn't know what she said. It felt like his hearing things underwater.

He was set down several seconds later. Nyx walked in front of him, blurry and out of focus, but it was definitely her. Alex would recognize her small frame anywhere.

She picked him up a second later. Alex nuzzled his nose into her head. She smelled so good. Grinning, he wrapped her in a hug as the world tilted around them. He thought he heard someone screaming, but it was probably his imagination.

Nyx's face swam into his vision seconds later. She was so pretty, and her lips were so pink and kissable. Kissing? Kissing. That was a great idea.

Alex kissed Nyx… and that was the last thing he saw.

4

The next morning was a bit hectic for Gabrielle, who was woken up early by Nim and told to get ready. Lancelot had arrived sometime last night and would speak to them after breakfast.

After taking a shower and getting dressed, Gabrielle headed for the dining hall with Nim and ate a nice breakfast. Morrigan had not been there. Gabrielle was grateful. She didn't much care for the girl, or her views, or her smile. In fact, she would be quite happy when they left this planet and she never had to see that girl again.

Sadly, Morrigan was the girl who escorted them to see Lancelot.

"And here we are!!" the girl announced with a cheerful smile as she opened a large set of double doors. "Big brother is in here!" The girl waltzed into the room, her voice echoing all the way down the hall. "Hello, Big brother!!"

Gabrielle walked beside Nim and her royal guard, who surrounded them both in a protective ring, weapons at the ready. She frowned. It hadn't occurred to her until now, but the royal guard's weapons were a bit outdated.

The large room was definitely an entrance hall. Most of the floor was marble, but running from the doorway they had entered to the throne on the opposite side was a red carpet. The roof was higher than she had expected. Gabrielle turned her head left and up, looking at the balcony upon which she thought several figures moved through. It was dark up there, so she couldn't tell.

A man sat on the throne. Shoulder-length blond hair was swept back. There were a few bangs framing his face. They hovered around his blue eyes. He was dressed like Gabrielle expected from royalty. He wore a really gaudy red outfit; his pants flared out at the knees, his doublet looked like velvet, and the shoulder cape was something that royals from most planets wore. His grin reminded Gabrielle of the girl, Morrigan.

She didn't like him.

"Princess Nimue," Lancelot greeted. "You are looking even more lovely than I remember. How is Arthur doing?"

"We have been better," Nim replied. "Camelot was recently attacked by Tristan, and we learned that you have taken over Winchester and driven out Bedivere. I've come today to demand an explanation."

"An explanation?" Lancelot cupped his chin. "Yes, I suppose an explanation is in order. You see, I did all this for the good of our solar system. Bedivere was plotting to overthrow Arthur. I merely wished to stop him."

"And I suppose Tristan's unprovoked attack on Camelot had nothing to do with you," Nim said calmly.

"Exactly."

Nim's right eyebrow twitched. "Do you expect me to believe that?"

"No." Lancelot smiled as he snapped his fingers. "I don't."

Several shadows leapt from the second floor. Screams erupted from the royal guards before Gabrielle could even figure out what was happening, blood erupted from some of the elite guards, who fell to the ground. One of them feel in front of her. Gabrielle looked down. There was a knife in the guard's neck.

Gabrielle froze as she tried to think of what to do, but her lack of action only lasted for a second, and then she was swiping her finger through the air and summoning an object from her D-space. Most people would have probably thought it was a gun. It was large and pink. The trigger was attached to the handle. Gabrielle took aim.

"DUCK!!!"

Her shout was followed by a loud *chug-chug-chug!* as she pulled the trigger. Nim and her guards were quick to duck, which was good because it meant they avoided being hit by Mr. Stick's goo-balls. The people around them weren't so lucky. Many of them were struck in the face, and the spheres exploded and covered them in a sticky substance that was impossible to break free from.

Gabrielle continued to shoot. Meanwhile, the royal guard recovered from the surprise attack and began their counterattack. They swung swords, slammed shields, and attacked with a zeal that Gabrielle had only seen in a few people.

She did her best to ignore the blood as it flew through the air, splattered against the ground, and created puddles. Gabrielle wasn't squeamish. There had been more than enough assassins after her life that she'd seen violence and death before, though she had never taken a life before. Plenty of people had died in front of her. Some of them had been kidnappers who Azazel or Papa had personally slain.

"Seize them!" Lancelot ordered. "I want Nimue and Princess Gabrielle alive!"

More guards were arriving. They came in through hidden doors in the wall, the balcony overlooking the first floor, and Morrigan even used geokinesis to create golems from the marble floor. As more enemies appeared before them, more of the royal guards fell. They were strong, but not that strong.

One of the guards fell to the ground in a burst of blood, their throat split open like a peeled banana. Another to her left went down in a hail of blaster fire. Steam rose from his body like it had been overcooked. To the left, a warrior was impaled through the chest with an energy sword, her body sagging forward before it was kicked off the weapon. It wasn't long before the half a dozen guards who'd gone with them were all dead.

Gabrielle grimaced as she summoned another device. It looked like an oval with exhaust ports on it, but it was actually Mr. Barrier, a device that she had made in an attempt to adapt light wave technology with Angelisian technology. Mr. Barrier was the result. Like all inventions that she made for the purpose of combat, it worked just as it was supposed to.

A bright blue barrier sprang up around her and Nim, a dome that could block any attack from all sides. Swords bounced off it. Blaster bolts were deflected and sent back at their attackers. While the color seemed off, the shield definitely worked just as it was supposed to. She could have congratulated herself on a successful trial run, but this was only the first part of her plan. Also, the barrier would eventually run out of power. They needed to escape before then.

"Morrigan!" Lancelot screamed.

"Do not worry, Big brother! I'll destroyed that barrier!"

Morrigan proved that she really could manipulate more than one type of energy when lightning sprang from her fingertips. She thrust her hand out. The lightning leapt forward and slammed into Gabrielle's shield. Fortunately, this shield was based on the lightwave barrier, which repelled all forms of energy.

Lightning was just another form of energy.

"Ah!"

The bolt of lightning bounced off the barrier and slammed into Morrigan. She screamed as what Gabriella calculated was around sixteen thousand volts of electricity coursed through her body. Lightning skittered across her skin. The scent of burning flesh made Gabrielle wrinkle her eyes. Morrigan's eyes rolled up into the back of her head and she started frothing at the mouth as she fell backward.

"MORRIGAN!!"

Lancelot finally raced down from the thrown and ran toward his sister, kneeling down and attempting to school the girl into his arms. But he couldn't. Morrigan was covered in lightning. He was zapped every time he tried.

"Hold onto me, Nim!" Gabrielle commanded as she opened her D-space again, this time to pull out Mr. Transporter. "We're getting out of here!"

Nim hugged her tightly as Gabrielle activated her device by pressing a button on the bracelet that was Mr. Transporter.

It happened in an instant. One second they were in the throne room of West Haven, and the next they were in a random room that appeared to be a shower room. It looked like someone was getting ready to take a bath. There was hot water filling a tub, steam wafting from the surface.

Mr. Transporter was the same device that she had used to escape from her bodyguards before meeting Alex. It worked using dimensional warping technology, another type of tech that Gabrielle had invented herself because no one else had done it. By shifting out of their dimension, Gabrielle could transport herself and anything she was carrying with her at the time, be that people or items.

"We… we just teleported, didn't we?" asked Nim, eyes wide.

"Yep," Gabrielle said.

"I've heard of dimension warping technology before, but I haven't seen it until now," Nim murmured. "That sort of technology is expensive… though I guess the creator of the Dimensional Gate wouldn't have to worry about that."

The Dimensional Gate was the device she created that allowed her to phase out of this dimension. Gabrielle didn't much care for that name. She thought her original name of Mr. Dimension was much better, but the politicians who forced her to patent and sell this technology made her change it. Stupid idiots. They were all idiots, but Papa was the biggest idiot for telling her to do as they said.

"Where are we…?" asked Nim.

"Hmm… don't know." Gabrielle placed a finger to her lips and looked around. The room was made of all tiles, there was a tub, and there was a shower head on the far wall with a stool. No one was there. "I didn't have time to set any coordinates, so the location we appeared was selected completely at random."

"Random, huh…" Nim frowned as she also looked around the room. "We were randomly transported into someone's shower…?"

"Seems that way."

At that exact moment, the door opened and a naked man with nothing but a towel around his waist walked into the room.

He stared at them, and they at him. Three. Two. One.

"IYYYAAAA!!! IT'S A PAIR OF PERVERTS!!!" the man squealed, holding a hand to his chest as though to protect his modesty. Sadly, since his hands were on his chest, there was nothing keeping the towel around his waist.

The sound of Nim's screams joined the man's as a white towel fell to the floor.

5

Hangover. Alex had heard of them before. They were the result of drinking so much alcohol that the body became dehydrated, and when the drinker woke up, the dehydration and poison from the alcohol gave them a massive headache. Seeing how he didn't drink, he'd never had one before.

Until now.

"Ooohhh…" Alex groaned. "Why does it feel like I was hit by a shuttle."

Everything hurt. Moving hurt, thinking hurt. He wanted to curl up into a ball and go back to sleep.

"Sit up and drink there," a voice said.

Alex groaned again. He didn't want to get up, but the voice wasn't taking no for an answer. Hands helped him sit up, and then a glass was placed near his lips, tilting and forcing a foul-tasting liquid down his throat. He gagged and tried to spit it out, but a pair of even bigger hands clamped his mouth shut and forced him to swallow.

"Drink," the voice commanded.

Left with no recourse, Alex drank the foul… whatever it was. Almost from the moment he swallowed, the pain in his head began vanishing, slowly at first but picking up speed. His mind soon cleared, and he was able to see who had forced him to drink the liquid.

"Nix," Alex hacked. His mouth was dry. "Where are we?"

"You don't remember what happened?" asked Nyx. Alex shook his head. "We're still in the tavern. I bought a room for us and dragged you here."

It was as she explained their situation that Alex realized he was lying in a bed. Nyx was sitting on the edge, turned slightly toward him. She was fully dressed, and so was he. His clothes were wrinkled.

"I'm sorry." Alex smiled at her. "It seems I was a burden to you."

Raven locks of hair whipped through the air as Nyx shook her head. "No. You did exactly what I needed you to do. I apologize for having you drink so much."

Alex hadn't realized that was what he was supposed to do. He couldn't remember what happened after a certain point, but he remembered choking on his drink, downing the second, a third, a fourth, and then everything went blank. Whatever happened after that, only Nyx knew.

"So… do you know what we're supposed to do now?" asked Alex.

Nodding, Nyx said, "we're going to meet with someone who might know the whereabouts of Bedivere… a man named Bors. I was told that he can be found at western bazaar around this time."

"Then we should hurry."

"Yes."

Alex stood up, and so did Nyx. The collar of her dress slipped. As she pulled it back up, Alex spotted a dark bruise on her neck.

"Are you okay?" asked Alex. When Nyx stared at him, he gestured to her neck. "It looks like you've got a bruise of some kind."

"Eep!"

"Nyx?"

"It's nothing." Nyx covered the bruise with her collar and moved toward the door. "Let's get going."

"Uh… okay."

The west bazaar was called such because the entire space was enclosed by a combination of archways and tarps. It was unusual to see something like this in such an advanced city. Even so, the place was crowded as he followed Nyx into the throng of people. Stall owners shouted about their great deals. Merchants and buyers haggled price. It was a threnody of chaotic order.

They were holding hands to keep from getting separated. Nyx's hand was incredibly small in his, yet the strength it possessed was undeniable. This very same hand had almost killed him at one point.

"What does Bors look like?" asked Alex, leaning into her ear and speaking loudly to be overheard by the numerous shouts.

"He has long blond hair, green eyes, and a goatee," Nyx said. "He's quite tall and will probably be wearing gaudy clothes and face paint. It will be hard to miss him."

Alex nodded as they began searching. It was hard to believe they would be able to find anyone in this crowd, but as he turned his head, taking in the sights, Alex soon came to realize that discovering Bors might be easier than expected.

Much easier.

"Is that him?"

Nyx looked at where Alex was pointing before nodding. "Yes, that is him."

The man in question towered over everyone else, wore a gaudy doublet made of vibrant purple with white piping, and face paint that made him look like a clown. No one else was paying him much attention. Either these people were used to this man, or weird people simply shopped here so often that no one cared.

With Nyx leading, they made their way to Bors, who was haggling with one of the stall owners. They waited for him to finish arguing over the price of some strange vegetable shaped like a butt. He looked less than pleased when the transaction was done, but they didn't care. They were on a schedule.

"Excuse me," Nyx said. "You are Bors?"

Bors looked at them. "Who wants to know?"

Nyx gave Bors the same seal that she had shown the bartender. The man looked at the sheet for several seconds, frowned, and gave the pair a scrutinizing look.

"This certainly seems authentic…" His eyes narrowed. "How do I know you aren't trying to trick me?"

Nyx shrugged. "Why would I bother tricking you? If I wanted information, I would just torture it out of you instead of using this roundabout method."

"True." Bors stroked his chin. "I also haven't seen either of you in Lancelot's court, though that doesn't mean much. Ha… very well. Follow me. I'll let you meet the person you are looking for, but you'll have to surrender any weapons you have before we head off."

It was kind of amusing how Bors made him hand over his whip, the only weapon not stored in his D-glove's dimensional space. What's more, Nyx had no weapons, but that was because she was a weapon herself. There was no sense in carrying a weapon when she could use alchemy to transmute a weapon from anything.

They followed Bors as he led them to a large building with a sign that marked it as an inn called *The Sleepy Sovereign.* Entering, Bors waved to the lady manning the front desk as he made his way through a door, gesturing for him and Nyx to follow. After traveling through a long hallway, they ended up at a door that Bors unlocked and entered.

It was a sitting room lined with bookshelves. Bors walked up to one shelf in particular, pulled a hidden lever, and stepped back as a passageway opened.

"Just follow the tunnel all the way to the end. You'll find Bedivere there," Bors said.

While Nyx nodded, Alex said, "Understood. Thank you for the help."

Bors shrugged. "I'll leave your weapon with the receptionist. Just get it from her when you return."

Alex didn't know if he would be returning, but the whip didn't matter since he had a lot of weapons in his D-glove, and his Aura of Creation was a weapon unto itself.

The tunnel they walked through was a lot longer than he expected it to be. He didn't know how far they traveled. However, they eventually reached a ladder that led to an automatic sliding trap door. As he stared at the metal door, deadpanning as he realized he didn't know the code to open it, Alex wondered what he should do.

"Should we go back down and ask Bors for the code or… huh?"

Alex almost missed the flashes of light that appeared before his eyes. He blinked, and then the door was split into several dozen chunks that crashed to the floor below. Turning his head, Alex looked at Nyx, who stared at him as though silently requesting that he keep moving.

He decided to do what her eyes said.

The room they found themselves in next looked like a regular bedroom. The trap door, which Alex realized was probably an emergency exit, was hidden behind a holographic wall. White carpet, white walls, white ceiling. Several decorations dotted the place, like a bookshelf filled with old tomes to his left, or the desk that sat against the far wall and the bed on his immediate right. He and Nyx walked further into the room.

The door on his left slid open. Alex and Nyx tensed before relaxing as a person walked in.

"Alex?" Gabrielle said, blinking several times.

"Gabby?" Alex also blinked, but not for the same reason. It was because of the way her boobs were bouncing.

Her bare boobs.

"Why aren't you wearing any clothes?!"

6

It wasn't long after arriving in that place that Alex and Nyx were able to meet the person they had been searching for. Gabrielle was dressed again. She sat next to Alex around a round table within a living room that only carried the basic amenities. There was some tea situated in front of everyone. Alex didn't know what kind of tea it was, but it had a floral scent.

Nimue was also present. She and Gabrielle had already told their story, about how they had gone to demand an explanation from Lancelot, about how Lancelot had attacked them while they were conversing via a sneak attack, and about how Gabrielle had used Mr. Transporter to teleport her and Nimue away. Alex regretted not being there to help, but there was little he could do or say.

"So, you're Bedivere," Alex said.

"That is correct," Bedivere said. "And you are Alexander Ryker, the one people are calling Gabrielle's Chosen."

"That's… a really pretentious name."

"I know."

The man called Bedivere looked nothing like what Alex had expected. He'd been expecting a thin and weedy looking man with cowardly eyes and no spine, but Bedivere was… well, Alex wouldn't call him handsome, more like… pretty.

His hair was a light blond, long, and tied into a brain at the back, while a fringe of bangs hovered over his green eyes. His face was effeminate. Were it not for his masculine build, Alex would have mistaken him for a woman. The cloak that he wore did a decent job of covering the fact that he had silver armor underneath.

"With Nimue and Gabby here, I'm sure you already know why we've come," Alex said.

"Of course." Bedivere reached for the small cup of tea and brought it to his lips. He sipped, set the cup back down, and then traced the lip of the cup with his index finger. "You have come to ascertain my location and discover why Lancelot is seeking the throne now. However, the answer to question two lies in the answer to question one."

"What does that mean?" asked Gabrielle.

"It means Bedivere likes speaking in cryptic riddles," Nimue responded.

"So, he's like a certain lecherous old man I know." Alex thought of his grandfather. "Great. This is just what I need."

"Don't be rude," Bedivere chided, his expression unchanging. "I was going to explain what I meant in just a second."

"Then hurry up," Alex said.

"I don't like waiting," Gabrielle added.

"Please just get to the point," Nym said.

Nyx just nodded.

"So impatient," Bedivere mumbled before getting to the point. "I'm sure you've figured this out already, but Lancelot and his sister Morrigan are merely puppets for their mother. Igraine is the one after the throne."

"Igraine is a very cunning woman," Nimue added. "If I am not mistaken, she was a bounty hunter at one point. She attacked Uther Pendragon's ship when he it was in transit between solar systems and was defeated, but rather than be executed, Uther had been impressed with her skills that he married her instead. There's always been a rumor that she seduced Uther, and that's why he didn't kill her."

Sitting on his left, Nyx tried to take a sip of her tea, but it was apparently too hot for her. She yelped and jerked the cup back. Trying again, Nyx blew on the tea several times to cool it off, and then took a tentative sip again. She frowned, drank some more, and made a face.

"Don't like the tea?" asked Alex.

Nyx shook her head. "I'm not a fan of arum tea."

"Regardless of what actually happened, there's no denying that Igraine is a cunning woman and that she's after the throne." Bedivere took another sip of tea, and then folded his hands on the table and leaned over to pin them with a look. "The reason Lancelot attacked me isn't because Winchester is the closest place to Camelot. It's because I found out what Igraine is after, and so she sent Lancelot and Morgan to take care of me."

Alex didn't know what he was talking about, and apparently neither did Gabrielle or Nyx. However, Nimue seemed to know. Her eyes slowly grew wide after several seconds. The princess and fiancé of Prince Arthur forced herself to calm down. Even so, her shoulders shook with repressed anxiety and perhaps even fear.

"You mean she's after Avalon, don't you?" Nimue asked.

"Indeed." Bedivere nodded several times. "She's after the Power of Kings."

Silence followed the remark. It was a very ominous proclamation, or it would have been, except Alex had no idea what they were talking about. Gabrielle and Nyx both frowned at Bedivere and Nimue, clearing expecting them to elaborate.

"What's the Power of Kings?" asked Gabrielle when neither of them said anything.

"It is the power that only the king of our solar system may wield," Bedivere said. "There's a legend that it's an ancient power unlike anything ever seen. However, those are only legends. The Power of Kings is an ancient device that contains the key to unlocking an alien device that's been around since before the founding of Camelot and the existence of the Pendragon line."

"So… it's like an alien super weapon?" asked Alex.

"We don't know," Nimue said. "There are no historical records of this device having ever been activated before, so we have no idea what it does. However, while no records exist, there is a story passed down among the royal family about the first Pendragon activating the device and using its power to become king. This is why it has been called the Power of Kings."

"What's more, the Pendragons exist to protect that power," Bedivere added. "The story states that when the first Pendragon activated it, he nearly eradicated all life in this solar system. Afterward, the key to unlocking that power was sealed within a stone, and a new legend came about, which stated that one would come to pull the key from the stone and lead our solar system into a new era of prosperity."

While a good portion of that story was unfamiliar to him, the last part about the stone and the key being sealed within it, and about someone pulling the key out, was familiar to him.

Their tea had grown cold by now. Alex hadn't drunk any of it. He placed his left elbow on the table and drummed his fingers against the surface.

"The key is Caliburn, isn't it?" asked Alex.

"Yes," Bedivere said.

"Oh, no!" Nimue stood up, knocking her chair back as she placed her hands on either side of the table and leaned over. "We can't stay here! Bedivere! Can you take us to Glastonbury?"

"What's wrong, Nim?" asked Gabrielle. "Why do we need to go to this Glaston-place?"

"Arthur went to Glastonbury!" Nimue said quickly, eyes frantic. "He was worried that Igraine would try to use our parents as bargaining chips, so he went there to check on them!"

Bedivere sighed. "He's probably walking right into Igraine's trap, if he hasn't already walked into it."

"That's why we need to go!"

"We can't," Bedivere said. Nimue opened her mouth, but Bedivere held up a hand to stop her. "Do not misunderstand me. It's not that I do not wish to go. When I say we can't, I mean we physically cannot do anything."

"Why is that?" asked Alex.

Nyx was the one who surprised him with an answer. "Because Winchester is under lockdown. No one is being allowed to enter or leave. The only reason Lancelot let Nimue land is because he wanted to hold her captive."

"If we could break into the palace, free my knights, and get them to their fighters, then we might be able to escape," Bedivere said. "But storming the palace is next to impossible. We simply lack the firepower."

"That isn't true," Alex said suddenly, and everyone looked at him, causing a grin to spread across his face. "You might not have had the firepower before, but you do now." Alex looked at Gabrielle. "After all, you have the greatest inventor in the galaxy on your side."

Gabrielle beamed at his words. She looked at everyone else, her smile not fading, and said, "I can definitely help you break into the palace, though everything after that will depend on you guys. I'm not much of a fighter."

"It is true that you could probably invent something to help us break in," Bedivere began, "but I don't have any equipment needed to build something that powerful."

"Don't worry!" Gabrielle cheered. "I already have several inventions that I can use. Just leave everything to me!"

7

When Gabrielle said to leave everything to her, Alex had understood what she meant, which was why he wasn't surprised by what he was seeing. On the other hand, Nimua and Bedivere looked like their eyes might fall out of their heads at any second.

They were standing several meters from the castle gate. Hiding behind a tree, he, Bedivere, Gabrielle, Nimue, and Nyx watched as several hundred robots stormed the castle. The guards hadn't stood a chance. The horde had marched right over them, trampling them, stripping them of their clothes, and leaving them more disoriented than if they had been hit on by a bunch of muscular men in speedos.

"Okay." Gabrielle walked out from behind the tree and moved toward the castle gates. "The guards are taken care of, so let's go."

Alex and Nyx were the first to follow Gabrielle. It took longer for Bedivere and Nimue to get over their shock, though they did eventually rush to catch up.

"I had no idea you had an entire army of robots at your disposal." Bedivere eyed the now naked and disoriented men and women who had been guarding the gate. There were six in all. Two had been standing on the outside, two on the inside, and two more inside of the station building. The building was no more, having been reduced to rubble along with a good portion of the wall.

"An army?" Gabrielle didn't look back as she strolled right on through the gates. Up ahead, screams and shouts could be heard as the robots continued to trample and strip everyone in sight. "Yeah, I guess you could call them that. I always like to keep my inventions inside of my D-space so other people can't use them for their own purposes."

"Ah." Bedivere's eyes lit up as though he understood.

"Where will we find your knights?" asked Alex.

"Probably in the dungeon."

"You guys still use dungeons?"

Bedivere furrowed his brow. "Is there something wrong with that?"

"I guess not," Alex said, though he personally found it weird. What sort of medieval fantasy was this?

The dungeon was located on the opposite side of the hanger. Alex and the others, using the distraction provided by Gabrielle's robots, ran through a number of artfully decorated hallways with portraits hanging from the walls and busts spaced in even intervals. Their feet thumped against the purple carpet as they followed Bedivere.

While the robots provided a great distraction for getting in, and their continued chaos kept most of the soldiers inside of the castle occupied, that did not mean they didn't have to fight. Six guards appeared from around a corner. They shouted something, but Alex didn't catch what they said because he and Nyx were already focused on defeating them.

Nyx slammed her hands into the ground, using alchemy to transmute the floor, which turned into a series of hands that slammed into three of the guards. As the three guards went down, the remaining three were distracted. Alex used that distraction to his advantage. He called upon his Aura of Creation and attacked from range.

Thanks to what he'd learned from the voices inside of his head, he knew that his method of using the Aura of Creation wasn't the only way to use it; there were other ways. Thinking on it, when he'd faced off against that simulation of Gabrielle's father, he'd been killed by a massive beam. Alex felt like kicking himself in the head.

Alex judged that he was five meters from the soldiers. Coating his hands in Aura of Creation, he threw several punches. Blue light erupted from his fists and slammed into the guards. Armor dented, cracked, and then shattered as the guards sailed backward. That didn't finish them off. They tracked to get up again, but Alex released several more energy blasts that knocked them upside the head.

They went down and didn't get back up.

"Oh! You're learning to use your powers like Papa!" Gabrielle exclaimed as they ran.

"Does your dad use his Aura of Creation like this?" asked Alex.

"Sometimes." Gabrielle scratched her chin as they turned a corner. "Papa likes creating big explosions. He's also really fond of shields and stuff."

"Uh huh…"

Alex wasn't surprised that Gabrielle didn't know much about her father's battle tactics. She might have been a genius inventor, but she cared little for anything outside of inventing and having fun.

He didn't blame her for that. Gabrielle had been isolated for a long time as a child, living in the palace on Angelisia with no one but herself, her guards, and her sisters. She hadn't been allowed outside. What's more, from what little Alex gathered during their conversations, it seems that several of her father's retainers had attempted to use Gabrielle to create weapons. With all that, it was no wonder she wanted to live a carefree life.

The dungeon were down a flight of stairs. Alex didn't know what to expect, but he supposed a dark and claustrophobic space filled with jail cells wasn't too far off the mark. It looked nothing like the Mars Penitentiary, which he'd had the misfortune of spending the night in before. There were two guards inside, but Nyx knocked them out before they could even blink.

Several people were inside of the jails, men and woman who looked bored. That kind of surprised him. They didn't appear worried. Some were doing pushups, others were meditating, and still others were just sitting on the floor and staring at nothing.

"You all look like you're having fun," Bedivere said.

Everyone stopped what they were doing. They looked over at him. There was two seconds pause. Then…

"My Lord!!!"

The group rushed toward the bars of their respective cells and clamored to get near him. All of them tried talking at once, which of course meant that no one could understand what anyone else was saying. Bedivere, wearing an amused smile, held up his hands and gestured for them to calm down.

"We're here to get all of you out of here," he said. "Camelot is in trouble, and we're going to need your help in getting to Avalon."

"Avalon?" one of them said.

"Yes. Now stand back. We're breaking you out of here."

The knights stood back Nyx used her transmutation to destroy the bars. Alex watched as she placed her hands on the metal and it simply… melted. It became liquid that flowed down into puddles on the ground.

Alchemy was composed of two aspects: deconstruction and reconstruction. First, alchemists broke down whatever they were transmuting—deconstruction—and then they rebuilt it into something of equal value—reconstruction. It looked like Nyx had simply stopped transmuting the bars at the deconstruction stage.

With the knights now free, the group made for the hanger. They didn't have to fight their way there, fortunately, but that was because Gabrielle's robots had already stripped every one of the soldiers. They passed by numerous soldiers who were naked and crying, or naked and unconscious. Alex knew well the "WTF?" looks of Bedivere's knights. He'd had that expression many times since meeting Gabrielle.

Just as Bedivere had said, there were numerous fighters sitting in the hanger. They were the blade fighters. Each one was smaller than he expected, about two meters in length, half a meter in height, and barely a quarter of one in width. There were a small bulbous cockpit protruding near the fore of the fighters, but the rest looked just like a sword.

"Come on," Bedivere said, gesturing for them to follow.

Alex, Gabrielle, Nimue, and Nyx walked with him to a much larger vessel, one that looked a lot like the ship that Prince Arthur had arrived on Mars in. Bedivere lowered the boarding ramp and had them all climb aboard. Already knowing what was expected of him, Alex went to one of the seats embedded into a wall, sat down, and strapped himself into the crash webbing. Meanwhile, Bedivere and Nimue went into the cockpit as Nyx and Gabrielle followed his example.

It wasn't long before the ship started up with a light thrum. Alex felt that unsettling moment where his stomach did flip flops as the ship began hovering in the air, but it soon settled. This vessel only had one viewport, but it gave him a perfect glimpse of the outside as they began moving.

"Wasn't that exciting?" Gabrielle asked as the ship began climbing out of Winchester's atmosphere.

"I suppose it was at that," Alex admitted. "It was more of a hassle than I expected as well."

"What do you think, Nyx?" asked Gabrielle.

Nyx turned her head to look at them both, and then went back to staring out of the viewport on the opposite side of the ship.

"I will be glad when we can go back home."

Thinking of homemade Alex remember all the people they had left behind. He wondered if they were okay. Was Alice keeping up with school? How were Ariel and Michelle fitting in? What was Jasmine up to? Was Kazekiri working hard? How was Selene doing? He wished he could see them, talk to them, but he knew that was impossible—at least, it would be until he could fix his Interdimensional Communicator.

I hope everyone is okay, was Alex's last thought as the ship entered hyperspace.

INTERLUDE

IGRAINE

Arthur sat in a single-man shuttle. His honor guard and Merlin had been against him coming on his own, but he knew that Igraine was a skilled sensor. Ten years ago, during the War of Jormungar, in which a neighboring solar system had tried to invade theirs, Igraine had sensed their imminent arrival despite them still being in hyperspace. She would sense if Merlin or someone else was with him and would suspect something.

With Igraine, it was better to be safe than sorry.

Glastonbury was a mostly water planet. Composed of about 95% water, there were only a few islands on the surface. The largest of these islands had been made into a castle for Uther and his wives. There they lived in the lap of luxury, traveling out on occasion for business or pleasure, but generally not getting involved with the day to day affairs of governing anymore.

They left that job to their kids.

It was all very lazy.

The descent through the atmosphere was a little bumpy, but the blade fighter he was using was his personal one. It had been upgraded with a number of modifications. The flight was much smoother than it should have been.

His comlink crackled to life. "Incoming vessel, this is royal capital control. Please state your name and business."

Activating his comlink, Arthur said, "This is Arthur, crown prince of Camelot. I'm here to see my family."

A moment of silence ensued before the comlink crackled again. "Roger that. We have you on our visuals. I apologize for the suspicion. Please proceed to docking bay eight."

"Will do, and don't worry about it."

Arthur piloted his blade fighter into the requested docking bay and set down. From even before he opened the hatch and exited, several workers moved up and began attaching fuel lines and calibration equipment. They worked very efficiently.

A man walked up to him, an older gentleman with a mustache and beard, who placed a hand over his chest and bowed to him.

"Sir Kay," Arthur greeted. "I had not realized you were still acting as captain of the guard for my parents."

"Indeed. It has been awhile, has it not?" Moving back up from his bow, Sir Kay offered him an amused smile. "If I am not mistaken, you have not been to Glastonbury in about four years."

"Something like that," Arthur said as he and Sir Kay walked out of the docking bay and into the hall. "How are my mothers?"

"They are doing quite well, from what I can gather." Sir Kay stroked his chin. "Though they have been acting a little strange recently. Not that I can blame them. It has been over a year since your father went missing."

Arthur smiled weakly. His father, Uther Pendragon, had gone missing over a year ago. King Lucifer, ruler of Angelisia and Emperor of the Galaxy, had requested him for a task. One did not deny a request from the being who controlled the galaxy. His father had left on the quest with Gadreel.

He had yet to return.

As he and Sir Kay turned a corner, they came upon a large door easily three times taller than him. Polished to a shine, the door gleamed a bright gold. Two guards stood on either side. Both guards saluted the two before opening the door. Arthur turned to Sir Kay, who gave him a polite bow.

"My Lord, I shall leave you here."

"Thank you for escorting me."

As Sir Kay walked off, Arthur squared his shoulders and entered the room.

Opulent was the first word he would have used to describe the room. While it was supposed to be a bedroom, the only thing about it that was bed-like were the luxurious beds resting underneath the shade of several trees. There was grass and various flowers, a stream that flowed into a crystal-clear pond, and several chairs and tables that rose from the ground as though they were trees shaped into chairs and tables. This entire place had definitely been created using life manipulation.

Only five women were in the room at the moment. A woman with purple hair lounged near the pond, reading a book. Iseult the wise. Two others, a fiery haired beauty and a femme whose smile reminded him of a devious fox, were having a battle of wits with a game of chess. Those were Morgause and Enide. Meters from them was none other than Igraine, and she was speaking with his mother.

Igraine's blonde hair trailed all the way down to her bare feet. Her white dress shimmered as she raised a hand and tucked a stray strand of hair between her ears. The woman sitting beside her looked a lot like him, or rather, he looked like her. She had blonde hair, but it was darker than Igraines. Arthur got his blue eyes from his mother. Unlike Igraine, she wore dark shorts and a sleeveless shirt.

Looks like mom still likes to pretend she's not royalty.

"Mother," Arthur greeted as he walked up to the woman.

It wasn't just his mom who stopped doing what they had been; Igraine stopped chatting as well, and so did the other three women sitting in the room. They all looked at him. While the three far away went back to what they were doing, his mother smiled widely as she stood up.

"Arthur!!!"

"Wa—goof!"

Arthur should have expected it, given his mother's personality, but he was wholly unprepared for her pounce. The wind was knocked from his lungs in a single whoosh. He blinked several times and stared at sunroof, which granted him a view of the sky.

"Oh, Arthur! How are you doing?! It's been so long since you visited me! You should do so more often!"

"Mom! I can't answer you if you don't let me!"

Arthur had forgotten how excitable his mother could be. She was always the type of woman who leapt first into any conversation, who liked to pounce on people she loved, and who was, well, a lot like Gabrielle in some aspects.

Perhaps that was the reason he found Gabrielle so suitable to be his wife. Not that it mattered now. Gabrielle was clearly smitten with Alexander, who complimented her better than he did.

"So, so? How are you? How's Nimue? Are you both doing well?" asked his mother after getting off him.

"Nimue and I are doing fine," Arthur said. "There are some problems with Lancelot and Morrigan, but aside from that, everything seems to be going smoothly."

"My son and daughter aren't causing trouble, are they?" asked Igraine, sounding legitimately worried. Arthur couldn't tell if she was being genuine or acting.

"They attacked Camelot."

While his mother gasped, Igraine held a hand to her mouth and her eyes widened. She looked visibly sick.

"I'm sorry." Igraine apologized. "I'll have a conversation with Lancelot and Morrigan as soon as I am able. Please forgive them. They are precocious children, but they mean well."

Arthur wavered, wondering whether or not she was acting or being honest. It was always hard to tell with Igraine. Even when he was younger, Igraine always seemed to speak with two mouths. It sometimes felt like he was looking at a distorted mirror, or listening to a radio that had overlapping voices.

He decided to keep things cordial. If he acted out now, then it would look like he was the villain.

"I would appreciate that."

His mother clapped her hands. "Since you're here, why don't you eat with us? We were just about to have lunch!"

Lunch did sound nice, and he still needed to ascertain whether or not Igraine honestly didn't know what her children were up to, or if this was all an act.

Everyone joined them for lunch. It was a simple lunch of sandwiches, though the sandwiches tasted like the stuff made from a gourmet. Even though it was merely simple spices with a variety of meats, the food tasted warm on his tongue. It was so good, he thought his tongue might go numb from the flavor.

Since everyone was eating from the same plate, including Igraine herself, Arthur didn't think she had poisoned it.

The conversation was mostly light. His father's wives got along decently well. If nothing else, they seemed to be close friends. Apparently, the five who were missing—those being Elaine, Gwenhyfach, Yvain, Isotta, and Esyllt—were actually searching for his father. He hadn't known that, but that wasn't so surprising. These women often stayed out of contact and did as they pleased.

"So you went all the way to this Mars in order to convince Gabrielle to be your wife, and then she turned you down?!" His mother laughed.

"It's not that funny." Arthur tried not to blush.

"It is extremely funny!" she shot back.

"Who is this Alexander person?" asked Igraine.

"He's a young man who ith marrying Gabrielle," Arthur said, pausing for a moment as his tongue tingled.

"Something wrong? The meal isn't too spicy, is it?" asked Igraine.

"No." Arthur shook his head and grabbed another sandwich. "Everything is…" he froze. The hand that had been moving fell onto the table with a clatter. He blinked and tried to move it, but he couldn't.

Beside him, his mother had already slumped forward into her seat, her head hitting the table with a loud thud. He feared she was dead, but then heard her loud snoring. That would have put him at ease. However, his mind was quickly growing dizzy.

All around him, the other three women slumped in their seats, shoulders sagging, heads lolling forward, bodies growing still. Poison. The word floated to him on irregular thoughts that flitted through his mind like ephemeral dreams. He couldn't grasp anything of substance. It felt like his mind was wading through cement.

He slumped backward.

"I'm sorry to do this," he heard a voice say. "However, I'm going to need you to sleep for a while."

"Wha…" was about as far as Arthur got before he was claimed by darkness.

CHAPTER 5

AVALON

The shuttle ferrying him, Bedivere, Gabrielle, Nimue, and Nyx arrived at Glastonbury in record time. According to Nimue, it should have taken six hours to get there. Thanks to Bedivere, it had only taken two. His knowledge of the space lanes was impressive. He directed them through numerous shortcuts that not even Nimue had knowledge of.

Flight control directed them to a docking bay that was unoccupied. As they emerged from the shuttle, it was to discover several people waiting for them. Four of them were women, but there was also an elderly gentleman with a strong build. He wore silver armor, had two blaster pistols strapped to his thighs, and carried a sword on his back.

"Princess Nimue," the gentleman greeted with a bow.

"Nimmy!!" one of the women rushed past the gentleman, a woman with blonde hair who looked a lot like Prince Arthur.

Nimue was prepared for the woman and only stumbled backward a few steps as she crashed into her. There was a loud cracking noise, like the sound of bones being broken. Alex winced, but Nimue didn't seem to mind.

"Claudia," Nimue said as the woman, Claudia, cried into her chest.

"It's horrible, Nimmy!! Arthur was kidnapped by Iggy!!"

"Uh…"

Standing in the background, Alex really had to wonder about this woman. He assumed she was Prince Arthur's mom. In which case, the other three women were likely Uther Pendragon's wives.

"You must be Alexander Ryker," the gentleman said. "My name is Kay. I am the captain of the guard here on Glastonbury. If possible, I would endeavor to explain the situation to you."

Alex glanced at Nimue and Claudia again. The poor princess was still dealing with the crying woman. He looked at Gabrielle and Nyx. While the pretty assassin was focused entirely on the man before them, Gabrielle didn't much seem to care, and was busy staring at some of the equipment.

"Please tell us what happened," Alex said, turning back to Kay.

"Of course."

Offering him another bow, Key proceeded to tell Alex, Gabrielle, and Nyx about what happened. He told them about how, several hours ago, Prince Arthur had arrived, went to see his mother, and was then kidnapped by Igraine. The entire explanation was very short, very concise. Time was of the essence, so Kay must have been hurrying to explain what he could with the time they had.

"To my regret, neither I nor anyone else suspected that Igraine would kidnap our crown prince," Kay finished.

"Do you know where Igraine is heading now? Do you know?" asked Alex.

It was not Kay who answered that question.

"We believe she is heading for Avalon," one of the women said as she stepped forward. Long purple hair glistened. Ruby eyes stared at him, set upon an enchanting and elegant face. She wore a one-piece dress, though it was on the short side, not even reaching mid-thigh. Thigh high boots covered the rest of her legs, ending in heels.

"That's the ancient device that the Pendragons are guarding, right?" asked Alex. Gabrielle attempted to move off, but he grabbed her hand to keep her from leaving. She probably wanted to take apart one of the other vessels in the docking bay.

"That is correct," the woman said. "She has everything she needs to activate it now."

"And that is?" asked Nyx.

"The blood of a Pendragon and Caliburn," the woman said seriously.

Because Avalon had been activated by the man who would go on to found the Pendragon line, it only activated for a Pendragon. Caliburn was the key. By having a Pendragon use Caliburn, Avalon would activate. That was what the purple-haired lady, Iseult, told them.

Avalon was not just a legendary and powerful device, they learned. It was a space station located between this solar system's binary stars. No one knew what it did, for it had not been activated in thousands of years, but everyone agreed that they could not let Igraine activated it. They had to rescue Prince Arthur and stop Igraine.

While Nimue communicated with the armada surrounding Camelot and the half-siblings that were allied with Prince Arthur, Alex and Gabrielle sat beside a quiet Nyx and waited for everything to start.

Uther Pendragon's four wives were also getting ready. They, along with Kay, were mobilizing the armada stationed around Glastonbury. The plan was for the armadas at Camelot and here, and the armadas controlled by Prince Arthur's half-siblings, to meet at Avalon and launch an attack. Since they didn't have any part in the preparations, Alex, Gabrielle, and Nyx just sat around a table in one of the unused guest rooms.

The door opened and Nimue entered the room.

"I just spoke with Dinadan and Gawain," Nimue said. "They will not be able to join up with us. It seems Tristan and Segwarides have sent their armadas to blockade Tintagel and Camelon."

"What about the ones who aren't allied with either Prince Arthur or Lancelot?" asked Alex.

Nimue shook her head. "They won't interfere with us, but they won't help us either."

"So, it's just us."

"Yes."

"Don't worry!" Gabrielle gave them both a thumbs up. "Even if it's just us, I'm sure we can rescue Arty! I have a lot of inventions that we can still use!"

Nimue smiled. "I don't doubt that. Anyway, both our armada and the one here on Glastonbury are being mobilized. I've also received a report that Lancelot has taken his armada and is now hovering around Avalon with a fleet of unknown origins. I'm guessing the unknowns belong to Igraine."

"Then there will be our two armadas versus theirs," Nyx said suddenly, speaking for the first time in a while. "I assume you'll lead one armada, while Uther Pendragon's wives the lead the other?"

"Wrong!!" a voice shouted as the doors were thrown open. Claudia stood in the doorway, now decked in black armor that made her look like a knight. She was even carrying an ominous looking black helmet under her left arm. "Iseult is leading the armada with Morgause and Enide. I'm going with you three."

"Huh?" Alex was the only person who voiced his shock.

Within the ringing silence, Claudia gave the entire group a grin that was more vicious than anything Alex had ever seen.

He almost pitied their enemies.

1

The fleet at Glastonbury was quickly mobilized and left for Avalon. Alex, Gabrielle, and Nyx went with Nimue and Claudia. Nimue had changed into a commander's uniform. It was basically just a form fitting unitard with a chestplate, shoulder pauldrons, vambraces, and greaves. Alex felt like he, Gabrielle, and Nyx were underdressed in their normal clothing. They didn't even look half as cool because their crisis suits were now invisible to make people underestimate them.

Thanks to Bedivere, it took them less than two hours to reach Avalon. Alex was in one of the smaller shuttles. It was called a Dragon-class shuttle. It wasn't as big as a Pendragon-class battleship. The Dragon-class shuttle could carry up to sixteen blade-class fighters and fifty soldiers. It was shaped, like, well, Claudia said it was shaped after a dragon, which was apparently a legendary creature in the Camelot system.

"That is a huge fleet," Alex muttered as he looked at all the ships surrounding them. He couldn't even count how many of them there were.

"Hmm…" Gabrielle was standing beside him, also staring out of the viewport. "You think so? I thought it was kind of small."

Alex glanced at her. "Erm… how big are the fleets of Angelisia?"

Gabrielle tilted her head, eyes squinting as she thought really hard. "Um… I think Angelisian armadas normally consist of one hundred thousand fighters, sixty thousand battlecruisers, ten thousand frigates, and a flagship."

"Uh…"

"Angelisia has the largest army in the entire galaxy," Nyx added from his left. "Not only are their battleships powerful, but they have more of them and more people to man them than anyone else. That's because serving in the military for at least five years is a requirement."

"Papa said that it's important for men and women to serve in the military so they can understand what the people who protect them every day go through," Gabrielle said.

"Uh huh…"

Alex had nothing to say to that.

The Glastonbury fleet soon hooked up with the Camelot fleet. Nimue should be heading over to the flagship, Camelot, at that moment. He wished her well.

"All right!" Claudia, helmet in hand, grinned at the three of them. "Let's hurry up and get moving. We're heading to the spear-class boarding ship! Follow me!"

Claudia gave them no choice as she spun on her heel and walked off. Alex, Gabrielle, and Nyx looked at each other before following the lady. The spear-class shuttle reminded him a lot of a trident. Most of the vessel was long, but the back moved into three fuselage thrusters that reminded him of a trident's blade.

"Welp! All aboard!" Claudia said.

"Uh… is it just us?" asked Alex.

"Aside from the pilot, yep," Claudia answered. "Now, come on."

The spear-class shuttle could hold up to a dozen soldiers—fourteen if they included the pilot and co-pilot. There were no seats. Situated against one of the walls was a bench that spanned the entire length of the shuttle.

"Sit down and strap in everyone," Claudia said as she walked over to the bench and sat down. He, Gabrielle, and Nyx did the same and strapped themselves in.

"Are you going to be okay, Gabby?" asked Alex. "I know you don't like fighting."

Gabrielle hesitated for a moment before smiling at him. It wasn't the usual bright beaming that reminded Alex of a shuttle's headlights. This one was softer, more genuine. It made his heart skip a beat.

"I'll be okay," Gabrielle said. "It's true I don't like violence or fighting or anything, but we're doing this for a friend. Besides, I'm already neck deep in what's going on here. There's no turning back now, you know?"

"Yeah, I guess."

"Although…"

"Although?"

Alex looked back at Gabrielle, who was still staring at him, though her expression somehow seemed more serious than he was used to.

"After all this is over, I want you to take me on a date."

"Well…" Alex dragged the word out to give himself time to get over his surprise, "I did promise you a date, didn't I? Once we get home, I'll take you out on a date."

"Yes! Thank you!" Gabrielle cheered.

"Oh, my." Claudia put her hands on her cheeks. "The glories of youth is great indeed."

Alex looked away from Gabrielle when he felt a tug on his sleeve. It was Nyx. She was looking up at him, her normally emotionless eyes containing something in them. They still looked half-lidded, just as always, but he could have sworn there was something imploring in them.

"Do you… wanna go on a date, too?" asked Alex. Nyx nodded.

"Nyx also wants to go on a date with you?" Gabrielle asked.

"Uh…"

"That's great!"

"It is?"

"Yes! It means that Nyx loves you, too, right?" Gabrielle leaned forward and looked at the pretty assassin on the opposite side of him. "You also love Alex, right?" Nyx didn't say anything, but she did nod after looking away. "Yay!"

"You children are truly in the springtime of your youth!" Claudia said, tears streaming down her cheeks.

"I don't even know what that means!"

It wasn't long before the dragon-class frigate they were in shook from explosions and blaster fire. Alex could see nothing outside. That somehow made him more nervous than if he could see what was happening. He wished he could have known what was going on.

"Lady Claudia!" a voice announced over the speaker. "We're preparing to launch, so please strap in if you haven't already."

"Who does he think they are?" asked Claudia with a pout. "Treating me like a kid is not cool."

Before Alex could do any more than contemplate facepalming, his stomach suddenly leapt into his throat as the forces of gravity pushed him into the seat. They had obviously just launched from the dragon-class frigate. That meant they were now soaring through space, during the middle of combat to boot. What made the whole situation worse was that Alex couldn't hear the battle that was obviously taking place.

Space is a vacuum. Because there was no atmosphere, sound did not travel through space, which meant he couldn't even hear what was going on. It sucked. Alex really hated it.

"We're nearing Avalon, ma'am," the voice said over the speakers again.

"About time." Claudia activated the comlink by pushing a button on her seat. "Show us."

"Bringing it up on screen."

A holographic display appeared in front of them, showing the group what could only be Avalon. It didn't look like much at first. The image was of a small long object situated between two stars. Two shafts of light were emitting from either end, traveling all the way to each star.

Then the image zoomed in, and Alex realized that they were dealing with something far more than just a simple object. Avalon looked was a space station shaped like the sheath of a sword. The shafts of light weren't really shafts nor were they light. It was plasma. That station was sucking up plasma from both suns.

"Ho…" Gabrielle murmured. "It looks like Avalon is using the power of the stars as fuel. It must have a plasma-based reactor inside."

"Is that similar to a solar reactor?" asked Alex.

"Yes, but it's many times more powerful, since plasma is many times more powerful than simple solar energy."

Alex knew how to build a solar reactor, but he had never considered gathering energy from the sun's plasma. He wasn't sure how such a thing was possible. To get plasma from a star into the ship, it would have to use some kind of tractor beam technology to pull it up. However, a regular tractor beam couldn't pull energy. That meant it was something different. What's more, the photosphere, a star's outer shell, had a temperature between 4,230 and 5,730 degrees Celsius. He didn't know of a material that could withstand such intense temperatures.

"The boarding shuttle is almost there," the pilot announced. "We'll be there in three."

Alex took a deep breath. This was it. They were about to jump into the belly of the beast.

"Two."

He tried to slow his rapidly beating heart, but it was difficult. His insides were squirming with nerves. Concentrating on anything other than how nervous he was, was proving difficult.

Two hands found his. Nyx and Gabrielle. They had both placed a hand over one of his. He turned his hands over and laced their fingers together, instantly feeling a little calmer than he had before.

"That's youth for you," Claudia said as she stared at them with a grin.

Alex would have said something to her.

"One!"

But in that moment, their spear-class boarding shuttle slammed nose first into Avalon and tore through the closed docking bay doors as though they were made of paper.

2

The interior of Avalon was like a twisting maze. Alex, Claudia, Gabrielle, and Nyx traveled down winding hallways, up durasteel stairs, over vast chasms by leaping across control pillars, and through several rooms with a number of strange contraptions that Alex didn't know anything about. He wished he had time to study them. However, not only was time of the essence, they were facing off against hordes of enemies.

They marched forward, their metal limbs reflecting light from the overhead lamp. Streamlined heads reminded Alex of these helmets he'd seen in a holodrama once. It had been a strange fantasy series about a group of warriors who wore knightly armor and fought galactic space worms. Their limbs were spindly, and they only had three fingers, but they could fire a blaster just fine.

Fortunately, for as many of these robots there were, they weren't very powerful. While Alex put up a shield using his Aura of Creation, Gabrielle, Nyx, and Claudia demolished everything in their path. Nyx was a monster. She used transmutation to create sinkholes in the floor or create giant hands that crushed her enemies like bugs. Claudia, with her black helmet that reminded him of a devil, mowed everything that came her way down with her sword. She swung the sword. Limbs flew. Heads rolled. Alex wondered how anyone could be so fast when they were covered from head to toe in heavy-looking armor.

Out of all the people fighting, Gabrielle was the most unorthodox, but also the most effective.

"Go! Go, go, go!"

She had two guns, one in each hand, and she pulled the trigger like a trigger-happy idiot. Her guns didn't fire blasters. They fired spheres that appeared innocuous at first glance—at least, until they bounced all around the room, struck something, and then created a black hole that sucked up everything within a certain radius.

Alex had never seen anything like it. The spheres were definitely propagating black holes. However, not only did the black hole not suck up everything in sight, it eventually disappeared.

The black holes did an excellent job of taking out the robots. For every black hole created, around 6 robots were sucked in, and Gabrielle was firing them off like a madwoman. She was even cackling like a madwoman.

"Mr. Black Hole is amazing! Mwahahahaha! Isn't this amazing, Alex!"

"Er… yeah, amazing…"

"Mwahahahahaha!"

Alex grimaced. "Hey, Claudia! Where do we need to go?!"

Claudia created a massive shockwave as she swung her sword in a horizontal arc. Several robots were torn asunder. Alex really had to wonder just what this woman had done before marrying King Uther.

"We're traveling up!" Claudia said.

While Alex had no way of knowing how long they fought, or how many enemies they destroyed, they eventually found their way to an elevator that took them up to a room. It was vast. Perhaps because this room took up the entire floor they were on, but the room was far larger than he'd seen so far.

Three people were in this room—four if he considered the person crucified to a cross.

Alex didn't know who these people were. All three of them had blond hair, blue eyes, and wore smug grins. The woman in the center wore a pure white dress. A sword was strapped at her hip. The male wore resplendent golden armor and carried a spear, while the girl was dressed in a black gown.

The person crucified to the cross was Prince Arthur.

"Iggy!" Claudia shouted as they stepped further into the room. "I've come to play!"

"Claudia." Igraine smiled. It was a pleasant smile, but Alex felt a shiver crawl up his spine. "How nice of you to join us. Perhaps you can convince your stubborn son to unlock Avalon for me?"

"Arthur!" Claudia called out. "How are you doing? Is everything okay? You're dizzy, are you? They haven't violated you, have they?"

"Are you ignoring me now?" asked Igraine.

Prince Arthur groaned. Even from this distance, Alex could see the blush on her face. "Mom... I wish you wouldn't be so... so..."

"Such a wonderfully concerning mother?"

"I was gonna say bat-shit crazy."

"How mean."

"Lancelot. Morrigan." Igraine looked at the two with her. So those were her children. Well, Alex probably should have expected that. "Keep those children occupied, would you?"

"You got it!" Lancelot grinned as he twirled his spear around his body. He was eying Alex, which Alex guessed meant this armor-wearing guy wanted to fight him. That was fine.

Alex activated his Aura of Creation and leapt away from the others as Lancelot charged at him. The spear impaled the ground where he'd been standing. Alex grimaced as it glanced off the floor, squealing as sparks flew everywhere. Lancelot wore a fierce grin on his face as he bent his knees and pushed off.

Holding out his hand, Alex launched a massive beam of energy at the man. Laughing like a maniac, Lancelot twirled the spear in his hands and swung. Light erupted from the spear. The beam of energy was sliced in half. As each half split off in separate directions and exploded against the wall and ceiling, Lancelot peeled his lips back and showed off his pearly whites.

"I see. You're not human. If I had to say, you must be an angelisian. Hehe, that's good. That's very good." Lancelot swung his spear around, twisting it and twirling it in complicated patterns that cut through the air. "This battle would be a lot more boring if you were just a human."

Alex thought several faster than he ever had as Lancelot charged at him again. He coated his arms in Aura of Creation, making a pair of vambraces that he reinforced and condensed as much as he could.

Lancelot came in, swinging his spear, which cut through the air with a loud whistling sound. Alex raised his arms and crossed them. Spear met vambraces. Alex grunted as his knees buckled, as his arms shook, as the ground around him cracked. Fortunately, his crisis suit had strengthened his limbs to ten times what it was with just his physique. Thanks to that, he was able to shove Lancelot through the air.

His opponent landed on the ground several meters away. He touched down lightly. Alex frowned as Lancelot twirled the staff along his back from one hand to the other.

"This is excellent. You're quite the fighter. I've never fought against an Angelisian before."

Alex took in a deep breath. "That so? Then this will be educational for you."

"What's going on here?" a voice yawned inside of his head. It was a familiar voice. He used to call it Voice Number One, but now he knew it had a name: Asmodeus.

"It seems there's a battle going on," Voice Number Two said.

"Battle? Oh! That must be why we woke up. Brat, you're using an awful lot of power. Is this twerp really so difficult to defeat?"

I'd appreciate it if you two didn't talk. I'm in a fight right now.

"Oh… so scary. Fine. We'll just sit back and watch for now."

"Good luck."

Alex pushed the voices away and thought about all of the people he loved, the people who were important to him, precious to him, who he would give anything for. He brought up images in his mind, memories of the times they had shared. He thought of Jasmine with her haughty laugh. He pictured Kazekiri as she petted animals at the store. He imagined Alice with her lazy expression and mannerisms. Gabrielle and Nyx. They were fighting Morrigan right now. Both of them had said they loved him. For them… yes, for them…

He could do this.

A snarl parted Alex's lips as he poured more energy into his next attack. The wind picked up around him, buffeting his hair as it swirled around him. Arcs of energy leapt off his body, striking the floor, skittering everywhere. In front of him, a massive ball of blue energy swirled, extended to one meter in length, then two, five, six, twenty. Alex raised his hands above his head. The Aura of Creation. It wasn't just a regular aura anymore.

It was a massive sword.

Lancelot whistled as he stared up at the sword, which almost reached all the way to the ceiling. He swing his spear and rested it against his shoulder.

"That's a lot of energy…" Lancelot took a single step back. "Are you sure you should be using that much power? You might destroy this entire station."

"I'm sure it'll survive," Alex said…

And then he brought the sword down with all his might.

3

Nyx and Gabrielle leapt apart as Morrigan sent several dozen spears of lightning their way. The spears struck the ground, exploded, and then chased after them. Gabrielle swiped her finger through the air. A rift appeared. She shoved her hand into it, and then pulled out a small sphere, which she activated and tossed into the air.

The sphere lit up, exploded, and then created another rift, this one much bigger. From within the fit, several dozen spears erupted, gleaming with a metallic luster. The lightning curved. It struck the spears and was negated. The spears went back inside the rift, which closed.

"Tch!" Morrigan clicked her tongue as Nyx slammed her hands on the ground and created several giant fists that tried to pound her into oblivion. She flicked her wrists. Light erupted from her fingers, bursting in a crescent that cut the hands apart. "That won't work on me."

"Then maybe this will!" Gabrielle cried out as she summoned a gun and fired. Red energy erupted from the gun and was blocked when Morrigan created an energy barrier. "That's aura manipulation. I see. So you really can use every form of energy manipulation."

"That's right," Morrigan said as the barrier disappeared. "I can use every form of energy manipulation imaginable, just like my mother. However, unlike my mother, I can use each form to its full potential!"

Morrigan raised her arms. A Massive ball of darkness crackled to life over her head. It was about three times the size of a person. Gabrielle wasn't much of a sensor, but even she realized that the amount of power being output by that ball was impressive. She could block it if she used her power, but…

I'd destroy this station.

"I was born for the sole purpose of defeating you! Of being stronger than you! My mother created me, cultivated me, raised me for that one purpose! You Angelisians are supposed to be the strongest being to walk this galaxy, but today I'm going to prove to the entire galaxy that you Angelisians are not all-powerful! Today I'm going to defeat you!"

"Hmm… I don't know why you want to defeat me," Gabrielle said, "but I have no intention of letting you beat me. Sorry."

Morrigan swung her arms down, which brought the sphere down. Gabrielle summoned another device. It was shaped like a silver disc. Throwing it at the descending sphere, Gabrielle took several steps back as the disc struck the ball of dark matter. There was no explosion, but something did erupt, a black hole that sucked the sphere right into it.

"W-what the hell is that?!" demanded Morrigan. "What sort of power is that?!"

"It isn't power. It's science," Gabrielle said. "And you should be more worried about yourself."

"Huh?"

Morrigan barely had a moment to realize the danger before several spears jutted from the ground and impaled her through the back and out her chest. That was what it seemed like at first. However, when Morrigan transformed into a human-shaped mass of dark matter that ate into the spears, Gabrielle realized that the Morrigan in front of them was just a clone created using Darkness Manipulation.

"Heh… how about that." Gabrielle pulled another device from her D-space. It looked like a sword, but it wasn't really used for combat. "She managed to swap herself out with a clone while talking to me."

"Princess Gabrielle," Nyx shouted. "Behind you!"

Spinning around, Gabrielle swung her sword… which was actually a quasi-dimensional precision cutter shaped like a sword, and sliced straight through a beam of bright red energy. It was undoubtedly chaos energy, but that hardly mattered. Her sword still cut through it with ease, and thanks to her crisis suit increasing her strength, she barely even felt any resistance.

The chaos energy that had been split in half suddenly transformed into swirling vortexes that tried to suck her and Nyx in. Gabrielle clicked her tongue as she let the vortexes take her. While Nyx stuck transmuted her hair into a set of spikes that speared the ground, she flew through the air began cutting the vortexes apart one by one, using their pull to draw her close. Each vortex that she cut disappeared as though it had never existed, until at last there were none left.

Gabrielle landed on the ground. A frustrated Morrigan clenched her hands into fists as Nyx joined Gabrielle.

"What sort of weapon is that?" asked Morrigan, scowling.

"It's not a weapon." Gabrielle held up her sword. "This is Mr. Cutter. He's a precision cutter that uses spatial distortions to cut through anything, regardless of whether it has mass or is made entirely of energy." Pausing, Gabrielle tilted her head. "Mr. Cutter actually severs things in this dimension by separating the space it cuts. Pretty neat, huh? I made him for when I needed to cut really large materials."

"So that's just a tool?!" Morrigan shrieked. "Who the hell uses such a powerful weapon as a mere tool!"

"Hey, Mr. Cutter is not a tool!"

"I'm through talking to you! Die!"

Morrigan held out her hands, palms spaced about six centimeters apart. A ball of chaos energy formed within the center between her palms. It crackled and pulsed. She launched the sphere at Nyx, who leapt to the side, avoiding it. The sphere struck the ground, and then rapidly expanded in all directions.

Nyx placed her hands on the floor and a wall rose from the floor as she transmuted it. That didn't stop the chaos energy, which continued to expand. Leaping back, Nyx tapped her feet against the floor, creating wall after wall after wall as she continued moving backward. It was not use. The expanding dome of chaotic energy continued growing.

Gabrielle would have loved to help. However, she had her hands full.

Immediately after launching her expanding chaos attack, Morrigan had created a really large missile from nothing. It was definitely made from energy. The entire thing was red and bubbling. It was Ion energy probably. That meant the missile was made from plasma. Since plasma was made from energy of this dimension, her sword would be able to cut through it, but that might also cause the missile to explode.

Hmm… this one is tricky. What should I use to destroy it?

Gabrielle leapt backward as the missile followed her. Even from this distance, she could feel the heat the missile was giving off. Plasma normally ran quite hot.

Flapping her wings, she took flight, twisting and turning as she did her best to avoid the missile, all the while trying to think of ways to destroy it without making it explode. She could always use a black hole… but no. It would take a stronger black hole than her usual ones, and that might destabilize the space, which could kill them all. What did she know about plasma. It cooled underwater, but she didn't have any water. What about space? If she exposed it to the vacuum of space, then maybe…

I've got it!

Swiping her finger through the air, Gabrielle summoned another item just as the plasma missile slammed into her and exploded.

4

Alex wasn't sure what happened, and it took him about sixteen blinks to realize that his giant sword was no longer in front of him. All that remained were the remnants, wisps of energy, which were dispersing even now.

Still standing where he had been was Lancelot. The man wore an amused grin as he lazily used the blade of his spear to trace patterns on the floor. Alex grimaced at the loud squeal that erupted.

"I forgot to mention this, but my spear is one of our most advanced close-range weapons, specifically designed to fight against Angelisians." Lancelot chuckled as he lifted the spear and pointed its tip at Alex. "I'm not sure how it works, but this baby can cut through any form of energy no matter how powerful. You're actually quite lucky that my first attack didn't cut your hands off."

A spear that cut through all forms of energy, including an Angelisian's Aura of Creation? Alex knew such technology existed. No matter how strong something was, even energy could be cut, severed, or destroyed if met with a force that was even more powerful. The problem was that this weapon clearly was not more powerful than his aura. That meant it used a different method of slicing through his power.

I need to know more about his weapon.

Alex called upon more of his Aura of Creation, hands forward, palmed pointed at Lancelot. The man wore a grin, which only widened when Alex swung out his hand and released a crescent of cutting energy. The son of Igraine spun his spear around as he danced, cutting through the first energy blade, and then cutting through a second one. A third. A fourth. Alex frowned as he continued throwing energy blades at Lancelot, only for each one to be cut in half as though it was nothing.

What sort of technology is that? It's not oscillation technology. It's not something that can sever energy either.

If it was oscillation technology, he would have seen the blade's minute vibrations as it cut through his energy. If it could sever energy, then it would have left a distortion in space. This was not doing either of those, which meant it was a different form of technology… but he didn't know of anything else that could cut through his blades like that. It was almost like…

"Here I come!" Lancelot shouted as he raced forward.

Alex had no more time to think as he spent the rest of it dodging thrusts and swings. The air around him sang as Lancelot tried to carve through his flesh, but his attacks, except his thrusts, were generally wide and easily avoided. His thrusts were another matter. However, Alex could judge when he was about to try and impale him by how Lancelot moved his arm back.

His Aura of Creation was useless. Alex didn't have enough control that he could generate the amount of energy needed to overpower whatever technology Lancelot was using. Maybe Azazel could, but he couldn't. That meant he had to find another method of victory.

Alex ducked under a swing, which sang as it carved the air above his head, and then rolled across the floor when Lancelot brought the spear back down. As the spear bounced off the floor, Lancelot pulled back up, spun on the balls of his feet, and tried to impale him with a swift thrust.

Activating his Aura of Creation, Alex coated his hand with the energy and tried to divert Lancelot's attack. He winced when the spear gouged a bloody furrow through his hand. Backing away, he ignored the way Lancelot flicked the blood off his blade. He looked at his hand, and then back at the spear.

It suddenly clicked.

"So that's how it is," Alex said, and then spoke louder. "Your spear uses a technology that negates all forms of energy."

"Like I said, I have no idea how it works." Lancelot slid his feet wide and held his spear in a two-handed grip. "I'm a warrior and a diplomat, not a scientist. I just know that your Aura of Creation is useless against this weapon."

That probably wasn't completely true. If there was a technology that could negate energy, then it would have to follow the principles that governed it. Law of Conservation of Energy stated that energy could neither be created nor destroyed. More than likely, this was absorbing the energy and dispersing it, thereby negating the energy of his attacks. However, such a technology would have a limit to how much it could absorb and disperse at the same time.

It's probably more than I can summon at the moment.

According to Gabrielle, Alex had a lot of power at his disposal, but the amount he could summon at any given time was limited thanks to the seal, which acted as a valve. Right now the valve was cracked but still closed. He could only summon a bit of power. Gabrielle's problem, consequently, was the inverse of his problem.

Either way, it meant he needed to find another way to defeat this guy.

"Perhaps I could be of assistance?"

No way.

"Hmhmhm. Don't be stubborn, brat. You are on the ropes. You can't generate enough energy to overpower that spear. I can help. My power is purely physical."

"Though it pains me to say this, with that seal keeping our powers at bay, your best bet is to use Asmodeus' power."

And go crazy?

"You needn't worry about that. I'd rather not have you destroyed this place in a power mad range and have us sucking vacuum. I need you alive. If you die, I die."

Alex wanted to debate the merits of using Asmodeus' power, but really, he didn't have a choice. Lancelot was already charging at him. If he didn't do something, he would lose.

Fine... but if you try anything...

"Don't worry... I can't do anything with this idiot angelisian watching me."

"Fear not. I won't let her control you like last time."

Alex had no choice but to trust the voices. As Lancelot ran toward him, Alex felt energy rush through his body. It was different from the Aura of Creation, which was like a calm river flowing over him. This was a raging torrent, an incredible storm that blasted through his body. It was fire. Hot and smoldering flames that caused his blood to boil.

Lancelot was now within striking distance, swinging his spear down as though to rend him from head to groin. Alex raised a single hand.

He caught Lancelot's spear.

"W-what the—!"

Alex yanked the spear forward, which resulted in Lancelot, still gripping the spear, being pulled with it—right into his waiting fist. Lancelot was blasted backwards. It was like being fired from a gun. One second he was there. Then there was a loud bang, like a detonation going off in his ear, and then Lancelot was gone, his body already embedded into a wall.

The spear that Lancelot had used was still in Alex's hand. He frowned at it. Raising his left leg, he took the spear in both hands and snapped it over his knee. Sparks flew from the inside, which was filled with circuits and wires.

He was amazed.

This is your power?

"Well, a small portion of it at least."

"Remember, both of our powers are sealed. That's why you can only use so much of our power."

Gotcha.

Alex looked over at Lancelot, who was kneeling on the ground, a hand pressed against his chest. Broken fragments of his armor clattered to the floor. Blood trickled down his mouth, signifying his internal injuries.

"W-what the hell was that?!" asked Lancelot as Alex walked up to him. "I thought you were angelisian! Even if you were wearing a crisis suit, there's no way you could generate so much strength!"

"I'm not sure what I am," Alex answered. "And I'm not about to tell you what I do know. This battle is over. You've lost."

Lancelot growled, but then he grimaced and coughed up more blood. Staring at him through half-lidded eyes clouded with pain, the spear-wielding warrior couldn't help but ask, "why are you even helping that brat? Arthur has done nothing to warrant you helping him, has he? Didn't he try to steal your woman from you? Why help him?"

"That's easy." Feeling a grin curl his lips into a smile, Alex pointed at himself with a thumb. "Because I'm going to be a hero." He paused, and then sheepishly added, "and Emperor of the Galaxy."

5

Energy shields were a trademark of starships. It wasn't something that starships could choose not to have. To enter hyperspace, ships had to phase into a region of space that existed within this universe, but a ship couldn't even enter that region without a shield. Ship chassis couldn't withstand the incredible acceleration that came from entering this region, which allowed faster than light travel.

Many shields were designed specifically for ships, and though there were a few personal defense shields, most of them couldn't withstand more than few shots from a blaster before running out of energy.

Except Gabrielle's.

"Hmm…"

Gabrielle mumbled as she watched the plasma wash over her shield. It licked at the edges of the large blue sphere that she had become wrapped in. It flickered like it was trying to find a crack that it could break through, but it wouldn't be able. Gabrielle nodded to herself. The shield was flawless.

Why are the inventions I make that work always things used to fight?

It was a question she had asked many times, but she was still no closer to figuring out the answer.

The plasma dispersed as it ran out of energy. Gabrielle deactivated her shield and landed back on the ground.

She looked for Morrigan and found her engaged in combat with Nyx, who had two curved swords in her hands and was swinging them at the blonde girl. Morrigan created several energy swords from chaotic energy. They hovered in the air and attacked Nyx, who leapt and spun and swung her blades. Gabrielle was impressed when the girl cut through the chaos energy like it was nothing.

Hmm... it doesn't look like she has realized that I'm not dead.

That meant she had an advantage. If she could launch a surprise attack, then she could capture Morrigan, but what invention should she use? Mr. Capture? Mr. Rope? She had many inventions that could theoretically capture and hold someone down. She just needed to figure out which one would work best in this particular situation.

Morrigan screamed as she raised her hands above her head and generated massive amounts of lightning, which struck at Nyx, who leapt backward, zigged and zagged. Nyx tapped the floor, and suddenly, a wall erupted from the floor. The lightning struck it. The wall was destroyed, but Nyx had already moved on, using the resulting dust cloud as cover.

I guess that's an assassin for you.

Gabrielle had been attacked by more than a few assassins before, but none of them were quite as good as Nyx. Then again, most of them never got past Azazel and the guards. Thinking on it, most were killed before they even got to the planet.

Papa was overzealously protective that way.

Nyx was able to reach Morrigan in record time, though she was spotted soon after. Morrigan held out a hand. An energy shield composed of white power appeared in front of her. It gushed into the form of an oval, flowing like water. It quickly solidified, and then hardened. That was ice manipulation. Nyx struck the ice. Her blade bounced off.

"Ah ha ha ha! Do you really think such a weak attack can penetrate my shield, alchemist?" asked Morrigan.

Frowning, Nyx transmuted her hair, which turned into several dozen hardened spear that she sent at Morrigan, who remained standing where she was. That was probably a bad idea. The spears pierced the ice shield one after another. Cracks formed along the shield before it shattered with a loud sound like breaking glass.

"What?!"

Morrigan hastily erected a barrier made of lightning. Nyx retracted her hair. Gabrielle thought it was a sound decision. While not conductors of electricity, Nyx would have been injured if she'd let her hair touch the lightning.

Watching the battle made Gabrielle finally realize which invention to use. She swiped her finger through the air and summoned Mr. Tentacles. It wasn't active yet, so it just looked like a long and squishy tube. Gabrielle squished it and tossed the tube into the air, high over the heads of Morrigan and Nyx, who still hadn't noticed that she was unharmed.

As the tube sailed through the air, it activated, and several dozen tentacles sprouted from it. Before Morrigan even knew what was happening, several tentacles had wrapped around her arms, legs, torso, breasts, and crotch. They squeezed her tightly and made sure she couldn't escape.

"W-what the hell is this?!" she shrieked.

"That's Mr. Tentacle," Gabrielle answered as she walked up to Nyx. "I made him a long time ago as a prank. I used to use him to trap my bodyguards when I was trying to run away. Don't bother trying to escape. My bodyguards were my test subjects, so Mr. Tentacle is resistant to all forms of energy manipulation and even cutting damage."

"Damn you!" Morrigan screeched. "I hate you! I hate you! Why are you so much stronger than me?! You didn't even use your Aura of Creation against me! Am I really so weak that you didn't even feel the need to use your powers to fight me?!"

Gabrielle frowned. "You seem to be under the wrong impression. I didn't use my power because I can't control it, not because I didn't want to. This fight would have been over before it began if I could use my power without destroying this entire station."

Morrigan's face turned red. "So, you're saying I'm just that weak?! That if you used your powers, I would have been destroyed instantly?!"

"Well, maybe not instantly, but…"

"I hate you! You're nothing but a spoiled princess who's been handed everything to her on a silver plate! Brains, power, beauty! You just have it all, don't you?! Just wait until I get out of this! I'll murder you, Gabrielle Angelise! I'll—"

"Be quiet." Nyx transmuted one of her bands into a ball gag, which she used her hair to shove into Morrigan's mouth, muffling the girl's screaming. "Princess Gabrielle, what should we do with her?"

"Let's leave her there," Gabrielle said after giving it some thought. "We should go help Alex—"

At that exact moment, Lancelot flew through the air, slammed into the wall, and fell off. Alex was walking toward him. It was a slow, steady pace, and it made her realize that Alex had his fight well in hand.

"Never mind," Gabrielle said. "We should help Claud—"

She looked over at Claudia, who was getting ready to help her son from the crucifix he was hanging from. Several meters from the stairs leading to the crown prince was Igraine. She was lying on the ground. Her dress was torn, and her face was resting against the cold floor, while her butt was sticking up in the air. It was a very awkward position.

"Huh, never mind." Gabrielle scratched the back of her head. Behind her, Morrigan continued to scream. "Does this mean the battle is over?"

"It seems that way," Nyx said as Arty's left arm was slung around his mama's shoulder. Before they could move, Arty suddenly jerked away from his mother as though he was a puppet being controlled by a string. He rushed over to Caliburn, picked up it, and then stabbed it into a slot inside of the pedestal standing before the crucifix.

Everything began to shake.

Art stared wide-eyed at Caliburn. "W-what did I…?"

"Hahahahaha!!" Everyone turned their attention to Igraine, who was no longer unconscious and sitting up. Her left hand was outstretched. Gabrielle noticed several threads attached to her fingers. The other ends were stuck to Arty. "I knew that if I just waited for you to let your guard down, I would be given a chance to make you do what I want. Now this station will activate! You're all too late! With this, my goal will finally be accomplished!"

"What should we do?" asked Alex, carrying an unconscious Lancelot over his shoulder.

"There's nothing you can do!" Igraine giggled. "Now that this station has been activated, all you can do is wait for Avalon to activate!"

"Let's get out of here!" Claudia said.

"Why bother?" asked Igraine as she stood up. "It's not like anything is going to happen to you. This station isn't just a weapon.

It's a station capable of creating a giant tractor beam that can move entire planets."

"What?" Arty gawked at her.

Igraine spread her arms. "Have you never wondered how our solar system could have so many planets capable of sustaining life? Most only have one or two, but every planet in our system is perfect for sustaining life. Do you not think that is just a little too coincidental?"

"N-now that you mention it…" Claudia mumbled. "It does seem weird… I think? I mean, all of our planets are so awesome."

Igraine rolled her eyes. "Your astuteness is astounding, as always."

Gabrielle frowned as she thought through what Igraine had said. This station was capable of pulling planets via a giant tractor beam. That was technically possible, but that sort of technology was advanced beyond anything their current galaxy had outside of her dimensional warping inventions. Igraine's knowledge also had several gaps in it.

To pull planets around required more than simply an overpowered tractor beam; the beam had to be capable of entering hyperspace. That also meant this station was capable of generating huge amounts of energy. For energy to enter hyperspace, the station would have to be able to generate nuclear, magnetic, and electric energy. There was also matters of what this station's operational range was, and a whole slew of other issues that she couldn't begin to think about at that moment.

However, there was something even darker than a simple station capable of creating a hyperspace tractor beam.

A tractor beam that powerful wasn't just able to pull planets. It would also be able to destroy stars and planets by collapsing their cores through massive gravitational fluxes. That meant this thing could easily be used as a weapon to shut the station down. Beyond that, however, was an even bigger problem.

"Where is the control room?" Gabrielle asked, silencing everyone.

"Excuse me?" asked Igraine.

"The control room. Where is the control room?"

"Why would I tell you that?"

"You just activated a powerful station that can create hyperspace capable tractor beams," Gabrielle said. "Do you think station's like this can just be reactivated after having been inactive for so long? A cold start like this is going to cause a massive influx of power to enter this station's core. What do you think is going to happen once all that power is shoved into the core without warning?"

Igraine suddenly paled. Gabrielle almost sighed as she realized that this lady hadn't even considered what would happen. She clearly wasn't much for engineering or science. This was why people who knew nothing about the creation of technology needed to not mess with inventions they didn't understand.

"If I don't shut this thing off, then this station is going to explode, all that energy is going to reverse course back into the stars, which will inevitably cause both stars to collapse and go nova." Gabrielle stared at Igraine. "I need to shut it off. Where is the control room?"

"I-it's this way…"

Igraine led them out of the room. Gabrielle used a remote to control Mr. Tentacle, having it follow her, the still screaming Morrigan wrapped up in its many appendages. Alex walked alongside her, while Nyx took up the rear and Claudia helped Arty walk.

Avalon was a massive station, which Gabrielle knew from the holographic feed she'd seen of it when they were getting ready to board, but a holographic display couldn't really give someone an accurate grasp of just how large something was. Now wandering through the station, Gabrielle realized that this thing even bigger than an Angelisian Dreadnaught, currently the largest vessel in the entire Angelisian Fleet.

As they ascended to another level via an elevator, Gabrielle looked out the glassteel tube.

Down below was a massive open space. It reminded her of the dome on Mars City in some ways, though it was a lot different. Far beneath them were numerous structures formed from geometric shapes. One could almost mistake them for houses, but that wasn't what they were.

High above the structures, floating in the air, was a massive black sphere that crackled with energy. Most would have mistaken it for a quantum black hole. Not her. That was clearly the power source. This area was obviously where all of the power from the binary stars was converted into a usable source of energy.

The elevator shook—the entire station was shaking, in fact. Igraine nearly fell. She grabbed hold of a handle, while Alex and Nyx bent their knees. Alex had a tougher time than Nyx because he was carrying Lancelot over his shoulder. Gabrielle used her wings to keep from falling.

"What was that?" asked Claudia.

"That's the station beginning to fall apart," Gabrielle said. "This station has been absorbing power for who knows how long, and now all that power is being sent to various systems required to activate it. Many of the systems are likely being overwhelmed with the surges of energy and breaking apart."

"In other words, we need to stop this before they break down completely," Alex said.

"Right."

There wasn't much time left. The shaking was only getting worse. As the lift door opened, Gabrielle rushed down the new hallway and used her own knowledge of technology guide her to the control room. She ignored the shouts from everyone else as they told her to stop.

Since the structure that converted plasma into power was down below, it meant the control room should be right above it. Finding it was easy. A locked blast door stood in her but, Gabrielle opened the valve that kept her power blocked and raised a hand. A beam of energy tore straight through the door. Sadly, it continued on and struck the next wall, tearing through that as well. She supposed it was good fortunate that there appeared to be several walls after that.

The control room wasn't large. She judged the room to be about ten square meters. In center, on a raised platform, was a large chair with an array of panels, levers, and screens. Gabrielle didn't hesitate. She leapt into the seat, wings folding so they wouldn't get squashed, cracked her fingers, and got to work.

She didn't recognize any of the characters being used on the panels, but that hardly mattered. All technology worked in more or less the same way. Gabrielle tapped several keys, watched them light up, and then tapped several more. The screens before her lit up as well. Symbols appeared. They were the same symbols that were on the panels.

Learning new languages was never my strong suit, but it seems like I don't have much of a choice now.

She would have to do this.

If she didn't, then the whole solar system was doomed.

6

Alex arrived in the control room with the others to see that Gabrielle was already hard at work, sitting on a chair located several steps above them. She was surrounded by an array of panels, levers, and screens. Her fingers were blurs.

The control room wasn't big. Shaped like a cylinder, the room was a flat ceiling several meters above them. Lights blinked all around. There were concentric lines that traced the room like the circuits of a matrix. Alex didn't know what they were, but he could tell from how they coincided with Gabrielle's fingers that each line of light performed a function related to the station.

"What is she doing?" Claudia stared at Gabrielle.

"She's probably trying to override the activation sequence," Alex said. "While Caliburn is the key to activating the station, the sequences themselves are controlled by codes and programs. If she can override the sequence, then she can take control of the station and shut it down before it explodes."

"Damn it," Igraine muttered. "All that work I put into activating Avalon. I even betrayed the crown for this, and it's all amounted to nothing."

"Why did you want to activate Avalon?" asked Claudia.

"Isn't it obvious?" Igraine gave her an aggrieved look. "I wanted to use it's hyperspace to locate Uther."

"I get it," Alex said as he set Lancelot on the floor. He ignored Morrigan's muffled screams. "This thing has a massive hyperspace tractor beam. However, to use that beam properly, it must have a highly advanced system capable of tracking planetary and solar bodies."

"Yes." Igraine nodded. "I was hoping to use this station's scanning abilities. With Arthur's blood controlling the station, it should have been easy."

"Why betray the crown for that?" asked Claudia.

"Because there's no way I would have been allowed to activate Avalon for something like this," Igraine said. "Would any of you have allowed it?"

"Probably not."

"And with good reason," Prince Arthur said. "Look at what's happened because you wanted to activate this station."

"Hindsight is always twenty twenty," Alex mumbled to himself. Nyx looked up at him, her eyes inquiring, but he just placed a hand on her shoulder. "It's nothing. Just an old human saying I heard once."

"Do you think she can stop this from blowing up?" asked Claudia.

"If anyone can do it, Gabrielle can," Alex said. "After all, she's the greatest genius ever born."

Alex looked back at Gabrielle as she continued to work. He could only really see her profile, but even so, her arms were moving like lightning, and he could tell from the minute twitches of her shoulders that she was working on decoding whatever programs were causing this station to activate.

A drop of sweat rolled down his face. The rumbling suddenly got much worse. Alex and the others almost fell to the floor, but then, all at once, the shaking slowed before stopping altogether.

It took a moment for everyone to realize that the shaking had stopped, but when the realization finally set in, Alex was looking back at Gabrielle as she stood from the chair and wandered down to them. The others were all looking shocked. They stared at Gabrielle like they couldn't believe what had just happened, but Alex knew Gabrielle was capable of. He'd had no doubts that she could do it.

"Alex! I stopped Avalon from blowing up." Gabrielle beamed at him as she held her hands, index and middle fingers extended to create a V-shape.

"Nice job, Gabby." Alex gave her a thumbs up.

Alex and the others breathed a sigh of relief. The threat had finally passed.

EPILOGUE

ALL'S WELL THAT ENDS WELL... OR SO THEY SAY

The battle around Avalon had concluded long before Alex and the others had emerged from the massive space station. Alex had learned that Lancelot's fleet had been rendered useless. There had been a few deaths, but surprisingly few people had died thanks to Nimue's decision to fire ion cannons instead of regular weapons.

The crew of every vessel had been rounded up and was now facing charges of treason, though Alex had reason to believe that most of the people would not be facing serious charges. A lot of them were simply following the orders of their ruler. Prince Arthur had confided that he planned on weeding out the individuals who were wanted to incite chaos and sending them to princess, while the rest would be redistributed to other fleets.

Alex, Gabrielle, and Nyx had been left to their own devices for much of that time. Prince Arthur and Nimue were busy regaining control of the solar system, but a number of things needed to happen for them to do that. The crown prince had to reestablish contact with the rest of his half-siblings. Furthermore, he had to make an example of Lancelot and Morrigan. Just what he had done to them was unknown to Alex, but he assumed the punishment enacted upon the pair had been harsh.

There was also Igraine. Even though she had done what she did to find her husband, it did not change how she had incited a war for her own purpose. Such an action, Alex had been told, would have normally resulted in her being executed.

Once again, however, there were circumstances that made execution unfeasible. The first was that Uther Pendragon, the king and ruler of this solar system, was not present. Only the king could order the execution of someone from the royal family. Prince Arthur might have been crown prince, but he did not have that authority.

There were other reasons, but Alex hadn't been made privy to them. The politics of this solar system was not his business.

With everyone else so busy, he, Gabrielle, and Nyx did not have much to do. They were free to wander Camelot, but after being there for nearly an entire week, the novelty had worn off. He had taken to sparring with Nyx or working on inventions with Gabrielle on his free time.

Both activities had their ups and downs.

His spars with Nyx were getting more intense as the days went by, especially after learning what he had about the Aura of Creation. Alex had been working out new ways to use his powers. He could create beams, energy blasts, bolts, cutting blades, vortexes, release energy from his hands, and create reflective surfaces. He could also attack through mediums, make shields, and even absorb energy and reuse it in various ways.

Energy absorption was probably the greatest ability he had discovered. It didn't require much of his own energy. He could absorb the energy of others through his palms, and then launch his own attack using the energy he had absorbed mixed with his own energy. This resulted in an attack many times more powerful than if he had used his own power.

Of course, because his spars with Nyx were so intense, they had destroyed the training hall and were told to spar outside of the castle. Then they had destroyed several fields and were told to stop. After that, they had stuck with hand-to-hand combat.

Working with Gabrielle was a lot of fun as well, but there were problems with that, too.

He and Gabrielle would often spend hours working on various inventions. Alex felt like he was getting the hang of Angelisian technology. He'd even managed to incorporate the anti-gravity repulsor fields into a robotic drone that could be controlled with a pair of gloves. The gloves also used a combination of Angelisian and human technology.

Unfortunately, his and Gabrielle inventions often went awry, and sometimes the problems they caused were quite large. One of their inventions had destroyed a lobby, another had demolished parts of the ceiling, and after a new cleaning robot had gone around stripping the clothes of all the butlers and maids, Prince Arthur had decided that enough was enough. He would no longer let them build their inventions within his palace.

Nearly a week after the battle around Avalon, Alex, Gabrielle, and Nyx were finally set to leave.

They stood in the docking bay with Prince Arthur, Nimue, and a cadre of royal guards, including Captain Tanner. The crown prince and his princess were dressed in pure white, a white gown for the princess and white slacks and a long-sleeved shirt for the prince. It made them look like an idyllic couple.

Claudia was also with them. Her clothing was still black, but it wasn't the crazy battle armor that she had been wearing before.

"Mother has agreed to pilot you two back to Mars," Prince Arthur said.

"You can cunt on me!" Claudia snapped off a smart yet somehow goofy salute.

"Did you just say cunt?" asked Alex.

"No?"

"I'm pretty sure you did."

"I said count."

"Anyway," Prince Arthur continued, "I would love to take you back myself, but there is still a lot of work that needs to be done."

"It's fine," Gabrielle said. "We understand."

"Thank you." Prince Arthur extended his hand toward Alex and, after a moment, Alex took the hand in a firm shake. "You've done a lot for my solar system. If you ever need anything, don't hesitate to ask."

Alex was about to tell him that there was no need for that, that this was what heroes always did, but he didn't say those words. It wasn't because he didn't want to. He actually did. Part of him had always wanted to say that corny line. The reason he didn't say those words was because he had just come up with a magnificent idea.

"Actually, there is something I'd like you to do," Alex began. "Have you ever heard of a planet called Jāhilīyah?"

AFTERWORD

Hey everyone! Thank you all for reading the latest volume of my sci-fi harem light novel series, A Most Unlikely Hero! If you enjoyed it, please consider leaving a review to help other readers decide whether or not this story is for them.

It is now the seventh volume of A Most Unlikely Hero, and Alex is finally stepping into the person I've always wanted him to be—a man willing to accept his harem. He's still a little tentative. However, the desire is there, and I believe he will grow as the story continues. He's only just confessed to Gabrielle, but I've got high hopes for our resident Harem King.

This particular volume took place in a galaxy far, far away… okay, it didn't. But it did take place is another solar system of the Milky Way Galaxy. This time, I had my hero and two of his heroines help a friend quell a rebellion staged by his own family.

I'm sure many of you have noticed that Arthur and his family are all based on Arthurian mythology. I think I have mentioned this before, but my idea for aliens in this story came from a thought I had: What if all the gods, heroes, and powerful historical figures we know were actually aliens from outer space? I sort of took this idea and just ran with it, and now here we are. It might not be a super original idea, but I have been having a blast writing it.

I can feel it…

… My chuunibyo power is growing!

Aaaaahh! Be still, oh black dragon that dwells within my right hand!!!

Er… no, wait. That's just my fap hand. Nevermind. False alarm.

Ahem. In either event, I plan to begin another arc in the next volume. You probably noticed how I set up the plot for the next story with the interludes. Kazekiri and Jasmine will be the main focus of the next volume. I hope you are all looking forward to it.

In closing, I would like to thank my copy editor and proofreaders for helping correct my syntax, grammar, and spelling. I am always grateful for the help they provide.

I would also like to thank XuaHanNin, who came through with more outstanding artwork. She's been doing an awesome job ever since I started this series. Her artwork just keeps improving and makes me want to do better as well.

Finally, I would like to thank you readers. Thank you for buying my books, for reading them, for leaving reviews on Amazon, and for just being awesome people in general. You all rock. I hope you will join me in my next volume of To Love Ru fan fic—erm, A Most Unlikely Hero.

~Brandon Varnell

SEE A SNEAK PEAK OF THE MANGA ADAPTION OF BRANDON'S AMERICAN KITSUNE SERIES!

HAVE YOU EVER EXPERIENCED ONE OF THOSE LIFE-CHANGING INSTANCES? AN EVENT SO MOMENTOUS THAT, YEARS LATER,
YOU'RE STILL MARVELING AT HOW IT CHANGED YOUR LIFE?

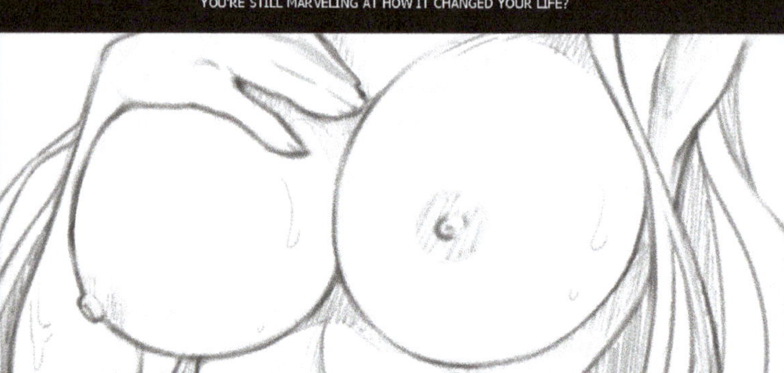

I HAD ONE OF THOSE. IT HAPPENED A WHILE AGO

EVEN TO THIS DAY, THROUGH ALL THE CHANGES THAT HAVE HAPPENED, THROUGH ALL THE EXPERIENCES THAT I'VE BEEN
THROUGH, I STILL CAN'T BELIEVE HOW THIS ONE MOMENT CHANGED MY LIFE FOREVER.

NO MATTER WHAT CAME AFTER, OUR FIRST MEETING IS SOMETHING THAT I'LL ALWAYS REMEMBER.

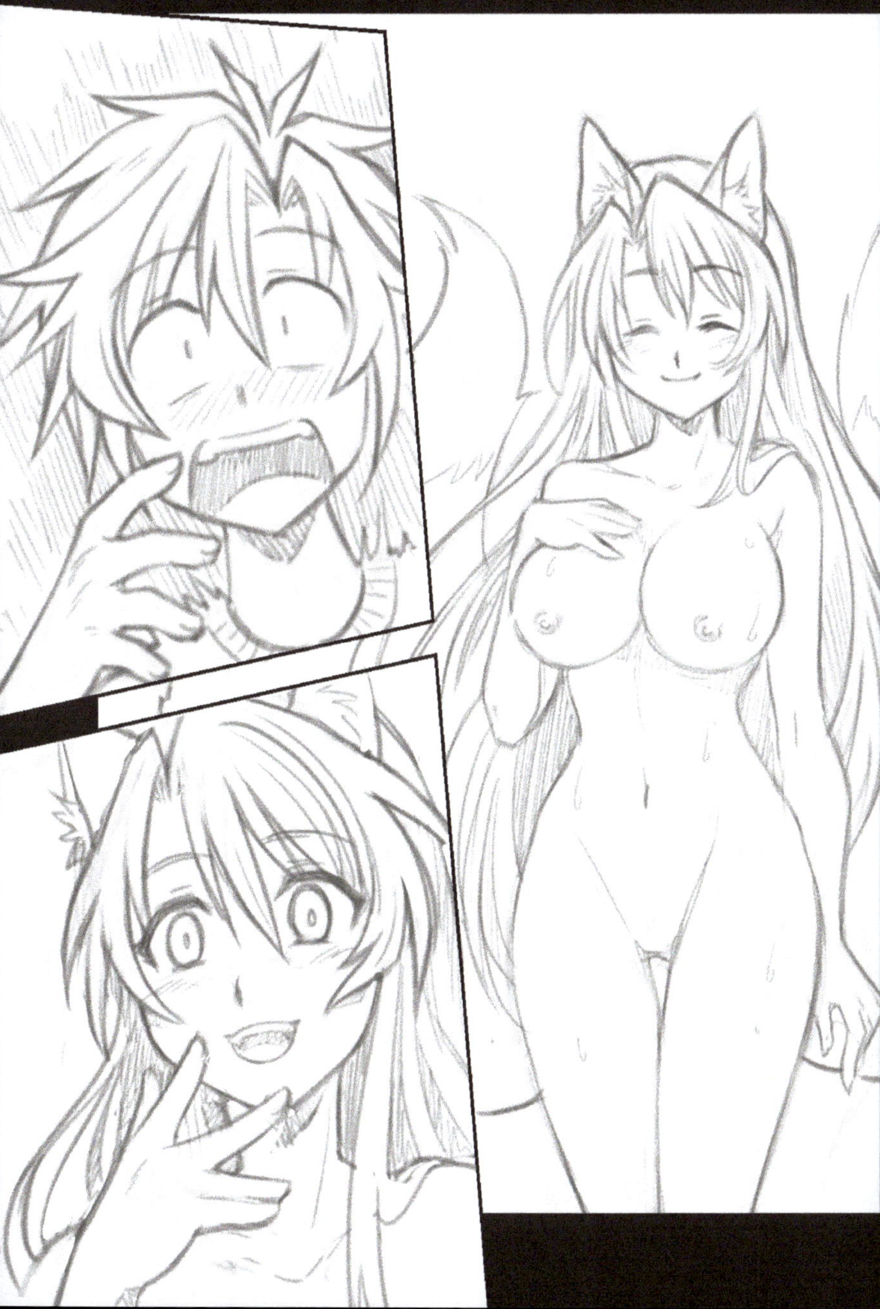

ESPECIALLY SINCE, AT THE BEGINNING OF THIS TALE, I THOUGHT SHE WAS NOTHING BUT AN ORDINARY FOX WITH, UNORDINARILY ENOUGH, TWO BUSHY RED TAILS.

LIFE

.

.

.

.

.

.

.

.

.

IT HITS YOU WHEN YOU LEAST EXPECT IT TO.

AMERICAN
KITSUNE

Hey, did you know?
Brandon Varnell has started a Patreon
You can get all kinds of awesome exclusives
Like:

1. The chance to read his stories before anyone else!
2. Free ebooks!
3. exclusive SFW and NSFW artwork!
4. Signed paperback copies!
5. His undying love!
Er... maybe we don't want that last one, but the rest is pretty cool, right?

To get this awesome exlusive conent go to:
https://www.patreon.com/BrandonVarnell
and sigh up today!

American Kitsune

volumes 1-12
are available now!

Arcadia's
IgnobleKnight
Volumes 1-6
are available now!

The Complete Series is available now on paperback and Amazon Kindle!
JOURNEY of a BETRAYED HERO

Volumes 1-2
available on Amazon and Kindle
WIEDERGEBURT
LEGEND OF THE REINCARNATED WARRIOR

The Executioner Series
The complete series
is available now!

Want to learn when a new book comes out?

Follow me on Social Media!

 @AmericanKitsune

 +BrandonVarnell

 @BrandonBVarnell

 http://bvarnell1101.tumblr.com/

 Brandon Varnell

 BrandonbVarnell

 https://www.patreon.com/
BrandonVarnell